ABOUT the AUTHOR

Chris Hare was educated at a boys' school in Harrow. Most of the time, he hated it. After he left, he trained and became a successful 'people' photographer, which he loved. He covered weddings from the local register office to St. Paul's Cathedral in London. During his career he was fortunate enough to witness many memorable events at weddings, not least the occasion when the bride's waters broke as she signed the register, and a Grandpa's 'famous last words' at the start of the wedding breakfast. (Slurp. 'Yummy. Nice soup!) Zonk.

Chris loves the theatre, French Impressionism, test cricket, animals, Luton Town FC and red wine. He also enjoys foreign travel and got the idea for this book whilst on a trip to America, and twenty years later, Geronimo! Here it is!!!

In 2002 he retired, and he and his wife Hilary moved to their lovely villa in Spain, she to paint, (water colours), he to write, (slowly).

Crabbe in all Innocence

by
Chris Hare

DEDICATIONS

For my family – Jay and Elaine, Julie and Paul, Jenny, Zoe, Tia and Maelie. And of course, for my long-suffering wife Hilary, who selflessly gave me the time and space I needed to complete this epic. (Only interrupting me when something really important came up, like when it was my turn to empty the dishwasher).

I also dedicate this book to my old friend Gordon Beattie, himself a published author, who just wouldn't stop nagging me to get this thing finished. Well, here it is, Gordon. It's done, so you can get off my case now.

ACKNOWLEDGEMENTS

I am indebted to these special friends for their help, advice and encouragement which rescued me whenever I got fed up with Crabbe, or just went into my shell. If I didn't always express my sincere and heartfelt thanks at the time – sorry, and let me put it right: John Ellison, Mike and Carole Newby, John Bibbings, Karen McKinley, Janet Bond, Gordon Beattie, Sandra Hare, Wendy Down and my brilliant editor, Amanda Bourne. I don't know if there's a Patron Saint of Patience, but if there isn't, there is now.

Crabbe in all Innocence

EPILOGUE

High, high above the skies in a secret place hidden even beyond the imagination of man, The Three Fates paused in their spinning of the tapestries of men's lives and looked down.

They smiled at the success of their labours. In a large deep hole among the graves lay the body of Lancelot Arthur Crabbe, poisoned, gassed and battered, but not quite dead.

The gods would miss him. Crabbe's innocent blunderings, his indiscretions and calamitous attempts at trying to please, had made the skies ring with laughter.

But now, it was nearly over, and the search would begin for a new Heroic Failure to take his place.

Crabbe's tapestry, like the millions of others they had created, was full of the bright innocent colours of childhood that slipped into shades of ever deepening black as the time and manner of his death approached.

It was all there, so intricately and carefully woven. The dates of his short life, his parentage, education, and all the events that would lead him to the place they'd selected for his demise.

However, in Crabbe's tapestry there was a significant difference. Once again, the deep, grim lines of the

7

weavers' ancient faces gave way to smiles, for here and there, particularly in the pattern of his teenage years, they had spun in some grey thread.

Grey. The colour of doubt, of the unknown, and of choice. The colour between the black certainty of death and the white purity of the innocence of life.

Not that Crabbe ever knew or ever suspected even for one moment, that he had been selected as a victim of *The Fates*, as their special plaything. It was a rare distinction (if 'distinction' is the right word) and *The Fates* had chosen well. Crabbe hadn't let them down.

In the countless tapestries they'd woven for ordinary human beings there was no grey. Everyone else's existence was predictable, unalterable. For the vast majority there was no choice. Their whole lives were determined, preordained.

But, for Crabbe, there had been times of choice. And, Crabbe, being Crabbe, usually made the wrong one. But it was almost at an end. He had travelled his path and his journey was nearly over.

As decided, he had suffered much during his final day on Earth. Now, he lay in someone else's grave, unconscious and unaware of what had happened and of what was due to happen very shortly. The final, fatal explosion.

His breathing was shallow, barely noticeable. In fact, he already looked dead.

Crabbe in all Innocence

It would appear to the casual passer-by that the 'arrangements', as a burial is so delicately termed, had been carried out in the traditional way. The body was lying on its back, with its hands clasped in supplication. The eyes were closed, although that detail couldn't be seen from above since the face was hidden deep in the shadow cast by the early morning sun.

This particular passer-by, being an Englishman, paused and doffed his hat, then bowed out of respect for the deceased before continuing on his way. He reached St. Mary's church at the top of the path before his brain gave voice to the doubts. Pausing again, he turned to look back at the churchyard and at the hundreds of gravestones and memorials and then at the open grave in particular. A questioning frown appeared on his brow and he stroked his chin in puzzled thought as he took in the scene.

All was not as it seemed. Not as it should be. This was England. There shouldn't be anomalies.

But there were.

He asked himself why, for example, the grave hadn't been filled in immediately. That was the usual practice, as far as he knew. Just as soon as the mourners left for the funeral tea, uncaring mud-encrusted strangers appeared with their shovels. That was how it happened when his granddad died.

The passer-by glanced round to make sure he was alone. His curiosity had been aroused and he wanted another look. He began whistling quietly to himself and arched his eyebrows, which, he thought, made him look like a picture of innocence.

Not that he had anything to feel guilty about, but he did think he might be accused of intruding should the gravediggers suddenly reappear to finish the job.

Still whistling softly, hands clasped behind his back, he strolled back down the path as nonchalantly as he could, righteousness all over his face as he approached the grave once more.

He looked down in prayerful contemplation even though his mind was racing as he tried to put his thoughts and questions in a logical order that would make sense of this mystery.

Presumably, he thought, this chap was laid to rest yesterday. Therefore, this man had been lying in his grave all night, exposed to the elements, and vultures, and fair game for a body snatcher.

He realised his imagination was running out of control and he forced his mind to concentrate on the known facts: body snatchers belonged in Scotland, in the reign of Queen Victoria, and so were a thing of the past. This was Harrow, 1932, King George the Fifth was on the throne. Were there vultures in Harrow? Or did they just fly round in circles over dead cowboys in American films? Momentarily his eyes darted to the sky, just in case.

Suddenly, something else occurred to him. Why was the body just lying there and not encased in a coffin?

Granddad's had been polished pine with brass fittings and a nameplate.

Then, there were the clothes. Nanny had insisted her late husband should be dressed in his best suit with a freshly starched wing collar holding his chins in place, with the help of his club tie. But he, whoever it was down there, wasn't even wearing a cheap shroud. Only a mismatch of old, stained and torn rags. The kind you wouldn't be seen dead in. Although, in his case…

A shiver ran down the passer-by's spine and he decided suddenly, it was high time he was somewhere else.

Being English, he did the English thing. He decided to ignore what he'd seen and pretend there was nothing unusual. After all, it was none of his business. They'd never been introduced. It would be different if it *was* Granddad down there. He would be concerned and would certainly report it. But it wasn't. Granddad was miles away in Potters Bar, safely planted in his best suit and starched wing collar, polished pine coffin, brass handles and nameplate.

The passer-by took up his whistling again but this time, a march, and resumed his passing by, only now with noticeably quicker steps. He drew a deep breath filling his lungs with the fresh morning air, feeling the need for a change of subject.

He glanced up to see if there were any rain clouds about, or vultures. There were none of either. It was going to be another perfect day. Free of clouds and birds of prey.

He returned his gaze to earth hoping to see another Englishman with whom he could discuss this fine weather, as Englishmen did when they didn't know what else to do.

Discovering he was still alone, he started at a run back up the path, anxious to get away and calling out 'Lovely day!' to the church spire towering over him as he made his escape.

The clocks of *The Fates* don't slow down as the time of death approaches. They just stop ticking as the thread of life is cut. Stops dead. Just like a human heart.

In the open grave, the almost late Lancelot Arthur Crabbe was totally unaware of anything as he dreamed dreams of memories. He gave an almost imperceptible smile as he remembered the first great love of life – Miss Peach.

1: THE NEW CRABBE

Given the strange nature of events that frequently plagued his formative years, it should come as no surprise to learn that Lancelot Arthur Crabbe was born on April 1st.

To be precise, he fought his way into the world at 3.25am on All Fools' Day, 1914, the eldest of four children born to Lillian Dorothy Crabbe, née Chadwick, a part-time librarian, and Frank Sydney Crabbe, bank clerk, of 59, Felbridge Avenue, Stanmore in Middlesex. His birth brought much joy to the neat and clean Crabbe household.

But it brought much disruption too. For after four years of marriage, Mr. and Mrs. Crabbe were well practised at running their lives and their home in an ordered way, because bank clerks and librarians are *ordered* people. The arrival of a demanding, ever hungry and usually wet baby who could (and frequently did,) scream and require immediate attention at any time of the day or night, did nothing to help the good order of their lives.

No amount of *shushing* into silence, an art Mrs. Crabbe had learnt and often used at the library, had any effect on young Lancelot. He wailed and screamed until his demands were met.

Mr. Crabbe, the infant's father, had for all the summers of his marriage, spent every second and fourth

Sunday afternoon on his hands and knees cutting his lawn (very neatly), with a pair of wood-handled garden shears, and the first and third Sundays up a ladder cleaning windows. But he found that as 'a family man', he was obliged to at least to speed up his weekend pastimes if not to abandon them, in order to devote time to his family, usually at the duck pond on The Green or on the swings at the local park.

Similarly, Mrs. Crabbe, who always did the washing on Monday mornings before going to work at Wealdstone Library for the two until five period, hadn't realised that a baby meant her doing washing *every* day, and further, his arrival reluctantly obliged her to give up her job in order to devote most of her time to her son. In those far-off days, working mothers hadn't been invented.

It all came as rather a shock. An unforeseen upheaval in their lives, but the proud parents accepted the enforced changes with good grace. For the eagerly awaited Lancelot Arthur was the apple of their eye.

But they soon learned, as millions of first-time parents before them, that it was against nature to expect their bundle of joy to fit in with the routine of their daily lives. *They* were the ones who had to change.

And change they did. To a degree, since they never entirely gave up old ways. Mrs. Crabbe, herself an ardent reader who discovered chivalry and romantic ideals on the *Myths and Legends of Britain* shelf at her library, read and reread everything she could on the exploits of King Arthur and his Knights of the Round Table. Obviously, it was from these tales that the forenames of her son came, and she secretly drew up a list of several other favoured Arthurian names, in case they should be blessed with another addition to the family.

Whilst the other mothers of Felbridge Avenue read their offspring bedtime stories from *Grimm's Fairy Tales* and Hans Christian Anderson, young Lancelot was treated to the exploits of the Green Knight and his heroic rescue of numerous damsels in distress whilst at the same time, vanquishing fire-breathing dragons by the score with his free hand.

Usually, he repaid his mother's endeavours by falling asleep within seconds, although it became apparent, as he grew from baby to toddler and then to a little boy, that his subconscious mind had absorbed the stories. Although it could never be thought that he'd been born and cast in the lion-hearted mould, he lived his life with a strong sense of justice, of chivalry towards females and of sticking up for the underdog, although, more often than not, it was he, Lancelot Arthur, who found himself in that role.

Unlike most new fathers of the time, Mr. Crabbe saw a great deal of his son. On July 14th, 1914 war was declared and soon after, Mr Crabbe received his conscription papers. He was sent to an army camp for basic training as a bombardier where, during his first week he inadvertently threw an imitation hand grenade in the wrong direction. Thereafter, he was transferred to the regimental kitchens where he succeeded in poisoning three captains with a ham salad in the Officers' Mess.

It was concluded by those in authority that with Frank Crabbe on their side, Britain would most certainly lose the war. They reviewed his qualifications and as a consequence, he was re-designated as a non-combatant pay clerk and tucked away in the vaults of the Bank of England. Those in authority felt a lot safer and were able to carry on with the war in peace.

Because of the shortage of barracks in Threadneedle Street and the relatively close proximity of Stanmore to the City of London, Private Crabbe was given a railway warrant and an extra shilling a day for subsistence and was allowed to spend every evening and almost every weekend at home.

As time passed it became obvious that Lancelot had inherited much from his parents. He was tall for his age, and thin, like his father. And following his mother's example he could often be found with his face buried in a comic – reading the words, not just looking at the cartoons and drawings like most other children. He was encouraged in his learning not only by his parents, but also by his class teacher, Miss Peach, at his first school, and this early interest in his education helped him develop an excellent memory.

Crabbe in all Innocence

Paradoxically, he could also be absent-minded, although at his tender age it was termed 'daydreaming'. He inherited the trait from his father, who demonstrated his forgetfulness all too frequently, on one occasion forgetting his own son.

The newly promoted Lance Corporal Crabbe had been sent by his wife to fetch Lancelot back from The Green where he was playing Good Guys and Germans with his friends from Felbridge Avenue. At the sight of the uniformed Mr. Crabbe marching towards them the other boys ran away and hid, leaving Lancelot tied to a tree where he was waiting to be tortured into giving away the Kaiser's plans.

Lance Corporal Crabbe, on seeing the knots they had tied to secure his son, called them back and demonstrated how to tie *proper* knots that wouldn't undo, a skill he learned in the Boy Scouts.

He had learned the skill well and was proud of the merit badge he'd been awarded. And he remembered exactly how to tie them now, as he found when he couldn't get them undone.

Leaving Lancelot tied to the tree, not that there was any choice in the matter, he returned home for a pair of scissors, and as his wife had just made a pot of tea, he settled down with a cup and began reading his paper, the scissors and his son having completely slipped his mind. Half an hour later, he was reminded by Mrs. Crabbe, who had by now realised her husband had returned alone.

But Frank Crabbe also had many good points. He had an inborn instinct for neatness, not only in columns of figures in his ledgers at the bank, but in all things, and he delighted in tidying up Lancelot's toy cupboard and lining up the tin soldiers according to rank, and in making sure the coloured pencils were always sharpened and pointing the same way in their wooden box.

Lancelot was, at least on the surface, a happy child. There was nothing particularly noticeable about him to indicate what *The Fates* had in store. No hint that he was destined to join the ranks of *Heroic Failures*. All that would come later.

As a young child he was always laughing but laughing longer and louder than his friends. Future generations would regard this characteristic as a sign of insecurity, a desire to be recognised and accepted. But, in his early years, if he was noticed at all, it was put down to showing off and something he would 'grow out of'.

In fact, when he laughed it was because others were laughing, not because he found a situation particularly amusing, but he wanted to be the same as everyone else and hid his lack of a sense of humour behind a happy façade. And so, he appeared to be a perfectly normal infant who, although born on a Wednesday, belied the traditional verse that 'Wednesday's child is full of woe'.

Crabbe in all Innocence

Through no lack of love or understanding but rather because of a lack of appreciation, Lancelot's inner needs weren't recognised and as a result he went through life trying harder. Not, it may be thought, a bad thing but in his case, it meant that if he found himself in a hole, it wouldn't occur to him that the obvious course was to stop digging. He would dig deeper.

His constant laughter was put down to having a happy disposition. His parents were therefore happy. Delighted, in fact, with their son.

With little Lancelot trotting beside them in his reins, Frank and Lillian visited their parents on alternate Sundays (the war permitting, which it nearly always did), Lillian's parents on grass cutting and duck pond days and Mr. and Mrs. Crabbe Senior on window cleaning and swings days. They gossiped, discussed the latest news from the front, sang around the piano and enjoyed one of the greatest of all British traditions – the Sunday roast. Each grandfather had 'contacts' so there was never any shortage of food.

In the following years, birthday parties were held for Lancelot with his friends from Felbridge Avenue and with his few friends from Belmont Junior and especially for his two grandfathers, who denied their advancing years by joining in gleefully with Pass the Parcel and Musical Chairs.

1918 arrived, a ceasefire was agreed, and the war ended. Acting-sergeant Crabbe once again became *Mr.*

Crabbe and resumed his peacetime job at the bank. But something was missing. At four years old, Lancelot was still an only child.

Puffing on their pipes in the garden of number 59, with slices of celebratory cake and bottles of brown ale within reach, Mr. Chadwick told Mr. Crabbe that since he was the father of the should-by-now-be-a-father-again, so to speak, it was up to him to have a word in his son's ear.

As an ordinary shop assistant of years before, Mr. Crabbe Senior would never have dreamed of approaching so delicate a subject with anyone, let alone his own son. But now, as *Manager* of Gillard & Co., (Ironmongers and General Hardware), he considered that since he had risen so far in the world, he should put his former sensibilities aside. He agreed to pursue the matter.

'Yes, Father, we'd dearly love another child,' Frank said, when his wife, mother and mother-in-law had taken Lancelot upstairs to try and rid him of the jelly and ice-cream he was wearing. Mr Chadwick remained in the garden, ostensibly sweeping up crumbs in the area immediately outside the window where he could easily hear what was being said.

'Trouble is, the walls of our house are so thin and when we get to the critical moment, if you follow, Lancelot always comes in and asks for a glass of water. It tends to put you off your stroke.'

'Have you thought of church?' his father asked.

17

'In what way? Praying?'

'Good Lord! No! By sending Lancelot to Sunday School. It will give you an hour or so to yourselves. Means you'll have to give up coming round Sundays for lunch, and there'll be no more cutting your grass and cleaning your windows on Sundays. You'll have to forget all that. You won't have the energy.'

'But it seems rather hypocritical,' the younger Mr. Crabbe replied, 'not to say, irreligious.'

'Nonsense, my boy! Sunday School's the answer. That's why it was invented. To give young people like you a little time to yourselves so you can 'go forth and multiply' – see? It's in the Bible. That's how we got your brother Robert.'

'And our Nancy!' called Mr. Chadwick, from the garden.

And so, the following week, Lancelot was taken by his mother to enrol in St. Michael's and All Angels sickeningly named junior branch, *St. Michael and his Little Angels*, and seven days after that, in the quietness and peace of their neat and clean semi, Frank and Lillian set about begetting him a neat and clean little sister.

It was not to be, however.

At least not until Galahad Tristram, and a year later, Percival Bedivere, had arrived.

But then, after three sons Mr. and Mrs. Crabbe were delighted to be blessed with a daughter. Throughout the latest pregnancy, both Frank and Lillian referred to

18

their unborn child as 'she' and went so far as to give her a name in advance, although Guinevere Iseult was actually christened Lucrezia Leonora as, by the time of her birth, Mrs. Crabbe had completely gone off books about King Arthur having read them *ad nauseam* at bedtime to her little boys and taken up reading about the Borgias instead.

Mr. and Mrs. Crabbe Senior and Mr. and Mrs. Chadwick, though equally delighted with the birth of their granddaughter, decided that 'enough was enough', that their children's semi was not large enough to accommodate further additions to the family, and that even though Frank had been promoted to Assistant Bank Manager with a salary commensurate with his status, it was decided Frank and Lillian simply must start practicing birth control. And it was left to Crabbe Senior to explain how to do it, whilst Mr. Chadwick once again applied his energies to sweeping up the spotlessly clean area outside the window.

The consequence of this further interview between father and son, (with a few hints from outside), resulted in grandsons one and two being withdrawn from the bosom of St. Michael's and his Little Angels, (number three and Lucrezia being too young to attend anyway) the lawn once again, being cut every second Sunday and the windows of 59, Felbridge Avenue being the envy of everyone who saw them.

As intended, it also called a halt to any further Crabbe productions.

The participants were, in the main, happy.

The exception was Lancelot, their first born, 'I don't want to give up Sunday School. I like it there,' he wailed.

'Well,' said Mr. Crabbe, 'you've still got your proper school, and on Sundays you can go to The Green with your friends. You like that.'

'I don't like Belmont Junior. I like Miss Peach, but I can't see the board.'

'Of course, you can! It's that big thing at the front.'

'Yes, I know it is, but I can't see what Miss Peach writes on it.'

Thus, it became clear that Lancelot had inherited another of his father's characteristics: he was short sighted.

Her husband being unable to get away from the bank during school hours, Mrs. Crabbe went to see Miss Peach on her own one lunchtime, leaving her three younger children in the care of a neighbour.

Miss Peach seemed far too young to be in charge of a class of twenty-five, but behind her pretty face was a concerned and caring common sense.

'Mrs. Crabbe, I am so sorry. I didn't realise. I thought Lancelot preferred to stay in at playtime because he seems to have developed a fondness for me, and I know he doesn't like to mix with the others. They can be rather rough, and your Lancelot is such a sensitive child. I now see he stays behind so he can get nearer the board to read what's written. He never said anything, and I'm afraid I didn't notice.'

'Can you move him to the front, Miss Peach?'

'Certainly, I can. But that is only a temporary solution. I think he should have his eyes tested, and if necessary, be fitted with a pair of spectacles. That apart,' she continued, 'I am glad to have this opportunity to speak to you. Please understand, Lancelot is a clever boy. He is intelligent and learns quickly, and he *remembers* what he learns. Obviously, he owes that to you and Mr. Crabbe. I wish all the parents of my other children took such an active role in their sons' education. But as we now know, he cannot see the board clearly enough and has devised his own strategy to overcome that. Others in my class do not read what I've written because they *cannot* read and as a consequence, I have to give most of my attention to them. That is why I think Lancelot should leave here.'

Horrified, Mrs. Crabbe said, 'You're *expelling* him?'

'No, no! He is the brightest in the class. But the others, who are slower to learn, are holding him back. It's my belief that Lancelot would do better – realise his potential, at another school. One that is more suited to develop his abilities.'

Within the week Lancelot had had his eyes tested, had been found to be suffering from myopia and was made to wear a pair of wire framed spectacles. With the cruelty of the young, he was called names and ridiculed by his classmates. But he didn't mind. He could see the board now perfectly, and as a result, soon left his class even further behind. He finished Belmont at the end of the term, and was glad to go, although his parting from Miss Peach was a tearful experience for both of them.

At White Gates, a small fee-paying school run by a stern and much feared Mrs. Helen, Lancelot prospered. He was not derided by his new friends for wearing glasses, but admired, because they made him look brainy.

He was, by no means, the brightest in his class. He was made to work, but he rose to the challenge, and whilst no longer top in every subject (and always bottom in art and games), he tried hard and pleased his parents by almost always receiving good marks and getting excellent reports.

But, in regard to his schooling, his parents faced another problem. Girls could complete their education at White Gates, but boys were only taught there until they reached eleven years of age and then were obliged to move on.

Mr. and Mrs. Crabbe were summoned to the school for an interview one evening. They found themselves sitting to attention and were careful not to fidget when Mrs. Helen addressed them in her mausoleum-like study.

'I have been considering Lancelot's future,' she announced, 'I have looked at all the other private schools in the area but can find nothing I think of as

22

suitable for him. I have therefore, cast my net wider. Particularly, I believe Lancelot would do well at a minor public school. *Major* public schools take boys from the age of thirteen, only lesser schools accept them at a lower age.'

Mr. Crabbe put up his hand and was granted permission to speak by Mrs. Helen raising her right eyebrow in his direction.

He stood, 'If you please, Mrs. Helen, whilst my wife and I are extremely grateful for your interest in our son's future...'

'Extremely grateful,' Mrs. Crabbe interrupted to emphasise her husband's words, but said nothing more when she received a look that informed her she had *not* been given permission to speak.

Humbled, she lapsed into silence as Mr. Crabbe continued, 'Err. Quite. *Very extremely* grateful indeed. But there is the question of cost. I believe fees at such schools can be quite expensive, and Lancelot has two younger brothers and a sister.'

'I have, of course, considered that aspect,' said Mrs. Helen, who spoke as if she had (naturally) considered everything.

Mr. Crabbe thought he was about to be ordered to sit down. So, he sat.

'Several of the lesser public schools offer a limited number of scholarships for the sons of people from the lower end...' she paused and corrected herself, 'from your type of background. It goes without saying that successful applicants must be above average intelligence, which Lancelot certainly is, and preferably *sporty*, which he most certainly isn't. Such establishments set great store by achievement in sport. They are wrong, of course.'

Mr. and Mrs. Crabbe both dared a murmured, 'Of course.'

'Quite. But there it is. As to fees, everything is paid for, normally from a bequest or trust set up by a former pupil, a successful businessman who wishes to be seen as something of a philanthropist, probably to help him become even more successful. All *you* need to provide is pocket money and the occasional cost of a school outing. Tuition fees, books, meals, uniform and lodgings are provided without charge.'

Mrs. Crabbe put her hand up. Mrs. Helen's right eyebrow rose in her direction.

She stood, 'Mrs. Helen, if I may...erm, did I understand you to say 'lodgings'?'

'Yes, you did. Public schools take in boarders. Lancelot will live at the school during term time. He will sleep in a dormitory.'

'But he's never been away from home before. Who will look after him?' She resumed her seat, lines of genuine concern appearing all over her face.

'He will learn to look after himself. It will be the making of him. Now,' she picked up some papers from her desk, 'after serious consideration, I have decided that *Chantry*, a public school in Wiltshire, would best

24

suit Lancelot's talents. An examination to determine who shall be awarded the scholarships is to be held there on Saturday the 25th. I have put your son's name down.'

Mrs. Helen stood.

Mr. and Mrs. Crabbe therefore stood, their mouths slightly gaping.

'That will be all,' her eyebrow indicating the study door.

It was only when they had walked halfway home that they realised, as was ever the case in matters concerning their eldest son, their opinion had not been sought.

2: RASPUTIN

The Reverend Walter Wilkes-Passmore (BA Hons), twenty-eighth Headmaster of Chantry, was a man of high standards and high principles, which is no more than you would expect from the Head of such a renowned seat of learning.

He also had a high-pitched voice, which was unfortunate, for when he got angry (a common occurrence with the Reverend gentleman), he didn't shout, he squeaked.

Paradoxically, the one thing about him that wasn't high was his height. He had been born with his left leg longer than his right, although he always claimed it was his right leg that was shorter than his left. It seemed to be a matter of importance to him, but whichever way you viewed the problem, the fact was, he was wonky. When he tried to stand upright, he leaned to one side as if being blown by a strong wind.

As a boy he had undergone three operations intended to balance him up. But the result was failure, as it so often was in the early days of corrective surgery. And so, he had been discharged from the Children's Hospital with a brown surgical boot which had an extra-high heel and a very thick rubber sole. He was also given a piece of paper signed by a senior surgeon which stated that he was in *prime physical condition* and a walking stick because, despite the surgical boot, he still had a pronounced limp.

As he grew into maturity, his feet also grew, and the brown boot was replaced several times. But *he* hardly grew, and he was forced to accept, albeit with very bad grace, that he was destined to live with the top of his head a mere five feet two inches above the ground.

As a boy, he was bullied at school, even persecuted. Other boys held competitions among themselves to see which of them could best imitate his limp, and if he were there to witness the proceedings, so much the better.

He fought back, using whatever non-physical means he had at his disposal. He became malicious and spiteful, vindictive and sly. But for all that, he was bright, quick to learn and intelligent.

He found that whilst on one hand, he was the object of ridicule by his schoolfellows, on the other, he was pitied and over-protected by the masters, a situation he exploited to its fullest advantage. Indeed, it didn't take him long to play one off against the other. He became manipulative and devious too. But above all, he became ambitious. He developed a determination to succeed at everything he attempted.

He would get to the top.

And he did. By fair means or foul, and after his marriage, with much whispering and threats in the correct ears by Mrs. Wilkes-Passmore, he rose to eminence. Not without problems and disappointments along the way, which he accepted, put behind him and carried on. And, as he progressed, he became a better person.

He was embarrassed by being un-tall, which he felt to be his only fault, apart from his uneven legs, and like so many of his diminutive stature, he had an innate need to prove himself. (Un-tall was an adjective of his own invention. He refused to think of himself as *short.*) With maturity, he was able to rid himself of some of the unfortunate traits he'd acquired with his un-tallness.

As success came his way, he stopped being malicious and spiteful and became pompous and self-satisfied instead.

He developed a code of conduct for running his life, *a set of rules*, which, he was convinced would help lesser men were they to adopt it.

He was proud of his rules, borne as they were out of years of experience and embellished with a considerable amount of imagination and invention. It was his intention, when he retired, to publish his code in a book of memoirs that would contain salutary lessons for the reader, based on *his* rules. Mankind would be forever in his debt.

Although he was presently alone in the School Chapel, one of his rules now forbade him from giving vent to a trapped pocket of wind he felt building up in the area between his waistcoat and spine.

28

Chris Hare

It was a regrettable fact that as an ordinary schoolmaster years before, in attempting to impress upon his pupils some of his own axioms of life, including the importance of good manners, he had unconsciously copied some of *their* rather uncivilised customs. They would have no compunction in releasing a trapped belch, and the louder the better. It would be a great relief to him now, were he to liberate it. He was sorely tempted. It was causing him considerable discomfort. With difficulty, he forbore. Not in here, not *in the sanctity of the School Chapel*, by far the most ancient of the many school buildings at Chantry.

He had, as many men do in middle age, developed a paunch. The cause of which was not only the passing years, but the taking of too many schools meals – huge fried breakfasts, and steak and kidney puddings for lunch followed by jam roly-poly; all the types of foodstuffs that helped adolescents build strong bones and develop muscles but did nothing complimentary for the over fifties.

Added to this ill-advised diet, there was the fact that he was physically unable to take exercise. Indeed, the only regular exercise he got was the beating of miscreant boys after Monday Assembly and his daily walk to the Chapel after luncheon.

He lowered his rotund frame carefully and wearily into his favourite pew, the one at the side of the altar behind the one that wasn't there anymore. It had collapsed two years before, when Mrs. Wilkes-

Passmore had sat on it. Surprisingly, it wasn't the bulk of Mrs. W-P, considerable though it was, that caused the collapse. The previous week, during a particularly long sermon, the structure had been severely weakened by the sixteen-year-old Honourable Bartholomew de Vere Llewellyn-Smythe's attempt at carving his name and title on the back of the pew with his Swiss Army penknife. Mrs. Wilkes-Passmore had been the final straw.

The heir to the Eighth Earl of Yeading had been made to stand for all meals and lessons during the following week as a penance. Not for carving his name, but for carving his title. Using one's title whilst still a pupil was not the Chantry way.

Bartholomew could not have sat in any comfort anyway. His sitting area being the target of the Headmaster's cane for a period seemingly longer than the sermon that had resulted in his misdemeanour.

The Headmaster gratefully removed his shoe and his boot and stretched out his legs, such as they were, in the space thus afforded by a future English peer with a long name and a Swiss Army penknife. *Is that all they have? The Swiss army? No rifles? Just little red penknives.*

Behind him, sunlight filtered through a stained-glass window depicting St. George slaying the dragon, the colours forming delicate patterns on his balding head. Of all the stained glass in the Chapel, the St. George was the one he liked the least. It reminded him of his wife, Harriet, who bore an uncanny resemblance, not to the dragon but to St. George. It was not that he didn't want to be reminded of Mrs. Wilkes-Passmore, indeed, he could hardly forget her, but just not in here, in his private place.

His eyes briefly scanned the black Honours Boards that were mounted at regular intervals around the cold, whitewashed stone walls, and proudly displayed in faded gold lettering, the names and brief details of the many men of Chantry who had, when the call came, given their lives in the defence of their country. Or, if not to defend their country, had answered the call to invade someone else's. A detail, he thought. They were all just as dead.

He saw the names and dates of 'Col. Angus M A McBeattie MC, Royal Highlanders, 1821–1857, Meerut, India'. The late Colonel had been the unwitting cause of a legal dispute involving Chantry with his bestowal of 'Two Scholarships for Two Sons of the Poor at Five Guineas a Term for Two Hundred Years'. His generosity ensured that the families from the lower end of society would be represented at Chantry so that the others, those born to privilege and wealth, would learn to tolerate lesser beings, which could only be a good measure in furthering the ambitions of the British Empire.

It was when the Colonel had gone off to Calcutta to slaughter the inhabitants, a hugely popular pastime during the early years of Queen Victoria's reign, and not all appreciated by the ungrateful natives who revolted and ended his days by hanging him from a banyan tree, that it was found that the terms of his endowment were irrevocable. In later years, no matter what exorbitant sums in the way of fees were extracted for the education of the sons of the wealthy, those 'Two Sons of the Poor' would receive what was arguably, one of the best educations in the whole of England for a few guineas a year from the late Colonel's estate.

The Reverend W-P had taken steps to ensure that such a state of affairs would never again be repeated.

His eyes moved away from Colonel McBeattie's inscription whose very name deeply offended the parsimonious section of the Wilkes-Passmore brain.

Glancing up and down the lists of the dead, he realised that there was hardly a country in the world that didn't have at least one Old Chantovian lying six feet below its surface.

Not Switzerland. Everywhere else, but Switzerland. *Was neutrality another word for cowardice?*

One of the Head's few regrets in life was that his own military career had been so brief. He would have loved to have been involved in something like the glory that was Waterloo or Blenheim. He pictured himself at the head of the troops, fearlessly charging on horseback with flashing and bloodied sabre toward the Russian guns at Balaclava, killing everyone in his path, and forcing the more intelligent ones to hide. Or, at Ypres in the last war. With W-P in charge, the Kaiser would have realised his defeat was inevitable. Immediate surrender from the Huns, and a statue of himself in Trafalgar Square.

Such were his musings as he looked up beyond the Honours Board to the hammer beam roof of the Chapel high above. For a moment he considered releasing the belch, just to see if he could hear it echo. Certainly, coughs echoed annoyingly in here, as did the sound of a hymn book being dropped, or a junior boy being clipped around the ear. He had read that the quack of a duck was the only sound that didn't produce an echo and that science was unable to explain the phenomenon. Perhaps science ought to try a duck or two in the Chapel, he thought.

But not now. Not during *his* time. During the week, the Chapel was strictly out of bounds to everyone: masters, pupils, scientists and ducks. He even privately resented it being used on Sundays for Divine Service. For this holy place, he had decreed, was *his private sanctuary* even if tradition dictated it had to be lent back to God once a week.

This was where, for a peaceful hour after lunch, he was able to get away from screaming boys, demanding masters, Mrs. Wilkes-Passmore, and the incessant rattle of Mrs. Pearl's dreadful typewriter.

The thought of lunch reminded him of that mysterious Sunday evening smell, and he interrupted his thoughts for a moment and sniffed, and for the

33

hundredth time wondered where it came from. And why only on Sundays, never during the week?

He looked around and smiled inwardly, forgetting about the strange odour for the moment (which he couldn't smell today, it not being a Sunday), as he thought of his little deception. It was assumed by everyone that this sacred time was to give the Headmaster an hour of peace to meditate and pray and to seek guidance from above. In one way, this assumption was correct, although God was rarely invited to intervene or help with his plans. For that, in fact, was what he did here. He dreamed, yes, but most of all, he planned.

For Doctor Wilkes-Passmore was a great planner. He never left anything to chance. Every tiny detail was considered. This had been his way since he was a young boy, and the practice had served him well. *If you fail to plan, you plan to fail* was a homily often quoted by his own Headmaster, and he'd never forgotten it.

In fact, he rarely forgot anything. His prodigious memory could effortlessly recall dates, names, lists, teams and almost everything he had ever read because he was a great reader as well. In his own opinion, he was great at most things.

Although, it had to be admitted, he had suffered from a Christian upbringing, and a dictum of that faith was that you were expected to be humble, on occasion. This, he found, didn't come naturally. He had had a successful career. He had come to terms with a physical handicap, endured ridicule, endured Mrs. Wilkes-Passmore's 'support' for many years, had become the most highly qualified curate in the whole of the Church of England, served his country in the army and had been an exemplary schoolmaster.

All of this he achieved practically by his own efforts (with, he allowed, a certain amount of bullying from Mrs. W-P). But whilst she was the brawn behind their marriage and his career, *he* was the brains, and consequently, he found humility a difficult skill to master. Not that he ever really tried.

Yes, he'd had a successful career, and to mix metaphors, which of course, he'd never do, he'd climbed almost to the top of his tree – still a few rungs of the ladder to go, but by his own ability and effort, he would make it to the very top. Even with the successes so far achieved, he still harboured an ambition to move on. There were *major* public schools and masterships of ancient universities.

He checked his watch. Time was moving on and he had yet to go over his usual welcoming speech for tomorrow. He reluctantly bent forward and replaced his boot and shoe. In so doing he compressed his stomach and almost released the belch in a far more undignified manner than releasing it through his throat.

Outside in the afternoon sun, he gazed at his kingdom. *All this, from such humble beginnings. All these acres. All these old buildings and the modern facilities. His staff, both teaching and support. Matrons for each House, gardeners, cooks, laundresses, cleaners, groundsmen – all under his command. Life was good. There wasn't a single cloud on his horizon.*

W-P was right. There wasn't a cloud on his horizon. But just below it, out of sight and it was coming to Chantry.

A dark cloud by the name of Lancelot Arthur Crabbe.

Chris Hare

3: FOUNDERS

The Colonel's bequest was not by any means the only one to cause distress to the Headmasters of Chantry, particularly in the early days. There was a 'sack of coal at Christmastide for the poorest widow in the village'. Who received that? There were so many claimants, some still waiting for their husbands to do the decent thing by dying.

There were 'Four fresh loaves of rye upon Lady Day to the poorest orphans', and strangest of all, 'A strong new hazel switch upon Easter Sunday with which to beat the poor vagrants so that they may be cleansed of sin'.

Fortunately, the endowments for these bequests had been used up within a few years of the benefactor's death, and thereafter the poorest widow went without her sack of coal and the orphans starved. The vagrants continued to be beaten on Easter Sunday and on any other day they were caught within the boundaries of the village, the 'strong hazel switches' being generously donated by the incumbent of the church who felt it was his Christian duty to ensure vagrants, beggars and anyone else to whom the vicar took a dislike, was given a severe bashing for the benefit of their eternal souls.

There were many other legacies, all equally bizarre and all referring to the poor. Such legacies fortunately ceased when either the money was gone or the time had expired, or they were conveniently forgotten when Chantry ran out of poor people, widows re-married or orphans were adopted (or starved to death).

The responsibility for this state of affairs, this obsession with remembering the poor people after the benefactor was dead, lay firmly on the shoulders of *Ye Ten Goode Men of Chantrie* as the founders of Chantry School were originally known. Though very rich themselves, they clearly thought their encouragement of others to be generous to poor people would smooth their own path to heaven when the time came.

It was interesting to note that in those far-off days, the philanthropist ensured that his beneficence came from the purses of his heirs and not from his own pocket while he was still on earth enjoying life to the full, completely ignoring the needs of the poor and needy.

In fact, there is no record of the *Ye Ten Goode Men* themselves donating anything at all – coal, loaves or beatings for vagrants. Given their penchant for changing sides to ensure their own safety, it may be assumed their generosity never went beyond their own front doors. The only record they left was the School Charter, an obviously ancient document, written on waxed vellum in Ancient Latin and hung with the seals of the Founders.

The Charter had been donated to the British Museum by Doctor Cholmondeley, Headmaster of Chantry 1801 – 1812, for an undisclosed sum, which, according to the

Principles laid down by the Founders, would have most certainly been passed onto the poor. Or not.

Hundreds of visiting Americans had admired the document in the Reading Room at the Museum. After all, it was almost older than America itself. *Admired* but not read since most of them had difficulty with English, let alone the flowery script of a long dead language.

The Founders of Chantry, everyone a diehard Cavalier who had sided with Charles I in the Civil War but who had changed sides to become fervent Cromwellian supporters when the King lost his head on that freezing January morning in Whitehall, changed sides once more when Charles II was restored to the throne.

Unsure of what the future may hold, or of which side they should be on when the future was *held*, they compromised, as Englishmen do when they don't really understand what is going on and decided to hide somewhere until more settled circumstances were re-established.

They discovered the out-of-the-way village of Chantrie in Wiltshire, a county that had supported Cromwell and his Roundheads in the Civil War. The village was close to the Wiltshire/Dorset border, and was thus most conveniently situated. Dorset had supported the King, and should Royalists question their motives in settling in enemy country, they agreed to say they'd got lost when they had moved *en bloc* from their manor houses and estates elsewhere in the kingdom.

On the southern side of Chantrie Hill they used their Christian Principles to evict the incumbent farmers, took over vast tracts of land and built larger and far grander houses than those they'd abandoned after the war. They founded a small school near the church on the summit of the hill for their sons' educations and endowed it with strict Puritan Principles in case the Parliamentarians should stage a successful counterrevolution. And, in case they didn't, they endowed it with strict Royalist Principles as well.

The resulting chaos ensured that nobody really understood what the Founders had intended, and so successive 'servants of the school' had read into the Charter whatever they wanted and whatever suited the political climate of the time. It was similar, in many ways, to the way most religions had started and evolved.

In time, the 'servants' became Headmasters. The school was greatly enlarged as it took possession of the houses and lands of the original Founders as, one by one, they were executed, incarcerated, transported or simply died, their homes being used as accommodation for pupils and masters or transformed into classrooms.

As the reputation of the school grew, so did the number of pupils, and boys from neighbouring counties were accepted into the fold.

It was deemed necessary to consolidate the lodgings into two of the largest houses. And, continuing the policy of sitting on the fence, the houses were named 'Cromwell' after Oliver Cromwell, the Lord Protector, should the Parliamentarians ask, or Thomas Cromwell, Henry VIII's Lord Chancellor, in case it's the Royalists enquiring too closely.

The other house, Charles, was named for Charles Fleetwood, a general in Cromwell's army, or Charles I or Charles II. It didn't matter which so long as they were both Royalists, which they were.

The system worked well, and as the school expanded it sub-divided again with the creation of two more houses, their names continuing the stratagem of self-protection so successfully espoused since the beginning. 'Henry' evoked either the memory of Henry Ireton, a signatory of Charles I death warrant or Henry Wilmot, Gentleman of the Bedchamber to Charles II.

The fourth house, and the only one that didn't need two interpretations of its name, was 'Keyes'. Sir Ambrose Keyes had been a soldier of fortune who had fought at different times for both sides in the Civil War, depending on which paid him the greater fortune. It was from this coat of arms that Chantry took its motto:

'CONSTANS ET FIDELIS'
(Constant and Faithful)

41

The village church was taken over and became the School Chapel. The churchyard where generations of dead villagers lay was levelled and turned into the Headmaster's garden. Because of the enriched soil all manner of flowers, vegetables and fruit trees were successfully grown.

At some time in the 18th century the Headmaster moved to a grander residence that had become available, and his former home was taken over by the four Housemasters and their wives. Their staff were given rooms in the lofts of the adjoining stables.

As it grew, the school prospered and became famous.

The gentry sent their sons there. Future Prime Ministers were educated at the school, and before long, the name Chantry came to be understood by everyone as being a school, rather than the village after which it was named. The Royalist Principles allowed and encouraged their sons to attend the school, but then the Parliamentary Principles entered the equation, and it was decreed that titles weren't to be used at Chantry.

The boys were known to each other and to their masters by their family name, although, most soon acquired a nickname. But it was a Principle, shared by both camps, that each boy should be treated as if he were of equal status to the next fellow, regardless of the next fellow's position in society at birth although, as the years went by, the son of an earl was considered more equal than say, the son of a baron.

Chris Hare

In the fullness of time, some of the descendants of the original inhabitants of the village, those who had survived the coming of *Ye Ten Goode Men*, returned and established their homes in the few areas of the hill not taken by the school. Some went back to farming, but others, those with an eye for business, opened shops which gratefully supplied all the school's many needs.

There was a gentleman's tailor, a hatter, bootmaker, two grocery shops and a general store, three tearooms, a bakery, and a butchery, supplying meat of dubious ancestry.

Thus, as is the way of the world, the village of Chantry grew. More housing was built, running water installed, a post office and a bank opened, there were two public houses, electricity and with the coming of the Great Western Railway, Chantry got its own station.

Although it was always referred to as 'the Village', Chantry had become a small town with a small Council and a large Mayor.

During late Victorian times, a mansion on the outskirts of the village was converted into a Catholic Girls' Boarding School, and so Chantry began the task of re-inventing itself again, with more houses being built and more businesses being opened to cater for the needs of St. Margaret's.

Contact between the two schools was limited. They were not only situated at opposite ends of the village: they were opposite in many other areas. One was a girls' school with mainly Catholic girls attending and the other was for boys, mainly Protestant, who were taught by masters wearing traditional mortarboards and gowns. St. Margaret's was staffed by a teaching order of nuns, who wore habits of rough black wool topped with large white headdresses of well starched linen.

Chantry's Catholic pupils were allowed to attend Mass at St. Margaret's, provided they behaved themselves, which they did, and also that they didn't talk to the girls, which they didn't.

The two schools exchanged polite Christmas greetings and apart from the occasional loan of books or equipment, there was rarely any dialogue between the two establishments.

A point of interest among many of the senior boys of Chantry was the window of the ladies' Haberdashery shop that had opened in the village and sold items of 'young persons' clothing. The purpose of certain female garments led to wild speculation from among the young men as to what exactly they were used to hold up or keep in place, when the said items appeared on display in the shop window.

A polite note from the Headmaster of Chantry asking that the 'items' be removed was completely ignored by the proprietor, a Mr. Abraham Silverman, who also laughed off the threat of excommunication by the Head of St. Margaret's, Reverend Mother Agnes, a distant relation of the 9th Marquis of Queensbury who had formulated the Queensbury Rules of Boxing. The

Reverend Mother, forgetting both her pedigree and vow of abstinence from violence, had called upon Mr. Silverman and, following a discussion on 'sinful objects' that failed to produce a satisfactory result (for her), she felled him with what the Marquis would have described as a 'low punch'.

In fact, it wasn't a punch but a knee. The result was the same and the offending articles were removed from the window display as soon as Mr. Silverman recovered the use of his legs.

Following the incident, relations between the two schools became, if not warmer then slightly less cold and distant. And what, nowadays, would be called 'dialogue' was begun, mainly by St. Margaret's, as they felt more benevolent because it was *their* Head who had won the battle of the 'items'.

Similarly, relations with the shopkeepers in the rest of the village remained peaceful. No one wanted to risk the wrath of Mother Agnes, and anything that could possibly be misconstrued, or might be considered a 'sinful object' was removed from window displays. Thus cucumbers, bananas and coconuts disappeared from public view.

The success of the school became self-perpetuating. Fathers, themselves educated at Chantry, had no hesitation in sending their sons there, who would in turn, send their own sons. It appeared at one time as if every noble or wealthy family in England was represented at the school.

But times change.

Families who owed their wealth to a long-dead aunt who had become the mistress of a long-dead king, and had managed to produce a child or two, were richly rewarded. The daughters of the union were married off to the sons of wealthy families who thought they would become even richer through a marital alliance with the king. The sons were given dukedoms, and they too made respectable marriages in the knowledge that riches and a title would be considered far more acceptable to society than being born on the wrong side of the blanket.

Usually, the children of these arranged marriages, because of the constant interbreeding, were stupid and were hidden away.

The boys were hidden at Chantry, where they were taught dancing, fencing and hunting.

They were taught everything a gentleman was expected to know at the time, which meant that when they left Chantry, they had no common sense and knew nothing of commerce or business. As a result, family fortunes were frittered to nothing, were invested unwisely, or were drunk or gambled away until all that remained was the title.

The school became less self-perpetuating. Those families thus affected were forced, because of their own financial difficulties coupled with ever-increasing fees, to seek other less expensive places of education for their sons.

To counter the ensuing loss of revenue, the Headmaster and Board of Governors sought to make up their losses by taking in the sons of the newly rich: people who had made fortunes from railways, mining, mills and slavery. And so, the pendulum swung back as more boys from lesser families swelled the ranks at Chantry.

An entrance examination was introduced to ensure that pupils were able to demonstrate a certain standard of intelligence but was abandoned when it was found that most of them couldn't. Consequently, the only requirement was one of money. If you could afford the fees, your son was welcomed with open arms.

But with the coming of the newly rich, an unforeseen problem arose. The boys, particularly those from the untamed north, from Durham and Scotland, were unable to speak to anyone from outside the areas from which they came. At least, they *could* speak, but they couldn't be understood, which was a difficulty.

It was solved by the simple expedient of elocution lessons, and studying the works of great poets, all for the extra charge of a guinea a term. Dancing and hunting were removed from the curriculum but fencing remained as it was still considered to be a 'gentlemanly pursuit'.

The Head decreed that every boy at his school should be taught to speak with the same accent so that there was no obvious division of class, *Ye Ten Goode Men of Chantrie* would have been proud of him. Further, he announced, the accent should be his own, Cambridge-educated one.

Making the boys put plums in their mouths – hence the expression and getting them to recite Shakespeare, accomplished this.

The idea worked brilliantly, and within a few months of a boy starting at Chantry he was able to enunciate with hardly a trace of his former, often rural, accent.

The unfortunate side of this was that when pupils returned home for the school holidays, their parents were unable to understand *them*. Fathers who had been 'pa' became 'pater'. Younger siblings, formerly addressed with phrases beginning with words like 'Now, you'm look 'ere thee', were deeply impressed when their older brother began a sentence with 'I say, old man…'.

Upon seeing how successful the experiment was, the Head decided to go a step further with his desire, in line with *his* version of the original Principle, of making everyone equal.

He introduced the unheard-of proposal of a *school uniform*, an idea that was soon copied by virtually every school in the country. Until then, boys had attended classes wearing whatever they wanted. Those from better off families, who wished to dress as dandies, did so. Whilst those from slightly humbler origins, unable to afford such luxury, dressed in far humbler apparel.

The Head, having rid his pupils of such a diversity of accents that betrayed the speaker's class, now accomplished the same ideal in the matter of clothing.

He did this by arranging for his son-in-law to open a gentlemen's haberdashery establishment in the village. Not only did he arrange it, he financed it in return for 50% of the profits.

He further arranged, with the father of one of the boys, a rich mill owner from Lancashire, for the purchase of vast quantities of broadcloth that he then had made into tailcoats, breeches and waistcoats. It was important to him that all the pupils, whatever their background, looked, sounded and dressed alike. To ensure this, he issued a further decree to the effect that *all school clothing* must be obtained only from Chantry Haberdashery, 'suppliers of fine clothing to the sons of gentlefolk'.

Thus, he ensured the closure of the original haberdashery and, in keeping with his usual practices, bought up its stock at a fraction of its true worth.

It was whilst planning to open a barber's shop, and on his way to bank a bagful of gold guineas, that he suffered a heart attack and dropped dead. His replacement as Head, a Cambridge graduate himself, continued the example of his predecessor by opening a small business in the village to be run by his wife, a gifted needlewoman.

49

Thereafter, the School Prefects were permitted to wear embroidered fancy waistcoats as a mark of their office. This produced a good income for the Head's wife and kept her working late at her little shop. The Head himself, was kept busy in the evenings giving French lessons to their parlour maids and cooks. He ensured his wife would remain at her embroidery a little longer each evening by inventing House Prefects, who, as may be guessed, were also permitted to wear fancy waistcoats.

This, it was said, was to follow the Principle of equality, making House Prefects equal in statue, but not in authority, to their School Prefect counterparts.

The business side of Chantry didn't stop with school fees, uniforms and waistcoats.

Parents of boys, deeply impressed with their son's upper-class accents (although not always understanding what was being said) wished to emulate the boys' obsession with being equal with each other, although in their case, it was necessary to be equal to *other* parents.

To accommodate this need, Mr. Johnstone-Lloyd, the immediate predecessor of the present Headmaster, opened two establishments in the village. One, for fathers, supplying suits of clothes in the 'gentleman farmer' style – flat check hats, tweed jackets with leather patches at the elbows, and plus fours. For the ladies, conveniently situated next door, there were also tweed jackets, tweed skirts and woollen dark brown stockings. All to be worn when the school was open to parents to check on their sons' progress, to speak to masters and to make sure that they were all being terribly equal.

Rolls-Royces were left with their chauffeurs in the car park of one of the public houses and parents walked the rest of the way to the school, trying to look as if they had just got off the bus.

It was nothing but inverted snobbery.

But it was the Chantry way.

4: WELCOME to CHANTRY

The Fates had decreed that Lancelot was to spend much of his future life at Chantry in a state of anxiety. And if not anxious, then embarrassed and often terrified.

He'd been told during his time at White Gates, that his forced laughter was nothing more than a pretence for getting himself noticed. The innocently conceived strategy had worked on Miss Peach and with his family while younger, but no longer. He was told, none too gently, to act his age.

The teaching staff at White Gates, though generally well meaning, suffered from a lack of understanding, as did so many in authority in those far-off days. When they told him to stop showing off, he stopped, but the insecurity he felt inside still remained, now exposed but unrecognised by those who should have seen, and clearly visible to anyone who cared to exploit it. Without the cover of his contrived laughter, his anxieties, embarrassment and terror were often exposed.

But he was never as terrified as were his parents when they accompanied him to Chantry two days before the start of his first term.

For Mr. and Mrs. Crabbe *were* terrified – terrified on his behalf, of what the future held for their eldest son.

Throughout the journey from Stanmore, via Paddington and on to Wiltshire, they displayed completely false expressions of confidence and happiness entirely for the benefit of Lancelot. They laughed hugely at anything and everything, chatted excitedly and pointed out interesting features of the landscape as the train sped through the English countryside.

Lancelot didn't join in with his parents' exuberance as he sat between them in the otherwise empty compartment, nose buried in his School Rules book, and only occasionally glancing up to see a windmill or a distant oak tree. Afterall, he had seen it all before when Mr. and Mrs. Crabbe had taken him to Chantry to sit the McBeattie Scholarship examination.

In other compartments up and down the train, the atmosphere couldn't have been more different. The parents of other new boys were also experiencing mixed, but different feelings. There was relief at the thought of getting rid of their sons for the next twelve weeks, and sorrow for the staff at Chantry who would be on the receiving end.

None of the other parents had visited the school before. They had arranged a place for their son by telephone, telegram or post, and having paid a term's fees in advance, considered that the sending of a large cheque three times a year absolved them from taking any further part or real interest in their sons' education thereafter, other than to deliver him to the school today.

Crabbe in all Innocence

Lancelot experienced conflicting emotions during the journey: an end to the familiar, the beginning of the unknown.

He was certainly excited at the prospect of starting his new life, but at the same time, was saddened at the thought of leaving the past behind, his brothers, his sister, friends from Felbridge Avenue, and of course, his parents. *Why were they so wildly enthusiastic? Were they pleased to be losing him from their lives?* They weren't. Last night, Mrs. Crabbe had cried herself to sleep.

Her husband had done his best to comfort her, and when at last she drifted off into a troubled, dream-filled sleep, he found himself still wide awake. He thumped his pillow, turned over, and tried counting sheep but in his mind, the sheep became schoolboys.

Little lost schoolboys in smart uniforms.

At midnight, he gave up, aware his constant tossing and turning might wake Mrs. Crabbe, and she would start crying again and Mr. Crabbe, like any other loving husband, hated to see his wife upset.

He looked in on his children, all sleeping peacefully. *What does the world hold for you?* he asked himself but made no reply.

He crept downstairs to make a pot of tea and then, in the stillness of the dining room and with only the mantelpiece clock making any noise, he decided to unpack Lancelot's trunk to repack it. It didn't need doing – he had already done it twice, but he did it anyway.

Under the neatly folded, clean and clearly labelled clothes he found Mister Red Ted, little Lucrezia's favourite teddy bear, which she had given her eldest brother as a remembrance. Even at her tender age, she *understood*. And there was Galahad's conker – a niner, no less. And Percy's lucky elastic band. Prize possessions. All given freely, with much affection. Lancelot had not wanted to take them, but when cautioned by his father, 'You must never refuse a gift from a child,' he relented, and was secretly glad he had.

Mr. Crabbe, by no means for the first time, realised he was a very fortunate man to have such a loving family.

He patted the brown cardboard box which contained a present he had bought Lancelot as a reward for gaining his place at Chantry – a Kodak 'Box Brownie' camera, then repacked the trunk and closed the lid, checked (again) that it was clearly addressed, finished his tea and went back to bed, where sleep eluded him for most of the night.

The windows of the coaches, as the train chugged seemingly exhausted into the pretty little station, were dripping rivulets of steam. Behind one, Mrs. Crabbe's face was running with tears. She had been building up her mental strength to cope with the parting, to show a brave face, but now as the moment drew closer her courage deserted her and she gave way to her emotions.

Mr. Crabbe, himself, having to fight back tears, put a consoling arm around his wife and whispered, 'There, there.' It was completely inadequate, but he couldn't trust himself to say more. Even those two words of comfort were punctuated by a barely concealed sob.

Lancelot, embarrassed by his parents' behaviour, stared unseeingly through the window as the train finally drew to a stop.

A whistle blew, a man with a handcart hurried by to the baggage car at the far end of the train, and a strangled voice announced over the tannoy system that they had arrived at Chantry Junction.

As one, twenty-three boys in twenty-three compartments closed their books of School Rules and put them away in their satchels. And as one, they rose and moved to the windows, hoping for a sight of their new home.

Most used a new white handkerchief to wipe away the steam from the glass, some used the backs of their hands, and a few wiped the windows clean with the sleeve of their school blazer. The latter received a swipe.

Doors began opening, and people who lived in Chantry or had business there started leaving the train.

Behind them, twenty-three boys were held in place with a firm grip on their shoulder by their mothers who, suddenly and tearfully, feeling pangs of guilt, now

56

decided they didn't want to lose their sons after all, and ignored the fact that their husbands had opened the carriage doors and were trying to eject their son by pushing his other shoulder, once more giving encouraging words such as 'this is it', or 'no going back now'. Or, in one case from a father who wore a bushy and obviously military handlebar moustache, 'over the top'.

But being English, they waited for someone else to make the first move. The Crabbe faction was first to get down from the train. And the rest, being the rest, followed and once on the platform, just stood there, looking at each other, looking up and down, looking for a Mr. Pinder.

'Yes, indeed,' said Mr. Crabbe, glancing at the letter he had taken from his inside pocket, 'Mrs. Pearl, the Headmaster's secretary, says we will be met by a Mr. Pinder. I wonder where he is.'

The man pushing the cart, now loaded with school trunks, made his way slowly past.

'Excuse me. You obviously have some connection with Chantry School. I wonder if you'd be able to point out Mr. Pinder to me?'

The man stopped, and gratefully lowered the handles of his cart.

'Certainly, I'm Ernie, groundsman,' he said with the soft burred accent of Wiltshire, at the same time withdrawing a filthy spotted handkerchief from his trouser pocket and dabbing at the sweat on his brow, 'See the booking office there?'

He pointed.

'Oh, yes. Yes.'

'And see that gent standing on his own holding a clipboard?'

'I do, yes. The gentleman wearing a gown and mortarboard?'

'That's the one. Well, believe or not, that there is Mr. Pinder.'

'Thank you very much, Mr. Groundsman,' replied Mr. Crabbe, pressing a penny into his open hand.

'You'm welcome,' he said touching a finger to his forehead, 'You'm from Lunnon?'

'From London, yes. Well, quite close to London.'

'Thought so,' he said, heaving up the handles of the cart, 'Lovely day.'

'It is indeed, and so warm. A glorious September day.'

Mr. Crabbe turned to his wife and son, 'That's Mr. Pinder, over there, by the booking office. Better go and introduce ourselves.'

He led the way, striding out as only a former acting-Sergeant could, completely unaware that behind him followed twenty-two sets of parents and their sons.

Mr. Crabbe was forestalled in introducing himself to Mr. Pinder by Mr. Pinder himself, who as they drew close, began to address the whole party.

'Welcome to Chantry. I am Mr. Pinder, Housemaster of Keyes and Head of English.'

He was in his early thirties, of middle height, and beneath his mortarboard he wore his black hair unusually long. *Obviously a rebellious type*, thought the military man at the back as he pushed his reluctant son to the front. He said nothing as Mr. Pinder continued, 'I do not usually wear my gown when away from School, but I thought it would be easier for you to recognise me.'

Mr. Crabbe went a little pink.

'We will begin by checking everyone is present. When I call your name, you will answer '*adsum*', which in Latin means 'I am present'. You will then come and stand by me.'

He glanced down at his clipboard.

'Crabbe.'

'*Adsum!*' said Mr. Crabbe smartly, and moved forward to stand by Mr. Pinder.

'Perhaps I didn't fully explain myself. It is the *boy* who answers '*adsum*' and moves over here.'

Mr. Crabbe turned even pinker, muttered, 'Sorry sir' and re-joined the party.

The others giggled at Mr. Crabbe's embarrassment, though in truth, they had all misunderstood and every father had been eagerly waiting to respond when their name was called. One or two had been silently rehearsing the word '*adsum*'.

'We will start again. Crabbe!'

Lancelot said '*adsum*' in his high-pitched voice and ran to join Mr. Pinder. The master extended his hand and said, 'Welcome to Chantry, Crabbe.'

Crabbe shook the proffered hand and looking up he saw a rather severe face. Severe, but with kindly brown eyes.

'Thank you, Mr. Pinder.'

'You call me 'sir'.'

'I beg your pardon. Thank you, sir.'

Mr. Pinder looked at his clipboard again, 'I see you have been assigned to my House, Crabbe. Do your best, work hard, and all will be well. Stand behind me.'

'Thank you, sir.'

A polite lad, thought Pinder, and obviously well brought up. He called the next name, 'Flint!'.

And so, it continued until each boy had been individually welcomed and had taken his place behind the gowned figure.

Mr. Pinder turned to face his charges.

'You will follow me in a single file. You will keep in step and there is to be no talking. We will go to the various Houses and you will be allotted your dormitories. Your parents will make their own way to the Hall, where tea will be served.'

He turned to the group of parents who were listening intently, 'The school grounds are large, and mindful of the possibility that you may become lost, prefects have been stationed at strategic places to point you in the right direction.'

Chris Hare

Mr. Pinder had suggested that a more sensible plan would be for a prefect to go to the station, collect the parents and lead them to the Hall. But the prefects themselves, at a meeting in their common room, said that having regard to the traditions of the school, they would prefer the system remained unaltered. Mr. Pinder, himself a great respecter of tradition, and without realising that the prefects actually made a profit from the exercise, therefore agreed.

He turned once more to the boys, 'After tea, the Headmaster will address you and you will be given ten minutes to make your farewells. Is that clear?'

'Yes, sir,' from all the boys and four of the fathers.

The boys followed Mr. Pinder through the booking hall, turned right, and made their silent way to one of the large houses on the far side of the hill, with not one single backward glance at the anxious faces of their parents, who stood silently and in sorrow, looking as if they were witnessing the Pied Piper kidnapping their children. They needed a leader. Someone who would raise their spirits.

They made a bad choice.

The poor innocent and now lonely souls formed a line behind Mr. Crabbe, who on seeing this, considered himself promoted to monitor.

Even though the chap at the back with the military moustache doubtless had a far greater claim to the position, it seemed that the other parents were looking to *him*, Frank Crabbe, to take charge. He was not the type to let anyone down, and so, in his acting-sergeant voice, called over his shoulder, 'No talking. By the left…'

They were an hour late for tea.

Having traversed most of the school grounds, Mr. Crabbe admitted to himself – but not out loud to everyone else, because talking was against school rules, that he was completely lost. He just couldn't remember from the tour they'd been given whilst Lancelot was sitting the McBeattie Scholarship exam, just which building was which, and none were signposted. Here and there he spotted a prefect, recognisable by his fancy waistcoat, but he felt it would be demeaning, as a true Englishman, to stop and ask directions. Then he recognized the art room because they'd passed it ten minutes before.

After further fruitless wanderings, he reluctantly accepted that there was no choice: he would seek assistance as his troops were beginning to make mutinous mutterings. He halted the column and approached a prefect who was nonchalantly leaning against the wall of the very building they were looking for. The prefect, gratefully accepted the penny Mr. Crabbe offered, gave precise directions, but to the School Chapel, 'Ah, yes. I remember now,' he said confidently to his waiting party, 'Follow me!'

At the Chapel they met another prefect who directed them to the science lab in exchange for a penny, and thence onwards and backwards. As they were going past the art room yet again, they spied the groundsman with the handcart who was trundling by with his final load of boys' trunks. He gave Mr. Crabbe correct directions, in return for a threepenny piece.

Mr. Crabbe addressed the column.

'Well, that was a fine invigorating walk on such a lovely day. I'm sure it's done wonders for your appetites. We will now march to the Hall, which is over there,' he said, vaguely indicating a building near the top of the hill as if he'd known where their destination lay all along.

'Let's smarten up a little, shall we? 'he said to Mrs. Crabbe, but took in the whole group, 'Must set a good example to the boys.'

Indeed, they were a tired and bedraggled group, unrecognizable as the smart, chattering parents who had travelled from Paddington earlier. Most of the ladies' makeup had been wiped away in the heat of the train, and the tears that followed had washed away what had remained. Stockings were laddered, hats awry. All the men had loosened collars and ties. The military man's moustache had been transformed along the way through constant angry twiddles to the ends of the finely waxed upwardly ended creation that it normally was. Now it was a drooping and pathetic semblance of its former self. But they did what they could, and having performed running repairs resumed their journey, noticing that all the prefects seemed to have vanished.

Mr. Crabbe, at the head of the column, politely knocked on the door.

5: TEA

'*Introeo*!' called a male voice, which Mr. Crabbe took to mean 'come in'.

He opened the door and saw before him an enormous auditorium with rows of seating. *Hall* was like a London theatre, with the floor sloping in a gentle gradient down towards a raised stage.

In the cleared level area in front of the stage, where the front stalls should be, at a long table sat the twenty-three boys, chewing greedily but silently on very thick jam sandwiches and drinking glasses of orange squash. To one side of them was another table, set at a right angle and empty of people but loaded with tea urns and plates of sandwiches. Clearly, this was the tea reserved for the parents, thought Mr. Crabbe.

The stage was crowded, not with theatrical props or scenery, but with a grand piano, a desk set up on a dais at centre stage, and a hideous brass eagle with spread wings that formed the top of the lectern. There were six human faces, all looking at him.

On the left was Mr. Pinder, now divested of his mortarboard and gown, sitting at a table with three other gentlemen. On the other side of the raised desk was another table with just a lady and a gentleman seated behind it. Mr. Crabbe seemed to recognise the lady from somewhere, but he was sure he'd never seen the gentleman before.

Crabbe in all Innocence

Embarrassed at not knowing what to do next, Mr. Crabbe glanced round, saw a carefully arranged collection of rusting swords mounted on the wall, and decided to take a deep interest in it.

The six humans on the stage rose as the party of parents edged forward. The boys stopped eating, glanced round to see that their parents had at last arrived then carried on with the business at hand.

Mr. Crabbe's party reached the back stalls when they were suddenly and rudely pushed aside by the military man, who marched to the front, climbed the stairs at the side of the stage and stood facing the four gentlemen before him.

Major Kirby had had enough! And to those on the stage it seemed they had been visited by a walrus.

Recognising Mr. Pinder, he took a step towards him and announced, 'I am Major Kir...'

He got no further as the gentleman he had just passed, and ignored, interrupted him. Standing on tiptoe, he said, 'Pardon me, but we don't use titles here.'

The major turned, bristling visibly from head to toe, except for his moustache, which remained where it was, ends drooping towards the floor.

'And pardon *me*, but 'Major' is not a title, it is a *rank*.'

'A moot point,' came the reply, 'title or rank, we are all equal here. We address each other by name only. It's a Founders' Principle.'

'Really and what is your name, if I may ask?'

'You may. I am the Headmaster.'

'Ah. Oh. Are you? Really?'

There was an awkward pause during which the Headmaster raised both eyebrows in the Major's direction, clearly waiting for a further response. The Crabbes noticed the gesture and were reminded of their interview at White Gates with Mrs. Helen. Possibly, the ability to communicate with one's eyebrows was a prerequisite of the position.

Mr. Pinder hid a grin behind the back of his hand, a mannerism of his, and the Major pulled at his moustache so that both ends were facing, albeit momentarily, east and west. It was a futile gesture as both sides gave up the struggle and resumed pointing down towards Australia.

'Ah,' the Major repeated, trying again to regain the high ground, but taking an embarrassing step backwards, 'and, if I may ask, err, is 'Headmaster' a title or rank?'

'It's neither. It is a *position.* A position of high authority.'

'Is it? Yes, I suppose it is,' replied the Major, crestfallen, and attempting a pathetic smile. 'Well, I thought I'd come and introduce myself. Maj..., er, *Mr.* Kirby,' he said, pointing at himself. After a further pause, and with the finger now trembling slightly, he pointed to Mr. Crabbe, who, with the other parents had neared the stage in order to listen, and said, 'That chap's in charge.'

Crabbe in all Innocence

He saluted the Head, smiled weakly at the four occupants of the other table, did a smart about turn, descended the steps and marched briskly back to stand by his wife, who swung her handbag at his pulled-in stomach.

The Major, who was wearing a corset, almost collapsed. His corset was a garment clearly designed to keep stomachs within, not handbags without.

The Headmaster raised an eyebrow in the direction of Mr. Crabbe who took the gesture to mean that he was being summoned to the stage. After the briefest hesitation, he climbed the steps and bowed.

'Good afternoon, Headmaster. I'm not really in charge, I just happened to find myself at the front. My name's Crabbe,' he said looking down at the nearly bald pate of the Headmaster.

Squinting upwards at Mr. Crabbe's eyes, nearly a foot above his own, the Head replied, 'Natural leader, like myself, eh? Good afternoon, Mr. Crabbe.' They shook hands, the Head squeezing rather too tightly both to inflict pain and to demonstrate his authority from the onset – despite his untallness.

Mr. Crabbe winced and withdrew his hand quickly as the Head continued, 'Dr. Wilkes-Passmore at your service.' He gestured towards the other table, 'Mr. Pinder, you've already met. I will introduce the three other gentlemen shortly, and this,' he said, indicating the lady next him, 'is Mrs. Pearl, school secretary.'

Mrs. Pearl was skeletal in appearance, in her mid-fifties, with white hair and white skin stretched tightly over her cheekbones. She smiled at him, which made her look like a grinning skull.

Mr. Crabbe bowed in the direction of Mrs. Pearl and then stepped forward to shake her bony hand.

'Yes, indeed, I remember now,' he said, 'I had the pleasure of meeting you a few weeks ago when my wife and I brought our son to sit the McBeattie...'

He stopped mid-sentence as Mrs. Pearl withdrew her hand and raised it, palm forward, to indicate firmly, he should say no more.

'Yes, I remember you, Mr. Crabbe, but...' she lowered her voice so the other parents could not hear, 'as the Headmaster just said, we are all equal at Chantry. It is of no concern to anyone whether your son is here through a scholarship or you are paying for his education. It is one of the Founders' Principles, and an unnecessary detail. Kindly remember that.'

'Yes. I will.'

'There's no need to apologise.'

'Sorry.'

'Not at all. Now, if you would be so kind as to ask your fellow parents to make themselves comfortable, I'm sure they will enjoy a cup of tea and something to eat.'

'That would be very welcome, Mrs. Pearl. We have all had a most interesting walk around the school grounds.'

69

Crabbe in all Innocence

He didn't say 'three times', he felt this was an 'unnecessary detail'.

The Head, Mrs. Pearl and the four gentlemen resumed their seats and continued eating as Mr. Crabbe bowed to them before turning to the other parents to indicate that they should take their seats at the long table. They did so, and by common unspoken consent left the chair at the top for Mr. Crabbe.

As he passed the Major, he whispered, 'Would you like to be Mother?'

'Certainly, certainly. Delighted.'

The Major, now recovered from his handbagging, busied himself at the tea urns, ensuring Mr. Crabbe received the very first cup.

All this was witnessed by silent, chewing schoolboys.

Lancelot saw his father, normally the mildest of men, in a new light. He was impressed. As was the boy opposite him who whispered, 'I'm Kirby, Toby Kirby. Your father's done a wonderful job in putting my father in his place. Mother's been trying for years.'

Lancelot was surprised the boy, albeit with his back to the stage and therefore unseen, should have spoken when they'd been forbidden to talk during meals. He tried to indicate with his eyes and by turning his palms upwards that it was nothing, but inside, he felt very proud of his father.

The Major, his moustache seemingly showing signs of recovery, thanks to his large intake of cucumber sandwiches, asked brightly, 'More tea, anyone?'

70

He instantly subsided to silence as a command from the stage, 'No talking during meals!'

Tea finished, the Headmaster rose and moved behind the desk, where he largely disappeared from view. Just his lower torso was visible through the desk legs. Then his head and upper body appeared gradually, as he mounted the wooden steps he'd had made specially to allow him to see over the top and *very importantly*, to be seen.

From an inside pocket, he took out his speech and smoothed down several sheets on the desktop. As he did, he glanced at the parents' table and said, 'Perhaps you would find it more comfortable in the stalls? The boys will remain where they are.'

The parents, as one, gratefully got up from their stiff-backed chairs and relocated to the theatre seats, twenty or so feet from the stage. Mr. and Mrs. Crabbe chose to sit at the back, at the end of the row, where they hoped they wouldn't be picked on.

'Sit up straight, don't fidget, and take careful note.'

Everyone immediately sat to attention.

'A very warm welcome to Chantry, and congratulations on winning places at the school – *your new home, your new family*,' began the Head. 'Chantry, like all ancient British institutions is steeped in tradition. The reasoning behind some of these traditions has, over the passage of time, become unclear. But that is not to say, they are ignored. *Certainly not*. One

71

tradition which is very relevant is to invite you to the school two days before the official first day of term to allow you and your parents to see where you will be spending the next few years, and to allow you,' he glared at the boys' table below him, 'to begin to find your way around...'

Mr. Crabbe did his best to listen, but he was tired – the early start, the long journey, the hike around the school grounds together with the heavy responsibility of leading the group, then too much to eat at tea, and now the most comfortable seat he had ever sat on. He leaned back and snuggled in. Within minutes, he found himself dozing.

He tried to keep himself awake by concentrating on the Head's speech but suddenly realised he was being stared at. By whom and for what purpose, he had no idea. But he was *aware* that someone was giving him their undivided attention.

A horrific thought occurred and surreptitiously, whilst looking straight ahead, he lowered his hand to check the state of his fly buttons. They were done up correctly, he was relieved to find and whilst fumbling around down there, he found the napkin he'd tucked into his trouser top at tea.

The Headmaster was introducing the four Housemasters at the other table on the stage. Each stood in turn as his name was announced, nodded and sat down again. Mr. Crabbe didn't take any of it in, but he noted that Mrs. Crabbe was giving the stage her full attention, so she could tell him about it later.

'And this, for anyone who didn't hear, is Mrs. Pearl, the school secretary,' continued the Head.

Realisation struck Mr. Crabbe! It was that brass eagle that was staring at him. He felt most uncomfortable, and stared back, determined to out-stare the creature. He furtively got up, whispered to Mrs. Crabbe that he'd got a cramp and moved to the other end of the row to see if the bulging eyes would follow him. They did.

He'd noticed this phenomenon in portraits at the National Gallery when he had visited with his parents many years before. He crept back to his seat and sat down again as the Head said, 'Chantry is a progressive school, embracing all that is new in modern teaching methods, and yet, conversely, we have one foot planted firmly in the past.'

'If he did that, he'd split himself up in the middle,' observed Toby Kirby in a whisper.

'You all come from different backgrounds; I have no doubt. But your origins are unimportant and irrelevant here. What is important is *not* where you come from, but where you want to go. And that is a question only you can answer. We will guide you, help you, advise you. Remember this: you can do nothing to change your past, but you can ruin the present by worrying about the future. Therefore, *do not worry about it*. Do your best, work hard and obey the rules. You will be kept extremely busy, and time will pass very quickly for you, if not for us.'

It was a rare thing for W-P to make a joke, but he thought he'd just made a good one, so he gave a small laugh. He glanced at the Housemaster's table and the four gentlemen smiled dutifully.

Mr. Crabbe missed it, since he was, by now, in a deep sleep. He woke suddenly on receiving a painful jab to his ribs from his wife's elbow.

He was awake in time to hear the Head's final words, 'I wish you all good luck during your years here, although, in reality, luck forms no part of the equation. To succeed in life, you need determination based on sound discipline, ability and obeying your betters. You will now take your parents to show them your House, you will say your goodbyes and then you will change for the Shells' Run.

Sport and regular exercise are held in high regard. You are here to broaden your shoulders as well as your minds, and the Shells' Run around the school grounds will help you get your bearings. That's all.' He clambered down from the steps and made his exit, stage left, fully knowing but not caring, that he'd just told a lie, albeit a white one.

The Shells' Run wasn't to get boys familiarised with their surroundings. It was to exhaust them. It ensured they got a good night's sleep, too tired to stay awake silently sobbing their hearts out.

The Fates, from their secret place high above, looked down. Everything was as they had planned. As it should be. Everything in its place – the school, the people, and Crabbe.

Not yet, but his time was coming.

Tick tock.

6: THE SHELLS' RUN

'I am James Russell, House Prefect of Keyes. Come this way.' Crabbe and Kirby, with two other new boys and their respective parents, did as they were ordered and followed in silence and trepidation.

Russell was a tall, muscular boy in his mid-teens. On the lapel of his school blazer he wore the silver enamelled badge of his office. Beneath the blazer he sported an embroidered waistcoat and, should anyone not be clear on how important he was, he carried a mahogany baton that he used as a pointer.

He pointed at a vast Elizabethan mansion.

'This is your House. There are five of them in Keyes House.'

It was an incongruous remark, because he was clearly pointing at one house, not five.

Seeing the puzzled expressions on the faces of his entourage, Russell attempted to explain,

'Allow me to explain. At Chantry, there are four Houses, each of which has five Houses. This is yours, and I am House Prefect of *this house*. I am, therefore, your House Prefect. It's all perfectly straightforward. Clear now?'

'Quite, quite,' said Mr. Crabbe, languishing in ignorance.

'Precisely so,' the senior Kirby nodded, still not understanding.

Without waiting for further comment Russell said, 'Follow me,' and marched towards the imposing 16th century edifice. They halted outside the huge open front door, which had probably used a whole oak tree in its construction.

Russell pointed, 'This is the entrance hall,' he said, unnecessarily. 'Parents aren't permitted to enter, but you can see from where you are standing that this is rather palatial.'

It most certainly was. There was carpeting on the floor, paintings of the walls and a display of silver cups and shields housed in a mahogany trophy cabinet.

The parents nodded in approval as Russell continued, 'Say your goodbyes now, then I'll conduct the boys to their dorm.'

It was a poignant moment for all of them, except Russell, who moved a short distance away, tactfully out of earshot.

Belying their inner feelings, they all adopted stiff upper-lip expressions, determined not to shed tears in front of other boys or parents. They hugged, shook hands, and kissed their mothers.

Mr. Pinder appeared, 'Have you said your farewells?' He didn't wait for a reply, but continued, 'Russell, take the Shells to their dorm and get them changed for the Run. All new boys are called Shells during their first year at Chantry, for obvious reasons.'

It wasn't obvious to any of them, but they felt it should be and didn't like to show their lack of understanding by asking Mr. Pinder to explain. Not that Pinder could explain since he didn't know either. They just *were*, that's all.

'Parents, if you'd be kind enough to follow me, I'll show you out of the school grounds.'

Mr. Pinder wasn't about to let parents find their own way. With Mr. Crabbe among them, he thought, they'd still be wandering around at Christmas.

As the boys, following Russell, passed through the oak door to begin their new lives, each glanced over their shoulder and gave their parents a final wave. The parents, lagging behind Mr. Pinder, waved back with Mr. Crabbe waving the white napkin, making him look like he was surrendering.

They were told not to dawdle.

'Right,' said Russell, referring to a list on his clipboard, 'you should be Crabbe, Kirby, Glover and Cartwright. Are you?'

'Yes, sir.'

'You don't call me 'sir'. You refer to me by name, and you stand up straight when you talk to me, shoulders back, chest out, hands by your sides.'

Crabbe in all Innocence

Russell was determined to set off on the right foot. A year before, as a newly created House Prefect, he had been too soft with the Shells, too affable and the little brutes had taken advantage of his friendliness and made his life hell with their constant demands for bedtime stories and glasses of water.

It was a mistake he would *not* repeat.

He led the way to the entrance hall and opened a door on one side. Pointing his baton at the large room, which was crammed with long wooden benches and one sofa, he said, 'This is your common room. It's where you relax. You do your prep in here and work on your extracurricular activities. You write home here, on Fridays. There's little time for relaxation. There are two staircases. That one,' he said, pointing, 'is the main one, which leads to your dorm in the attic. The other, at the back of the house, is the servants' stairs to the attic but also descends to the cloak and boot rooms. They were originally the servants' hall, the kitchens, the butler's pantry and the laundry. Any questions?'

'Do we have a butler, Mr. Russell?' asked Cartwright.

'Just 'Russell', and no. There's no butler these days. Any butlering you require will be undertaken by yourselves. The laundry is still in use. It smells, particularly on Mondays, which is laundry day. Sorting the laundry is a punishment reserved for Shells. Let us continue,' he said, leading the way up five flights of stairs.

The dormitory was sparsely furnished, four iron bedsteads, with a night table and single wardrobe each. A lone naked lightbulb hung down from the ceiling. No curtains on the window, no carpeting on the floor. No bars on the window either, otherwise it would have been a prison cell.

Crabbe looked around in disbelief, 'Oh glory,' he whispered.

'Your school trunks have been stowed beneath each of your beds. Change into your running kit now, and then join me and the rest of the Shells downstairs by the main entrance in ten minutes.'

Russell departed, and in silence the four dormers opened their trunks and took out their white shorts and tops which were embroidered on the front with the name of their House in Keyes colours of green and yellow.

Outside, all the new boys formed a straight line in front of Browne.

'I'm Digby Browne, School Prefect. *School* Prefect.' he said, emphasising his superiority over Russell, 'Pay attention.'

He was dressed in a similar fashion to Russell, although the baton he carried was a foot longer, and had a silver point and the badge on his lapel was enamelled in gold.

'You will find that at Chantry, we are very competitive. We never give in. We don't cry at Chantry and we always contribute 100% at the very least.

Except on this single occasion. This is not a race. It is a run. You will follow the paper trail that has been laid out. You will not deviate. You will not explore. And take special note, (here Browne decided to put his own stamp of terror on the Shells,) no one is permitted to die during the Shells' Run. It is not allowed. Therefore, if you feel like dropping dead after the first few miles, do NOT do so. Slow down. Walk if you must, finish the course, return to your House, give your name to the prefect in charge, retire to bed and recover. Is that clear?'

There were several nods, a few murmurs and a grunt or two as the Shells absorbed Browne's words. It was then Browne noticed Crabbe's black shoes.

He pointed his baton, 'You boy, you're wearing running shoes. Why?'

'I'm going running,' came a rather high-pitched reply.

'Don't answer me back! I'm a School Prefect.'

James Russell smiled.

'Russell, why didn't you check that this Shell was wearing the correct apparel?'

Russell stopped smiling. He didn't care for being corrected in front of a bunch of new boys.

'If you remember, Browne, you asked me to ensure there were sufficient quantities for the prefects' late tea. And so, I was, er, elsewhere.'

'Ah, yes. Quite. Now you, boy. Name?'

'Erm, Crabbe,' Crabbe replied, going red.

'Right, Crabbe. You are wearing black running shoes, with spikes, which are worn when running on a cinder track. As the Shells' run is mainly on grass, you should be wearing plimsolls, like everyone else.'

'Sorry,' he replied, hugely embarrassed at getting something wrong.

'Never mind. Cut back to the dorm and change. Then catch us up.'

Crabbe mumbled something incoherently and hurried back to his dorm. He quickly changed into his plimsolls, and determined not to get anything else wrong, charged back down the stairs.

He found himself alone. Everyone had gone.

Crabbe didn't wake up the next morning. At least, not in the literal sense. It would be more accurate to say that he became, very gradually aware that he was still alive, which surprised him since the run around the school grounds the previous evening had almost finished him off. It had left him gasping for breath, his heart thumping furiously and his lungs, he was sure, about to burst. But he hadn't given in. And he hadn't broken a rule by dying.

James Russell had waited patiently by the main door, clipboard in one hand, pencil in the other. It was his job to tick off the boys as they arrived back.

He looked at his watch, a gold half-hunter presented to him by his father as a reward for being elevated to the rank of prefect. Then he looked at the list again. A

single boy remained unaccounted for, one Lancelot
Crabbe, whom he remembered as being the one
wearing the wrong shoes. It was exactly half an hour
since he had noted the arrival of Kirby, and Russell was
starving. He was worried that he might miss out on the
bacon and eggs being prepared for the prefects' late tea.

He decided to give Crabbe another twenty minutes
before going in search of him but after ten minutes he'd
realised what must have happened. He'd been a little
late taking up his position as it had taken longer than
usual to smuggle the bacon out of the kitchens. This
lad, Crabbe, Russell decided, must have come back
first, way ahead of the rest of the field, while Russell
was liberating the bacon. Yes, that was it. Crabbe had
beaten the others back and gone straight to the dorm.

He supposed he ought to check, but Crabbe's dorm
was in the attic. It had been a long day, and he was due
on the drum early in the morning. And he was hungry.
So, he put a tick by Crabbe's name and flicked off the
master switch behind the front door enveloping the
house in darkness.

In fact, as Russell turned off the lights, Crabbe was
still out there, blundering around and trying to keep his
eyes on the paper trail which was getting more and
difficult to see. Besides which, much of it had blown
away and Crabbe ran wearily in the wrong direction,
following false leads. But he didn't give in.

His run had turned into a trot, then a slow walk. He
was ready to start crawling when he spied his House at

long, long last. He finally staggered through the front door and with a last supreme effort, he summoned his remaining ounce of strength and groped around until he found the stairs. Being both physically and mentally exhausted, he was grateful for the banisters that showed him the way up.

In turn, around midnight, he got into bed with each of his sleeping dormers who each fought back viciously. Cartwright even hurled a pillow at whoever it was invading his space.

He stumbled around in the blackness until he found his own bed and just managed to kick off his plimsolls before collapsing. He wondered, briefly, if this was what death was like: an endless dark enveloping a disembodied mind. His last thought before sleep claimed him was that this was where he would spend his last night on earth.

But he didn't die. He couldn't. It wasn't his time. *Yet.*

As dawn broke, his eyes shuddered open, and he saw faint streaks of daylight laid out across the ceiling. He heard the sounds of a cat being strangled somewhere far away as he groped for his glasses on the nightstand. They didn't help, he could still see very little. In the faint gloom he looked down the length of his bed and found his sheets were severely awry. It was apparent he'd been in a violent battle with something, and that he had lost.

Crabbe in all Innocence

Crabbe screwed up his eyes and stared hard at the other beds.

As the room lightened, he saw that each of the other occupants, still soundly sleeping, had been fighting the same demons, and with equally dire results. Kirby had turned himself around so that his feet were on his pillow and Cartwright didn't seem to have a pillow, whereas Glover had two.

Crabbe blinked wearily, slowly remembering where he was, and wondering about the thumping sound he could hear coming up from the centre of the earth. The shrieking noises of the cat being murdered got louder as the thumping got closer.

Gingerly, he tried to move. It hurt to bend forward. It hurt to sit up. It even hurt to breathe.

The dorm door was flung open and Russell stood there, holding a drum. He screamed 'Wake up!' and thumped it a few more times.

Crabbe sat bolt upright and swung his legs over the edge of the bed, shocked into complete consciousness and covering his ears.

Kirby leapt up from his bed and started jumping up and down on the spot, flinging his arms wide and trying to count to three as he did, 'One, two three. One, two…' After about ten such manoeuvres he subsided back onto his bed, breathing heavily.

Cartwright and Glover just stayed where they were, awake but with mouths wide open agape at Kirby's antics.

Chris Hare

'This is the Keyes morning drum. You get up when you hear it. Each House has its own musical instrument for sounding the *wake up*,' said Russell, as he gave the drum a final extra hard bash. 'Charles House has bagpipes', not a cat then, thought Crabbe, 'and Oliver uses a cymbal and Henry a bugle.'

The whole school was woken at the same time, so why it was deemed necessary to have *four* different sounds for wake up, he didn't know. It was one of many traditions at Chantry that everyone followed without quite knowing why.

'You boy,' he said, indicating Kirby with a drumstick, 'What was all that about?'

'Sorry, I forgot where I was. I was doing my morning exercises, if you please. My father makes me do them the moment I wake up. He says it will make me fit for when I join the Army.'

'Well, I'm not your daddy and this isn't the Army. This is Chantry and I am the duty Keyes Prefect for today. Now, pay attention. You must obey me instantly or face the consequences.'

He didn't add what the consequences were. There was no need – whatever they were, they would be horrible.

In any case, after some hours of drifting in and out of sleep and trying to keep warm, the four dormers were in no state to question anything.

Russell caught sight of Crabbe, still wearing his running kit from the previous night. His severe manner

85

lightened, 'Hello. You're keen. Getting dressed for another run? Excellent spirit. I wish there were more like you. You other three should take your example from...erm...What's your name again?'

'Crabbe.'

'Shame.'

'No. Crabbe.'

'Ah, Crabbe,' he remembered, the missing boy from last night, 'you show a lot of spirit. Well done.'

Crabbe smiled weakly but couldn't think of anything to say.

'Anyway, no running this morning, no matter how keen you are. But you did very well on the run yesterday.'

Crabbe, misunderstanding, found his voice and muttered quietly, 'Sorry.'

'What's that? Speak up!'

'I'll do better next time.'

'Excellent, excellent. Now, buck up! Ablutions,' he ordered.

Like sheep, they herded into the bathroom where they were instructed to strip and shower. There was no hint of heat in the water and when they emerged, they were ordered to the sinks for two minutes vigorous tooth brushing.

Afterwards, they were taken back to the dorm, where they dressed in their school uniforms, made their beds and sat silently, still shivering from the effects of the shower and teeth chattering uncontrollably, while Russell went off to check on something.

He returned a few minutes later.

'You have late breakfast this morning. I'll take you to your form room first where you will be introduced to Mr. Finney, your form master for the coming year. You will also meet Miss Griggs, who is one of the matrons at Chantry. The school bursar will also be there to open an account in your name for spends at the tuck shop. Bring whatever money you have and give it to him for safekeeping.

Mr. Finney will allocate a desk for each of you, and you will be given a term timetable which you will learn by heart. Always remember where you are and where you are supposed to be. After today it will be your own responsibility to find your way round the school and the grounds and to know at what time you should be there, wherever that is. Lateness, for any reason, is a sin and is not tolerated at Chantry. The consequences for being late are dire. Follow me. Keep in step.'

He turned and marched out in time to the beating of his drum.

7: THE SOLDIER

The Headmaster watched from his study window as the Shells were marched around the school grounds by the prefects.

He tut-tutted to himself. Not because of the actions of the prefects, who were performing their duties perfectly well, fully aware they were under the Head's eye. It was the new boys who looked half asleep – which indeed, many of them were. The Shells' Run had tired them, but it hadn't completely stopped them from being the horrors they were.

They slouched along, yawning and jostling each other, not listening to Russell who looked about to use his mahogany baton to crown some of them. The Head fully appreciated why some animals chose to eat their young.

'This will never do,' he said to the window under his breath, 'I didn't put up with this sort of slovenliness from the servicemen I had the honour of leading during my time in uniform, and I don't intend to put up with it now. These boys must learn to *discipline* themselves. Smarten up. *And I am the man to make sure they do it!*'

He realised he was addressing his thoughts to a piece of glass, turned, forgot the Shells, and reminisced on his military career. The Head's experiences in warfare were legendary.

88

They were also completely imaginary.

Many years before, the Reverend Doctor, when curate at All Saints', became disenchanted with life in the Church and lost his faith, such as it was. He even began doubting the existence of God, which is not a good sign in a clergyman.

His faith was restored, however, one bright sunny day, when his father-in-law, the Bishop, whilst conducting a Christening and in the act of begging the Almighty to receive the infant into His church and eventually, after a full and fruitful life, His bosom, the Right Reverend dropped dead.

Mrs. Wilkes-Passmore was desolate. Walter Wilkes-Passmore tried his best to console her even though he couldn't get his arm around her shoulders. He attempted endearments, whispering from as near as he could get, including 'I'll do your father's funeral for nothing,' and more unfortunately, 'Now there's a See without a Bishop. I could apply for the post.'.

The Archbishop attended the funeral, listened, smiled, sympathised and drank a considerable amount of Wilkes-Passmore sherry. And recommended another candidate to Number 10.

The Wilkes-Passmores were obliged to leave the late Bishop's Residence. *Mr.*, because he had stopped using his Reverend Doctor title in protest at being thus overlooked, resolved to leave the church.

He did. And there was much rejoicing at his departing.

Crabbe in all Innocence

Mrs. Wilkes-Passmore was in full agreement with her husband's decision. She firmly believed that the church, now sadly without the guidance and wisdom of her father, was a spent force anyway.

In his will the Bishop remembered his only daughter to the tune of £500, and they were able to afford the cost of taking rented accommodation. He hadn't, however, remembered his son-in-law, so Walter had no compunction in claiming his five-guinea fee for conducting the funeral, and a further three shillings for the Archbishop's sherry.

Whilst Harriet went daily to the graveyard to commune with the shade of her late father, Walter sat at his desk and plotted and planned. He took two sheets of paper and headed one 'Good Points' and the other 'Not Such Good Points'. He didn't believe he had any bad.

By the end of the morning's exercise of very serious self-analysis, he had completed both sides of the 'Good Points' page, and both sides of two more pages as well. The 'Not Such Good Points' paper remained blank.

Indeed, by 'Good Point' 47 he could see the direction this was all taking: he was obviously born to take charge. He was a natural leader of men. He had always believed it so, and now here it was before him; twelve columns of evidence in black and white. Proof, if proof were needed, of his innate abilities.

He went back to believing in God for a while. It was clearly His purpose that he, Walter Wilkes-Passmore, was destined for great things. He felt himself above the ordinary man – not in the literal sense, of course. But intellectually. He knew he was far, far superior.

With that fact being fully understood and accepted, he considered the next problem. How best to make use of this abundance of unique talent to his benefit and also the benefit of mankind, he added after a moment of hesitation.

But of what and of whom, should he *take charge*?

A simple enough question, but an answer requires much more deep thought. He lay down his pen, clasped his hands behind his head and leaned back in his chair, closing his eyes in the hope of receiving divine guidance from above.

He ruled out becoming a Chief Constable of Police because he knew there were height restrictions, and in any case, you were expected to pound the beat for at least two years before you could even begin to work your way up. Pounding the beat most certainly didn't appeal. Besides which, he'd prefer a profession where he could start at the top of the ladder.

He tried prayer.

Not for the first time he wondered why those who spoke to God through prayer were seen by the rest of humanity as being good men, but those who claimed to have been spoken to *by God* were regarded as poor hopeless imbeciles.

As it was, inspiration did not come from above, but from slightly below him and to the left. There on his desk lay his yet unwrapped birthday present to Harriet, a leather-bound copy of *Slaughter in Moscow*, the history of Napoleon's defeat in the winter of 1812. Mrs. W-P loved that sort of thing. The more gore and brutality the better.

He was planning to leave it on her bed among the teddy bears. This, he knew, from experience, was the best way to present it. It precluded her from becoming overcome with emotion and flinging her arms around him in gratitude. She had done this once one Christmas, on being given a book about Capital Punishment. He'd been lucky to escape with bruised ribs. Here, in the guise of Harriet's present was inspiration. The Army!

He would enrol as an Officer Cadet at Sandhurst. Not exactly 'at the top', true, but well on the way. People would call him 'Sir' and salute. He would have a batman to look after his uniform. That definitely appealed. He might have to march a bit in the early days, just until they promoted him.

He was sure there were no rules about how tall you had to be. Nelson, a naval man, was diminutive in stature and only had one arm. At least W-P was complete, despite his inclination a few degrees starboard, to use the naval vernacular.

And now glancing through the first few pages, he'd found that Napoleon himself was fairly untall.

He grew more and more excited about the idea and started to read *Slaughter in Moscow* in earnest. He made notes in the margin of where Napoleon had gone wrong, consequently spoiling the book. He'd have to find something else for Harriet.

When she was informed, Mrs. Wilkes-Passmore was in two minds. She liked the idea of being posted abroad and having a servant sitting on her veranda pulling a piece of rope that kept a fan moving – she was currently reading a history of Indian Mutiny and the executions that followed and hadn't come to terms with the fact that the world had moved on since those days.

On the other hand, she had been born in England to a mother who had died with the effort, and she thought she owed it to England to stay there.

They agreed to delay the final decision. Before enrolling in Sandhurst, W-P was required to attend a 'suitability assessment course', living under canvas for three weeks in Wiltshire. After this, they decided, they would reconsider their options once they knew what rank he would start off with.

He travelled to Wiltshire, and within two hours of reporting in at the main gate, he was back reporting his departure.

It appeared the MO, a Captain and some sort of doctor apparently, had noticed his walking stick, and consequently the big brown boot, and finally the disparity in the length of the W-P legs. When asked to march up and down in bare feet, he obliged, but went in a curve and not the straight line the MO was expecting.

'And of what use, may I ask, would you be to the great British Army in a war marching in circles?'

'I could surround the enemy on my own.'

'Sadly, the Army will have to try and get along without you. Failed!'

'But Captain, I thought the Army was desperate for officers.'

'Not that desperate, it isn't. Next!'

Crestfallen, Walter Wilkes-Passmore, BA (Hons) and from now on, Field Marshal of the British Army (failed), realised his number was up – there was no way out of this one. He would have to go home and confess to Harriet.

Not normally a man to be downcast, on this occasion he was deeply depressed on the train journey back to Civvy Street. He felt he was the victim of a cruel fate, and there was nothing he could do about it. It was by no means the first time he'd stared defeat in the face, but it was the first time he hadn't been able to talk, or cheat, his way out of a difficult situation.

Alone in the carriage he allowed himself to become enveloped with feelings of inadequacy, of despair and self-pity. He had been so certain that having left the Army of the Church, the Army of England would have welcomed him with unconcealed joy.

But alas, it was not to be. He had been denied the chance to rise to a position in life where he could mould lesser men's minds and characters – where he could serve as a shining example for all mankind, be admired and, yes, looked up to. In short, to make others as himself, in his image; decisive, fearless, reliable and capable. All virtuous words from the list of 'Good Points' he had made just a few weeks before.

'You worm!' shouted Mrs. W-P when he broke the news. 'You mouse! You should have punched that Captain on the nose. You should have complained to a General, not accepted defeat. You should have fought them. I would have!'

And with you as the enemy, the Army wouldn't stand a chance. Wisely, he kept his thoughts to himself as she continued to berate him. It was the first time she had behaved like this in all their years of married life, and Walter cowed under the onslaught. For all that, she was a loyal wife, brought up to believe that it was a married woman's duty to support her husband *in word and deed.*

'I can see I should never have let you go on your own. I should have been with you. They would have listened to me. Well, what do you intend to do about it about it, pray?'

Walter mistaking the meaning of his wife's final word, answered, 'If you think prayer would help.'

'Of course prayer won't help! Not without Daddy. He could have thought up a prayer for you. I'll ask him tomorrow.'

By that, Harriet meant that she would, on her visit to her father's grave, ask her father to compose something suitable. Not that the late Bishop would reply being too busy decomposing.

Crabbe in all Innocence

The following afternoon, she burst into her husband's study, her stockings torn, her dress flaked with mud and decorated with tiny pieces of dark shiny stone. She was flushed, as if she'd been running, although it wasn't likely that someone of her size could run without causing an earthquake, and W-P hadn't felt a single tremor.

Nevertheless, she charged in, a huge smile on her huge face and excitedly and breathlessly announced that her father *had replied*, or rather, that he had miraculously indicated the way.

'There I was, kneeling next to dear Daddy's grave. Well, really, I was kneeling on someone else's grave. They don't leave enough of a piece of no-man's land for the purpose.'

Actually, they did. There was ample room for a person who wasn't quite as ample as she to kneel in prayer, if they wished to.

'Anyway, after I'd spoken to Daddy and explained the difficulties, I used the headstone of the man on who's grave I'd been kneeling to help myself to my feet. It was made of black marble but it's obviously faulty, because it broke into pieces even though I'd hardly touched it.'

Wilkes-Passmore could imagine the remains of the marble headstone, crushed under the enormous pressure of his wife using it to lever herself up.

She continued, 'I was picking up the larger pieces when I happened to glance down at the inscription on one and it was a message from Daddy.'

He regarded Harriet through a narrowed eye for a moment and said, 'Your father was certainly capable of doing great things, but to engrave a message to you after he was dead?'

'No, Walter. He didn't engrave it. But he made sure I received the message into my own hand.'

'I see. And what was the substance of his message?'

'It said, *'Teach me the way, O Lord, and lead me in the right way, because of mine enemies'*. It's from the Book of Common Prayer.'

'Yes. I *know* it's from the Book of Common Prayer. It's part of my job to know the Book of Common Prayer from beginning to end and backwards. How though, was the inscription of significance to our present circumstances?'

'Well, isn't it obvious? You said you wanted to *guide* people. To teach them to be more like you. You've tried the church and were unhappy in it. You've tried the Army and they were unhappy with you in it. Look. Look at the first word, Walter. *Teach.*'

The light of inspiration suddenly flared up brightly inside the W-P brain.

'Of course, Harriet. Of course. You, with the help of your dear departed father, and the chap in the grave next door, have solved the dilemma. *I will teach!*'

Crabbe in all Innocence

Chris Hare

8: THE ROAD to GREATNESS

Having made the decision to join the teaching profession, whilst the Reverend Doctor, as he once more styled himself after what he came to refer to as his *Honourable Discharge* from the Army, went again to his study to list the subjects he was good at, Mrs. Wilkes-Passmore set about finding a school at which he could teach. One worthy of his talents.

She was aware, naturally, of her husband's penchant for exaggerating his achievements, but she didn't consider it wrong. In fact, she started to copy the practice. Her father, whilst dead, was promoted from Bishop to Saint in short order. No one, not even those who had known him in life, thought for one second of contradicting Harriet, for her very presence prohibited everyone from voicing an opinion that differed, even slightly, from her own.

It didn't take long for W-P to complete a list of 'Subjects I'm Good At'. He was simply confirming what he already knew. He was good at everything.

That is, he was good at and therefore able to teach, English Grammar, English Literature, Mathematics, Geography, History, Art, Science, Physics and Latin. He didn't list anything that contained any physical exercise, for obvious reasons. Equally, he had had enough of religion. He also decided against mentioning

French, a language in which he was fluent, because he hated France and all things French with a passion.

At eleven years of age, after Wilkes-Passmore had spent a considerable amount of time in hospital where he was heartily disliked, he was returned to the bosom of his family to parents who absolutely loathed him. They considered Walter's surgical boot an embarrassment not to be seen by their friends in church and they did all they could to ignore his existence, akin to the mad uncle locked away in the attic. But they were Christians too, and didn't lock him away but sent him to a boarding school in Suffolk.

It was a good school with a record of high academic achievement but it wasn't suitable for Walter since all forms of sport were held in such great regard and he was unable to participate, although he took a keen interest, sometimes acting as scorer at cricket matches, and on Sports' Day he could be found holding one end of the tape at the finishing line of the track events.

But for the rest, when the others in his form were out running, fielding or kicking, he was made to stay in school for extra lessons. On occasion, he was moved up a form for the afternoon and set work that would normally be beyond what was expected for a pupil of his years.

Far from objecting, he accepted the challenge and relished these extra lessons. He became *bookish*, and while others spent their evenings after prep reading comics or playing schoolboy games, more often than not, he was in the library continuing his studies.

This did nothing to help his popularity among his schoolfellows, who regarded him as a *swot*, and far from showing compassion for his disability, they picked on him and made him the object of their ridicule.

W-P was affronted. *It was not to be endured!*

But with the unfairness of the young, instead of seeking revenge upon his tormentors, he picked on a boy who was even smaller than he was. An innocent and likeable lad who happened to be French. Walter kicked him hard with the reinforced toe of his surgical boot.

His victim picked himself up and behaved most unexpectedly even for someone from France. Rather than burst into tears and run away to find someone smaller than himself to bully (thus perpetuating the accepted code of behaviour among schoolboys), he squared up to an amazed Walter and punched him firmly on the nose.

Such a cowardly act, unworthy as it was, turned Wilkes-Passmore's mind against the French forever. He never forgot it, and from that moment hated everything even remotely connected to the French including, polish, windows, chalk, mustard, beans and dressing and most of all, the people.

But there was a good side to the incident, according to Walter's rather twisted way of reasoning, in that the punch, but not the kick that preceded it, were observed by Mr. Hossack (Modern Languages), who happened to be passing and, grasping the French boy's ear, he marched him to the Headmaster's study for 'correction'.

This appealed to Walter's natural sense of justice. He viewed it as an example of Divine Retribution, and with his bloodied nose, saw himself something of a martyr. It was then, ten minutes after deciding that hating French people and French things would be added to his growing list of rules, that he decided since God had taken an interest in him, he would take an interest in God. He set his sights on becoming holy. He remembered from his months in hospital that his only visitor, the chaplain, dropped by very occasionally, spoke a load of rubbish and ate all his grapes.

He would do better. Would Walter Wilkes-Passmore be the Third Coming? No. Not even close.

After a largely indifferent period of being God's representative on Earth, he realised that marrying a few parishioners who were dead from the neck up, and burying a few who were dead all over, and having the Bible quoted at him constantly, did nothing in his quest for greatness.

He further realised that, although he was married in the sight of God, and happily married at that (thus proving the adage that *opposites attract*), the whole concept of religion and monogamous marriage was pure theory, based on writings thousands of years old and regularly altered since to adapt to the latest ways of thinking and political expediency.

Even the tract for engaged couples he had written himself, '*Correct Principles and Ideals of Married Bliss*', was largely only theory, particularly the sections covering the joys of 'bodily union', as was his statement that the husband, as head of the household, should make all the important decisions.

Mrs. Wilkes-Passmore made several appointments for interviews on behalf of W-P but didn't trust him to attend in person following his seemingly ready acceptance of defeat in the Army, and so during the following fortnight, she went herself to six possible schools where *she* interviewed *them*.

She settled on a small private school in East Sussex where accommodation was provided, her husband being appointed, *in absentia*, to teach fifteen-year-olds Mathematics, English Grammar and English Literature.

The Headmaster, Mr. Thompson, a tall, thin gentleman who was clearly terrified of her, was also clearly embarrassed when he asked her if she thought W-P might be willing to give the occasional lesson in the Birds and Bees, as he coyly put it. Harriet, who thought he meant Nature Studies, said her husband was very good at that too, and would be delighted.

The truth was that the Reverend Doctor's knowledge of that subject only came from what he had learnt in books borrowed from the vicar of All Saints'. The vicar had several dozen books on the theme, which Walter had been obliged to read in order to lecture engaged couples about the 'night-time' side of marriage.

These engaged couples probably knew more about it than he did. The fifteen-year-olds of the Lower Third certainly did. Where the Orchestra of Love was concerned, the Reverend gentleman was but a piccolo whereas *Mrs.* Wilkes-Passmore was the grand piano.

Far from being the demure, shrinking violet of a Bishop's daughter that one might expect from reading the novels of Thomas Hardy or the Bronte sisters, Harriet was built as if she had been conjured from the mind of Bram Stoker whilst he was having a very bad dream. To say she was large would be a gross understatement. It's more accurate to describe her simply as *gross* and leave it at that.

He had proposed marriage, not out of love or any form of attraction, but because he thought a clergyman *ought* to be married. And he was, after all, the most highly qualified curate ever to emerge from Theological College. More importantly, because she was the daughter of his own Bishop, he could see how an alliance with her family would increase his own chances of advancement within the church.

She accepted his proposal at the first time of asking, again, not because of love or attraction, but fearing she might never get another offer, and she thought a Bishop's daughter *ought* to be married.

Chris Hare

There were no children, as unsurprisingly, Walter Wilkes-Passmore had given up on the attempt to procreate after two minutes of undignified fumbling in their room in a small hotel in Great Yarmouth where they spent their honeymoon. Truthfully, he had gone off the idea of a physical union when the newly married Mrs. Wilkes-Passmore emerged from the bathroom wearing what he assumed, was a blue tent.

And so, during that fortnight of inactive physical exertions on his part, and no apparent desire on hers, Walter Wilkes-Passmore had spent his time doing what he did best – plotting and planning. Mrs. Wilkes-Passmore, however, having accepted with considerable amount of gratitude and not a little relief, that the 'rude' part of married life was to pass her by, spent hour after hour at Great Yarmouth fun fairs, winning fluffy teddy bears by the score at those attractions that required brute strength, which she had in abundance. Afterwards, several of the attractions required repair but the 'I Speak Your Weight' machine was declared beyond restoration after it had been dealt a right hook.

Within months of their return to the home they had set up in a small flat adjourning the Bishop's Residence, Walter found himself replaced in the marital bed by his wife's collection of fluffy teddy bears. An arrangement that suited Reverend Doctor and Mrs. W-P admirably.

Whether it suited the bears is unknown, but it could be imagined that had the little fluffies been blessed with

105

the power of speech, they just might have voiced an objection to being crushed by a human steamroller night after night.

The couple settled happily in East Sussex, and W-P found he was happy in his new career. He had never been, and never would be, happy in the *laughing* sense. He hardly ever laughed, and even a smile was rare. But he was content with his lot. He rapidly learnt that being deceitful, spreading rumours and covertly letting others know of their shortcomings, misjudgements or mistakes, as well as lying and cheating, were all part of everyday life in English public schools.

It's not the way you would expect teachers to behave, but there it is. It's the accepted path for gaining recognition and promotion.

And the Wilkes-Passmores, particularly the Reverend Doctor Walter, became experts. He understood the *political* side of school life and kept in mind another homily: *keep your friends close, but your enemies closer.*

He learnt that progression was not at all dependent on hard work but, to gain advancement, you had to be noticed by the right sort of person, by the Headmaster, by the Governors. You had to mix in the right circles, whisper in the right ears and subtly heap praise upon your own head. No one else would do it for you.

In a very short time, many things about W-P grew (not his height, although he always did his best to sound taller when speaking on the phone). Harriet grew in the same way as her husband, not physically, which in her case was a blessing for humanity. They grew in imagination, memory and importance.

When speaking to a new acquaintance, should the topic come up, which it invariably did once he found an opening, his service in the Armed Forces stretched in length from a few minutes to several years. His rank, if he had one, rose and rose, as he would say with a mixture of pride, modesty and creativity, the actual colour of his hat could not be seen beneath the vast quantities of gold braiding.

There were the medals he had been awarded, never worn – he didn't want to be accused of boasting, the campaigns he had fought in – details too ghastly to bring to mind, let alone speak of, and the dispatches in which the name Wilkes-Passmore had been mentioned – 'Nothing really, just doing my duty'.

None of it held a shred of truth, but the more he told his tales, the more he came to believe they were true. His claim to have invented an ultimate weapon for the sole use of the British Army, he meant his idea of being able to surround the enemy on his own, was altered so his listener might believe he was talking about a devastating bomb. The point is, he never went into details, thus giving the impression that his invention was very much still on the hush-hush.

Often, his listeners completely misunderstood his meaning, and thought the Wilkes-Passmore ultimate

107

weapon he referred to, was actually *Mrs*. Wilkes-Passmore. Which, in some ways, perhaps it was.

After two terms, she decided it was time to move on. To take another step up the ladder. She found a larger school with an improved salary, bigger accommodation, and better prospects for advancement, and they moved on.

And on.

Each time they moved they climbed another rung. He became Senior Master, then a Head of Department, and then a Housemaster.

And now, as Head of Chantry, he had the opportunity once again, to fulfil his ambition. He would be demonstrating his military genius to the whole world. Well, *his* world.

Next year, he would direct the Fourth Year in the battle scenes from *Macbeth*. He was anticipating the opportunity with pleasure. But of course, he didn't realise at this time, his army would include a Heroic Failure, one Lancelot Arthur Crabbe.

Chris Hare

9: THE FIRST YEAR

Like any journey into the unknown, the first steps were cautious, tentative and often in the wrong direction, but so began the defining part of Crabbe's journey through life. With repetition came confidence and some small successes.

Mr. Finney, Crabbe's first form master, looked like a relic from the Victorian era, and as such, blended in with the embellishment and decoration of the form room which, like their dorm, was spartan in the extreme. A raised dais was at one end of the room on which the master's desk was sited in front of the blackboard. There was a map of the world on one wall, shelves of books on another and rows of ink-stained wooden desks aligned on ink-stained wooden floorboards. The walls were painted in an uninviting sludge and the ceiling an equally dull cream from which four bare light bulbs dangled. The whole effect was reminiscent of a classroom from a Dickens' novel, except for the presence of electric lights and the (apparent) absence of cockroaches.

Crabbe was ever the optimist. He didn't mind if the school was a Victorian horror. Whilst many of the other Shells had spent their entire school lives as boarders and no doubt, bemoaned their lot, Crabbe rather took to it. He didn't feel homesick, *even* after two days. He felt

109

safe, secure and decided he was going to enjoy being a Chantovian.

But he hadn't met the Keyes matron yet.

Mr. Finney though, was a kindly-looking middle-aged man, clearly a bachelor, who sported leather patches on the elbows of his jackets and more often than not, a hole in the heel of his socks. He carried a very ancient and battered briefcase which in some way matched the rest of him. He was a friendly soul who smiled a lot. Crabbe saw him as a kindred spirit and took to him instantly.

Mr. Finney's contribution to the education of the boys of the middle school was History. On the first day he told the class that there was a joke circulating among the prefects, one he wasn't supposed to know, that History was his subject because he'd lived through most of it. Russell, who had escorted the Shells to their classroom, went a little red as he exited quietly.

'Ah, well. We are what we are,' said Mr Finney. 'To continue, I also run the Photographic Society, one of the extra-curricular activities you may like to consider joining. Photography is a most interesting hobby and I do advise you to think about it. The only condition of membership is that you own a camera.'

Crabbe *did* own a camera. The Box Brownie his father had given him was in his trunk. It had been a moment of inspiration for Mr. Crabbe – the idea had just popped into his head, from nowhere.

110

Chris Hare

Nowhere? This was an essential part of the Crabbe tapestry. The idea didn't just randomly 'pop in'. It was very carefully, woven in.

The Fates ordained that Crabbe should spend his first year or so at Chantry in relative peace but with some seeds sown to facilitate future disasters. These were carefully hidden under a cloak of subtlety. There was never a hint as to what was to happen, either to Crabbe or the unfortunates destined to cross his path.

During their first week, the Shells were given a physical examination by their respective House matrons. For Crabbe it would prove to be one of the most embarrassing events of his entire life. So far, that is.

Miss Griggs looked to be in her eighties, but, in fact, was not yet fifty. Dressed in an ash-grey uniform, she had grey hair, grey stockings, and a stern grey face. She smelled of carbolic.

'Strip to your underwear and line up to be examined.' she ordered.

The Shells did so. Quickly and in silence.

Miss Griggs looked each boy up and down, staring intently, aggressively searching for some serious defect.

She seemed to find something particularly unpleasant with Crabbe, possibly some loathsome disease she hadn't yet encountered. She prodded and poked in a most ungentlemanly manner. Crabbe tried a pleasant smile, but it wasn't reciprocated.

111

Crabbe in all Innocence

'You're far too thin, and much too tall for your age,' as if it was his fault. It wasn't. He was just gawky, like every other male in the Crabbe family. Even so, he said he was sorry, and that he'd try harder.

She sniffed with disapproval and took a pace backwards so she could take in the whole ghastly sight in one go. Clearly, this boy was a weakling. It was obvious he wouldn't be able to hold his own in sporting activities. And they were hardly onerous for Shells – plenty of running, some simple gym exercises and friendly inter-House sporting competitions. Nothing beyond the capabilities of an ordinary adolescent. But this Crabbe?

After the inspection was over, she climbed onto the dais and Mr. Finney surrendered the floor and took a respectful step back. He knew what was coming.

'Now, new boys, attend to me!' She kept her eyes closed as she spoke. Perhaps she didn't want to look at them. That was alright, because the boys certainly didn't want to be seen.

She spent five minutes talking about hygiene, which Crabbe found immensely embarrassing. He allowed his eyes to wander, trying, metaphorically, to close his ears and shut out the rude words.

Mr. Finney kept his eyes firmly on Miss Griggs as she spoke, hanging on her every word as if her views on hygiene were meant just for him.

After an age, she finished the lecture and told the Shells to line up again to have their statistics taken.

112

Russell returned, pushing some apparatus which he wheeled over to in front of the dais. It looked like portable gallows.

Each boy was weighed, and a note taken of his height, and all carefully entered by Miss Griggs into her book. She made little comment, just the occasional grunt.

Until it was Kirby's turn, 'You are too short for your weight. Either limit your intake of food or grow,' she instructed.

'Yes, Matron' replied Kirby because it couldn't be denied he'd inherited his father's rather ungainly figure.

Miss Griggs turned as she reached the door.

'You, Crabbe,' she said. 'By looking as if we are starving you, you are letting the school down. I will examine you again with next year's intake of Shells, by which time, you will have put on at least a stone in weight. Mr. Finney and I will be keeping an eye on you. Understand?'

'Yes, Matron,' replied Crabbe, and Mr. Finney.

Looking in a mirror Crabbe had to admit Miss Griggs was right. 'Oh glory,' he said to his reflection. He had no strength, and he had no stamina.

Seeing a photograph of Crabbe lined up with the others for a race on games afternoon, one would think he was the ideal candidate for middle-distance running. He was, by far, the tallest in his Year, with long legs that should have sent him striding to the finishing line way ahead of the others.

There was nothing wrong with his appetite: food was always a priority with him, as it was with every boy throughout the world. But where others put on muscle, growing outwards as they made the journey from boyhood to adolescence, Crabbe put on inches, just growing upwards.

That photograph would show a row of healthy, fit and eager white-clad athletes, waiting to burst into action at the report of the staring pistol. But included in their midst would be a giant, a white-clad, short-sighted stick insect wearing wire framed specs.

As threatened, the following year he was examined again. He *had* put on a little weight, but he'd also grown, despite being told.

Miss Griggs decided to take the matter further and shift her responsibility by reporting it to Mr. Finney. Mr. Finney agreed, and although a caring and considerate teacher, didn't feel that he should get the blame if something dreadful were to happen to Crabbe. He therefore consulted Mr. Pinder, who also agreed. During his tenure as Keyes Housemaster, he hadn't lost a single student through death, and sincerely wished to maintain his record. Consequently, he felt obliged to report the matter to the highest authority and had a quick word with the Head. He also agreed and made a phone call.

Chris Hare

The weeks passed and being of a gentle nature Crabbe presented no threat to anyone. He made friends easily. His fellow dormers – Kirby, Glover and Cartwright soon became Tobes, Gloves and Carters, while Crabbe himself was generally referred to by his initials. He didn't mind not having a nickname like the others and felt that L.C. was far more grown up than a childish version of his proper name. And so, with his full knowledge and agreement, he was known by most of his fellow Chantovians and by several members of the teaching staff, as 'Elsie'.

He worked hard and earned a 'brainy' reputation, only too happy to come to the aid of his classmates if they were stuck on a mathematical problem or needed help with their Latin. Crabbe gained good marks in every subject, except art, at which he was useless, and sports, as has already been noted, he was worse than useless. He wasn't worried unduly about art – he thought either one could draw, or one couldn't. He just accepted that he was one who couldn't and left it at that.

As for sports, he didn't mind coming last all the time, he'd grown used to it. But he *did* mind looking so thin, looking like a bespectacled collection of bones. He stood out in a crowd, for all the wrong reasons. He *minded* that, because he'd never been one to court notice or popularity. He was happy just *being* there, being part of Chantry, but standing at the back, preferably in the shadows.

Crabbe in all Innocence

Everything was so competitive, that was the trouble, and Crabbe wasn't competitive by nature. The boys were encouraged to set themselves targets and do all in their power to achieve them. Not just in sports, but in everything. To better the mark they received last year in a particular examination, to read a book in a week, then then the next in six days. Apparently, it was all to make them fit in with the outside world. Although in Crabbe's case, he just wanted to be *fit*.

'*Fit*' meaning *strong, able bodied, athletic*.

And so, at the next sports afternoon, Mr. Pinder waited patiently at the finishing line for Crabbe to (eventually) struggle across, and as they walked together towards the changing rooms, Mr. Pinder himself struggled to find words of comfort.

'Never mind, Crabbe. The race is not always won by the swiftest.'

Crabbe, for once having a disrespectful thought, wondered if Mr. Pinder had gone round the bend.

Later, after experiencing more of what life had to throw at him, he came to understand what Mr. Pinder had meant: the winner wasn't necessarily *only* he who crossed the line first. Perhaps, he who came last in the field could be called a winner too, if in doing so he'd managed to overcome a disability or handicap not shared by the rest of the competitors. He might not have won the cup, but because of his endeavour, he had won respect.

116

Chris Hare

10: ASSEMBLY

It may be thought a rare, if not impossible coincidence for some hundreds of souls from different backgrounds and different parts of the world to be sharing the same thoughts, the same opinions, all at the same time.

Yet, such coincidences do happen, and at Chantry it happened every Monday during term, in Hall and at 8.30am.

And, despite the diversity of ages between the masters and boys and indeed, the diversity of ages between the pupils themselves, which ranged from terrified Shells to great muscle-bound Sixth formers, they were as one: standing, *bored beyond belief* as James Russell (duty prefect again) fought his way through the Lesson, reading from the huge School Bible which was open between the spread wings of the solid brass eagle lectern.

The malevolent features that organised the eagle's face included hypnotic, bulging eyes that stared down into Hall, daring anyone to move on pain of being ripped apart by its wickedly curved beak. It had the effect of making everyone stare back, eyes never moving from the stage, where could be seen the lectern, Russell, the Headmaster's desk on the raised dais, and through it, part of his legs. His face and upper body, and from his knees downward were concealed behind the desktop and the set of wooden steps he'd had constructed to see and be seen over the top.

Had anyone paused to consider the eagle's feelings, which no one ever had, it could be thought that this monster, this gift from a former Chantovian, was itself in all probability, bored out of its mind by the stilted, stuttered efforts of someone who didn't want to read from those interminable pages to people who didn't want to listen.

After all, the eagle had occupied the same spot on the stage for over fifty years whilst Russell, and generations of prefects before him, had struggled with in the main, unpronounceable names from an era they learned of in Ancient History.

No prefect had ever had a problem with the name 'Moses', which was a sensible name. Less sensible, and the cause of much ribald speculation in the dorms after lights out by thirteen-year- olds and upwards, was the story of being *found* in the bulrushes by the Pharaoh's daughter.

Was it relevant? Did Old Testament stories of who begot whom thousands of years ago really matter? Was who smote who of any concern, or any interest, to modern day man? They were always smiting each other in those days.

Collectively, such was their thinking as Russell droned on.

But it was a fact that not a single one of those present would ever dream of giving voice to their thoughts.

119

That would be sacrilege – not the sacrilege of commenting adversely on cadences of Holy Writ, but *blasphemy* – the implied criticism of an ancient, and therefore revered, School Tradition.

This latest brass eagle lectern had doubtless been presented to replace an even older bored-stiff brass griffin lectern, that had probably collapsed under the weight of an even older Bible going back to the days of the founding of Chantry in the Civil War.

The pupils of Chantry did their best to listen, just in case during the day one of the masters should fire a question at them. It was a favourite trick, designed to keep boys attentive, *at all times*. But the drawback this time, was that the masters had to listen to the Lesson too.

Listen they all did, knowing full well that occupying centre stage, a few feet to the right and slightly behind Russell, the dread figure of the Head was standing with an expression on his face that made the brass eagle look positively lovable.

The Head would be paying strict attention, they knew. He would be concentrating and noting every badly pronounced name and thinking what an uplifting experience this was for them all. *No better way to start the week than by listening to a couple of chapters read aloud from the Good Book.*

In fact, he was barely awake.

Had any part of him, apart from his legs, been able to be seen, it would have been natural to think that the

120

Head was meditating hard on each word of the scripture, head bowed in reverence, eyes closed in concentration. The reality was very much otherwise.

Since being appointed to the Headship of Chantry three years before, the Reverend Wilkes-Passmore had learnt, during the tedious parts of school life such as this, to adopt the guise of a tripod.

His left foot firmly planted on the ancient oak planking stage, eighteen inches from his right encased in the surgical boot, and to the front, forming the apex of the triangle, his ebony walking stick which bore most of the Headmaster's weight. This particular stick was acquired shortly after his wife, as a second line of defence, and was topped with a silver horse's head handle.

Years ago, as a young curate from Theological College, he had spent many long hours studying the Bible, and committed vast tracts to memory. He had held Bible study classes in the Church hall, and taught Bible stories to youngsters at Sunday School. Parishioners thought it was their duty to deliver an apt quote whenever they saw him, and he was expected to come back with a suitable response. All in all, he became heartily sick of the Bible, which is not something you would expect a reverend gentleman to admit. Even to himself.

But admit he did, and realised the Church held no future for him. It wasn't just the Bible. It was the *people*. His colleagues at the College had been, without exception, sanctimonious earnest young men who would never make a success of anything. He'd long ago convinced himself that if you fail at everything else, your only option was to become a vicar.

And then there were the people who *went* to Church. The congregation. After a few weeks delivering his Sunday sermons he realised that those attending could be divided into two groups; those who were asleep, and himself. Though not particularly gifted at perceiving changes in atmosphere, he could not deny the snoring.

Most of his parishioners were elderly, living out their final years and going to Church in the belief that, when their moment came and they departed this life, because they had been regular worshippers ever since realising they were not immortal, in some cases, barely six weeks, they would be welcomed into heaven with open arms.

Such had been his brilliant academic success and achievements at Theological College, it was acknowledged by those in authority that it was only a matter of time before he'd be offered a bishopric. But even before he was promoted to vicar, he'd resigned his curacy, joined the army for a brief and unmemorable career and became a schoolteacher.

And he loved it.

First, as an assistant master in a small private school, from which lowly, two guinea a week position, he had rapidly climbed the ladder, made sensible and timely changes in his teaching appointments, until by 1930, he had reached the top. Or so he thought at the time. But now he had dreams of Eton or Harrow.

For the present, here he was – Walter Wilkes-Passmore, BA (Hons), still a Doctor of Divinity, still a Reverend, but now, and this was very important, the Headmaster of an English public school. Certainly, Chantry was a little on the small side compared to some and considered 'minor' since they rarely got any royalty, even so, it was just as ancient and just as renowned.

Russell came to the end of whatever he was reading, and politely waited for the Head to say the 'Amen' so the massed ranks of staff and pupils and staff before him could say 'Amen' in return.

They went through the ritual. Russell closed the Bible, bowed to the Head, and returned to stand in his place at the end of the row of Fifth Years towards the rear of Hall.

Dr. Wilkes-Passmore climbed his three wooden steps and his top half appeared to the school.

'Let us pray. Oh Lord,' and he squeaked his way through some prayers of his own composition, raising his voice so those at the back could hear. They came to an end with a more or less, simultaneous 'Amen'.

He looked down severely through the *pince-nez* spectacles balanced on the end of his nose and glanced at the list of names in the punishment book.

It was ironic that every Monday morning at Assembly, after a hymn of the uplifting variety, sung with gusto but little regard for the tune, the Lesson, which they had all just endured, and the prayers led by the Headmaster himself, which always included something about forgiving your enemy, came the list of boys he was going to beat.

Would they ever learn? Would they never come to accept that rules were rules for obeying, not breaking?

He began, 'Wildman, Elames-Turner, Bond Minor. My study, after Assembly.'

Only three names? Not bad, he thought, before continuing with those listed for lesser punishment.

'Upper Third, class detention for the pillow fight after Sports today in your classroom. The following boys are on the Housemaster's Report, to be worked this Sunday morning, after Chapel.'

He got to the end of the list and looked up, 'Wildman, Elames-Turner and Bond Minor, prepare yourselves. This will be the third occasion this term that each of you has been sent to me for a beating. I intend that you learn your lesson. You will remember this morning, I assure you.'

The three guilty boys, all from the Second Year, grimaced at each other. Dr. Wilkes-Passmore had a strong and practiced right arm. It was a known fact that the Head, before taking up his appointment at Chantry, had trained in torture with the Spanish Inquisition.

There were several other known facts about *Rasputin*.

One was his limp. It was undisputed by the whole school, or at least the whole Lower School, that the

124

limp was the result of being hit in the leg by an arrow at Agincourt.

The Head tapped the top of his desk to emphasise his words, 'Listen carefully. An important part of your education is learning the meaning of discipline. When the Great War started in 1914, young men were conscripted into the army. Many were not much older than our own Fifth and Sixth formers. They had to learn the meaning of discipline the hard way, by instantly obeying orders, without question. The slightest hesitation or challenge to authority meant their death – shot by their own side instead of going 'over the top' to be shot by the Germans.

It is your good fortune that when the war ended in 1918, the victorious powers agreed that it had been the war *to end all wars*. Such a huge conflict could never be allowed to happen again.

But, in order to keep peace in this world, we still have to fight small wars, and it is not impossible that you might be called upon to *do your duty*, should the need arise, and don your uniforms to fight for King and Country.'

He paused and gave his audience a meaningful stare. He enjoyed putting the fear of God into boys, as well as beating them.

'It would be better for you to learn to obey *now*, whilst you are young and safe at school and have myself and your masters to guide you. I do not relish the thought of having to flog you for your

125

misdemeanours,' he lied, 'but it seems to be the only way. It is a necessary part of my position as Headmaster of Chantry, and I will not shrink from my duty. But if you shrink from yours by disobeying orders, you will discover to your cost the awful punishments that await wrongdoers in uniform.'

The silence in the Hall, as five hundred pupils took in the Head's words, if possible, became even deeper.

'Finally, this afternoon's sporting programme.'

Sport was still a most important part of life at Chantry. All around the hall were more black honours boards displaying the names of sporting heroes rather than dead ones. Over the years, the school had produced many great sportsmen who had become household names, but, as Doctor Wilkes-Passmore took up his lists, he doubted any of the present pupils would ever run for their country or row for Oxford or Cambridge.

Because of his limp, the Head had never been able to take the field, but that didn't prevent him from being a fervent supporter. In winter, he could be found on the touchline of the rugby pitch every Saturday afternoon, screaming encouragement to the school team and urging them into greater efforts. And, because he was the type of man he was, also threatening them with the most savage beatings if they failed.

As today was a Saturday in the Summer Term, there were no lessons after lunch but there was cricket.

'The two Sixth-forms against each other,' W-P read, 'The Colts to take on, and beat, the visiting Ridfield County team, and the combined Fifth Year Eleven to win away at Byngham Hall.'

Unlike rugby, cricket was a far quieter game. A game to be played and watched by a gentleman. One didn't cheer, one politely clapped. Exceptionally, if there was a particularly fine six or a humdinger of a ball bowled, then it was permitted to call out 'shot, sir' or 'great ball'.

And so, to ensure the English way of cricket was observed, no more than fifty spectators were permitted to watch each match.

The Head read out the names of those boys selected to play, and then, replacing his papers and picking up his walking stick from the top of the desk, he concluded morning assembly by announcing that the pupils who were not playing or watching, would take part in a paper chase in and around the village.

'Except for you, Crabbe.' He pointed his stick in the general direction of the tall boy with glasses and the pale face, a face that turned crimson at the mention of his name. 'You will go to St. Margaret's to play tennis.'

Crabbe's jaw dropped, and he felt beads of sweat form on his forehead. He glowed crimson.

The Reverend Doctor turned and climbed down the steps, unaware or ignoring the number of boys behind him who were stabbing their hands in the air begging to be allowed to play tennis too.

Crabbe in all Innocence

Crabbe just stood there, reddening deeper by the second and gaping stupidly at the vacated dais. He heard nothing. Not the please, sirs, let me play tennis, and not the loudly whispered, good lucks to Wildman, Elames-Turner and Bond Minor as they went, reluctantly, to receive payment for their sins.

Chris Hare

11: THE LITTLE SISTERS of GREAT MERCY

Crabbe stood there, staring blankly at the now empty stage. He was at a loss. He felt picked on. *Victimised.*

Why? He had never been summoned to the Headmaster's study for correction. He had never knowingly or deliberately broken any school rules. He'd never answered back to a master and was always polite and respectful. He'd done his best to look like the others. He'd eaten his greens and drank gallons of milk. He'd even joined in with Toby's morning exercises. All to no avail.

And now, this. He knew what was behind it, but he wasn't the only skinny boy at the school. And he wasn't the tallest. But he *was* the thinnest of all the tall ones. It just wasn't fair. Was he really going to have to suffer this humiliation? Could he appeal, resign, or perhaps, run away? Mouth open and sweating, he desperately tried to think through his options.

In his heart he knew he had none. No choices. The Head's word was law. It was decided, and that, was that.

In deep despair, he made his way back to the dorm, hands thrust deep in his pockets, head down, avoiding eye contact. After changing into his cricket whites, he paused in front of the full-length mirror and stared. Reluctantly, he had to accept that those in authority were right – he was an embarrassment to the school. A beanpole.

Yes. They were right, and so it followed that he, Lancelot Arthur Crabbe, must be *wrong*.

Another thought followed. If they were correct, and his reflection proved they were, perhaps their solution to *his* problem was also correct.

With that thought, he suddenly brightened. Perhaps, perhaps…

There was a spring in his step by the time he had made his way to St. Margaret's playing fields on the other side of the village. He felt invigorated, confident and even ebullient. It really was as if the proverbial millstone had been lifted from around his neck. He climbed the steps to the sports' pavilion and heard the high-pitched laughter and chatter of younger boys coming from inside.

Boys! Juniors. Yes, but at least they were boys. He knew little of girls and had absolutely no idea of how to go about speaking to one. It also occurred that, although tennis was as yet a mystery to him, because he was older and probably far taller, he might, for the first time ever, win at sports!

This last idea brought a wide smile to his face, and with that happy prospect in mind, he pushed open the door to the pavilion and stepped inside, throwing the loose end of his scarf nonchalantly over his shoulder as he did so.

As was often the way, he found wearing glasses something of a nuisance. To be accurate, it was not the actual wearing of the glasses that caused this problem, but the removal of them when they steamed up in humid atmospheres, such as that in a changing room.

Without registering who was in there or what was going on, he took them off to polish the lenses with the end of his scarf, still beaming in a way that displayed the air of confidence that had only so recently descended upon him.

He could vaguely make out the suddenly silent out-of-focus lads in front of him and hoped they were beaming back.

He put his specs back on, and in the instant before he was deafened, stabbed and throttled from behind, he saw he had been beaming widely at several young ladies in various stages of undress.

His already red face turned redder. He opened his mouth to scream. Whether or not he succeeded will never be known as another scream was more loudly vented from somewhere behind him.

A tremendous force on the other end of the scarf sent him bending backwards and Crabbe was unable to resist. Dragged out through the door in reverse he felt the point of the knife pressed into the small of his back. His assailant let go of the scarf in the doorway but before Crabbe could straighten up or try another yell, a strong ungiving hand grabbed at his throat, the fingers threatening to push his Adam's apple out through the back of his collar. Through eyes screwed in pain, he had a final glimpse of the young ladies who had stopped whatever they were doing to glance at him briefly and then carry on as if nothing at all out of the ordinary was happening.

Going backwards down the pavilion steps was particularly painful. Breathing difficult, shrieking impossible. The knife was still pressed into his spine. It hadn't punctured him yet.

He stopped at the bottom of the steps and the iron grip was released, and Crabbe found himself being spun round to face his adversary, who landed a punch on his hip. In front of him and a foot or so lower, was an enormous white headdress and beneath that, an enormous nun, short, powerfully built, and not holding a knife to Crabbe's back, but a pointed silver crucifix.

The punch she'd thrown was intended for his ear, but she couldn't reach. She was able to reach Crabbe's tie, and did, pulling it down until his face was a mere six inches from her own snarling features. Crabbe could see every strand of her moustache.

She didn't hit him again, for which he was grateful, but contented herself with berating him in such a venomous fashion that spittle gathered in the corners of her mouth before being sprayed over him.

'You disgusting little pervert!' she began.

Crabbe, hardly able to speak because of the damage to his Adam's apple, with possibly his final breath, croaked, 'I'm not a pervert, or a convert. I'm Church of England.'

The nun spat back, 'Same thing. You are a disgusting, depraved, hideous and degenerate little monster,' and she used the sharp end of the crucifix to punctuate each syllable.

Although in pain and completely terrified, Crabbe was nevertheless aware that he'd been called 'little' twice, which he certainly wasn't.

'How dare you spy on my girls? Have you no shame?'

Crabbe opened his mouth to protest, but she raised the crucifix like a dagger and looked about to deliver a fatal blow. Because of the height difference, the sharp end hovered threateningly in the area of Crabbe's navel.

'But…'

'Silence!' she screamed and continued haranguing the unfortunate Crabbe, who had no choice but to listen and be spat at, whilst being strangled with his own school tie and threatened with death at the hands of a silver crucifix – or rather, the feet thereof. And besides these factors, he was worried as to the state, and current whereabouts of his Adam's apple. The restriction of oxygen was making his mind wander and he felt giddy.

From Biology lessons, he remembered that the Adam's apple was an important part of the mechanism for speech, and felt that should he survive the encounter, he would need his Adam's apple to speak an

133

apology even though whether this was really *that* important also crossed his confused brain. Could the Adam's apple be like the appendix, there in one's body but serving no purpose other than to be cut out by a junior surgeon who needed the practice? He would ask Mr. Davis on Thursday. Or was Science on Wednesdays?

And why didn't girls have them? He was of an age to wonder about girls, a mystery to him. The subject of females was taboo in Biology lessons, but still, he wondered. He'd been wondering several things to do with girls since his last birthday. Until now, the absence of an Adam's apple hadn't been one of them.

But, he thought, as he started to feel he was floating, females certainly talked a great deal, as evidenced by the one presently killing him. Had she got an Adam's apple? If she had, it wouldn't be like a chap's bulging forth from his throat. It was probably fitted in reverse, bobbing up and down unnoticed, pointing into the neck, instead of out of it.

He peered through hazy eyes at the flabby area below the chin of his murderess. It was impossible to see anything other than the folds of angry quivering red flesh that dangled and swung there. Just before passing out, it occurred to him that had she been possessed of an Adam's apple, it would probably win first prize in a fruit and vegetable show. Then he collapsed.

Although he was sure he was at the point of death, Crabbe thought he ought to get up from where he'd landed when he was so ordered. Anyway, had he been unable to get up, though dying, his corpse would because it was being hauled upwards by means of its tie.

'Go and stand in the corner and do not move. I have eyes in the back of my head.'

Once, he had read a book sent to Cartwright by his godmother that had dead people called zombies who could walk around. He walked like that now, zombie fashion, to stand in the corner, *but there were no corners.*

He was on a playing field that seemed to drift on and on forever, corner-less. But there was an oak tree, so he went to stand by that, bowing his head to reflect upon his sins, which, he thought was appropriate in the circumstances.

Not that he felt he had committed any, but realising that since he was obviously still alive, it might prevent him from being murdered again.

Behind him, the nun blew a whistle and roared at the pavilion for silence and for the girls to come outside instantly and form two lines. This they did and without a sound. Crabbe took some small comfort in knowing that he wasn't the only one terrified of her.

Then he heard her footsteps behind him.

Another of Cartwright's godmother's books had been about the devil coming to Earth and walking about on cloven hoofs. A clearer minded Crabbe would have dismissed the possibility. A Roman Catholic nun in league with the devil? Impossible! But a tortured and beaten woolly minded Crabbe?

The footsteps got nearer. He bunched his fists, readying for more pain, and lowered his head still further. He put on an expression he hoped would be taken for remorse.

'Turn around,' came a command.

He turned, his face twitching slightly in anticipation of a fresh assault.

'You look like you are chewing a wasp.'

Crabbe stopped twitching and went for the look of an innocent Christian martyr. The face in front of him was now a watered-down shade of carmine, but the voice was the same.

It boomed, 'I am Sister Rosemary of the Order of the Little Sisters of Great Mercy. The Sisters are a charitable, teaching institution. It is out of charity that we agreed to take you for games.'

There didn't seem to be a single feature of her glowering face that could remotely be considered charitable. Crabbe had felt a fish out of water about being sent to play tennis, but this lady behaved like the creature from the Black Lagoon.

'Madam,' he said.

'Sister!' she barked.

'Sister, I must ask your pardon for blundering into the changing room. It was quite unintentional, an innocent mistake. Allow me to explain. My name is Crabbe, I'm from...'

He got no further. She held up a stubby finger and screamed, 'Silence!' It seemed to be her favourite word. 'I know who you are, what you are doing here and where you are from. The Lord moves in mysterious ways. My girls are studying the works of Jane Austen. This,' she said, turning towards the girls and jabbing a finger into Crabbe's ribs at the same time, 'is the Wuthering Height you were warned of. It is a boy.'

He felt himself colouring up as thirty sets of eyes inspected him.

'He will partner me in a doubles match against Koshkai and Cassandra on the main court.'

She bent over and lifted the skirt of her habit. Crabbe immediately averted his eyes. He had no wish to glimpse the nun's underwear which he suspected was made of asbestos. From somewhere out of the depths, she extracted a piece of paper and read out the names of the girls who were to play on the other courts and those who would play rounders.

She blew her whistle again and the two rows broke up into a babbling disorganised swarm, all moving and talking at once with nobody listening.

Another blast restored peace and the girls were ordered to their allotted games, leaving Cassandra, a stocky brown-haired girl who looked to Crabbe as if she was built for a successful career as a nun, and Koshkai, a slim Japanese girl who smiled at him warmly and bowed from the waist, her long black hair falling either side of her pretty pale face.

137

Crabbe in all Innocence

Crabbe was captivated. Enchanted.

His face lit up in a smile and blushing, he returned the bow slowly, thinking that when he was upright again, he would say something to her. Perhaps ask her something about her Adam's apple?

He didn't get the chance. At about an incline of two feet his right ear came within range and was clouted. He staggered, clutching at the side of his head and hearing the rushing sound of wind careering through a cave thinking that whoever it was that named this nun's order had got the wording all mixed up. *Great Sisters of Little Mercy* would be far more appropriate.

With an effort, he straightened up. He didn't want to look unmanly in front of Koshkai.

'No fraternising!' came the scream from Sister Rosemary, 'You are here to play tennis, nothing more. Do you hear?'

Despite the throbbing ear, he heard. Anyone who wasn't totally stone deaf would have heard.

'Go and change!' ordered this devil incarnate.

'But Miss, err, Sister, I have nothing to change into. I didn't think. I am wearing my cricket flannels. Will they not suffice?'

'Of course not! You can't play tennis inappropriately attired. Find some shorts from the brown locker then return here to line up.'

Crabbe rooted through the brown locker and found several pairs of shorts, and some other garments he dared not touch. He held the different sized shorts up in front of him, and eventually decided on a pair that were long enough to reach down to his knees. He glanced round for a private place to change. He didn't want someone blundering in like he had.

Having locked the toilet door, he removed his flannels and put on the shorts. He discovered two problems. Though longish in length, they were too wide in width. There was at least nine inches of waistband surplus to his shape. They must have belonged to a giantess, or a nun. So, how would he keep them up? He decided that wearing his braces from his cricket whites would be considered 'inappropriate attire' and he was sure he wouldn't be allowed to play in his white cricket sweater which normally concealed them.

Inspiration struck and he used his tie as a belt and then fluffed his shirt out over it. He looked well enough, so he faced his second problem. The legs of his shorts were three inches shorter than the legs of his underpants.

He took hold of the left leg of the shorts and tugged it down. The right leg shifted up by the same distance and he found himself wondering if Archimedes had ever pondered on this point. Probably not. They didn't wear shorts in those days. They wore togas and doubtless had a slave to ensure the hem was level. Did they wear underpants?

Crabbe in all Innocence

He realised he was deliberately wasting time, putting off the moment when he would have to go out and face the she-wolf.

Outside, Sister Rosemary was getting impatient. She pointed her whistle in the direction of the pavilion and gave a shrill blast.

Crabbe heard and jumped back to the task in hand feeling like Sydney Carton about to have his head removed and having rolled up each leg of his underpants so that they were covered by the shorts, he unlocked the toilet door and marched forth to bravely meet his fate with Madame Guillotine.

But, when putting on a confident, eager expression, he said, 'All present and correct, Madame Defarge. That is, Sister...' His voice trailed away to a tiny squeak and his assumed confidence trailed away along with it.

Fortunately, she was not holding knitting needles, but tennis rackets. She handed one to Crabbe, who was surprised by its weight. Obviously, he thought, Sister Rosemary was powerful enough to have thrown a cannon ball at the Armada, Cassandra too. But Koshkai? He doubted she had the strength to even hold a tennis racket. And he tested his theory by dropping his.

'Weakling! Pick it up and follow!'

He did, with both hands, and staggered along behind the nun.

The two girls followed, giggling.

Crabbe thought their amusement came from the idea of playing tennis with a boy. He was unaware that his left underpants' leg had rolled down and was flapping somewhere around his knees as he trotted and tried to keep up with Sister Rosemary. His mind, now clearer, was focused on the woman in front. Did she really intend to play tennis in her robes and that great white headdress thing that made her look as if she'd been landed on by a passing swan?

Apparently, she did.

The girls were directed to one side of the court where they warmed up by gently knocking the ball back and forth to one another. Crabbe was surprised to see Koshkai handling her racket as if it were balsa. He set himself a target. If Koshkai, a mere girl (albeit the most beautiful and charming girl he had ever laid eyes on), if she could handle the heavy racket so easily, then he would make sure he did it just as well.

He listened intently as Sister Rosemary bawled out the rules and rudiments of the game.

'Pay attention. The game is quite simple, so you should take to it readily enough.'

Crabbe thought he was being complimented, so he risked a darting smile.

'You will stand on that line and serve,' she indicated the baseline and Crabbe went and stood on it obediently. 'You will throw the ball up and then hit it with your racket, using both hands if necessary, over the net towards Cassandra, who will return it and then there will be a rally which will probably include all four players. Do you understand so far?'

Crabbe said that he did, which was partly true. He couldn't see the *point* of the game, but daren't mention it to Sister Rosemary. The last thing he wanted was another dose of crucifix.

In cricket, he reasoned to himself, there were tactics, stratagems that would bring about the defeat of the opposition. He'd thought tennis would be the same, but no, tennis he found out, was all about brute strength.

Sister Rosemary continued, 'as to scoring, whichever side wins the first point gets fifteen points and the other side gets love. Then it gets a little more complicated.'

Crabbe set himself another target. He would win. The thought of love with Sister Rosemary filled him with renewed horror.

In any case, who would win was a foregone conclusion. He had a height advantage and although Cassandra was built on a grander scale, he knew from painful experience that beneath her voluminous habit, his partner simply bulged with muscle. As for Koshkai, she looked as if she wasn't strong enough to hurt a fly. If he served to her, he would be very gentle.

But, to begin with, he was to serve to the prowling Cassandra opposite. At least, that was what he was instructed to do and what he intended.

But the road to hell is paved with good intentions, as he soon found.

Sister Rosemary stood by the net, her back to Crabbe, 'On my whistle, serve!' and she blew a single blast.

He threw the ball into the air and as it came down, hit it with a mighty, two handed blow. He put in every ounce of effort, his feet even leaving the ground as he smashed the ball.

It was a glorious shot. It left his racket with the speed of a bullet and Cassandra would have had no chance of returning it, had it reached her.

But it didn't. It didn't even get over the net.

As it flew, Crabbe thought it would take six-inch armour plating to stop it. Or the back of Sister Rosemary's neck. The ball made for the unsuspecting nun. As it struck, Crabbe thought she must have six-inch skin that prevented her head from being removed.

He also remembered her saying she'd eyes in the back of her head. If this had been true, she would have seen the ball coming and ducked.

For a few moments, total silence. The only parts of Sister Rosemary that were able to move were her chins which moved of their own accord, pulsating in agony.

Crabbe also found himself unable to move. He stood, rooted to the spot, rigid with fear at the realisation of what he had just done. Cassandra stopped prowling on her baseline when she saw she wouldn't have to return Crabbe's serve, and it was Koshkai, nearest the battered nun, who eventually broke the silence by calling out, 'Are you alright, Sister?'

Crabbe in all Innocence

Sister didn't answer but slowly turned to Crabbe who knew beyond doubt that his end was now in sight. The crucifix was aimed at him. *Was it loaded?*

Blood drained from his face as the nun took two or three faltering steps towards him. He looked beyond her at the now strangely white face of Koshkai. He suddenly and desperately wanted hers to be the last face he saw before he died. Not the crimson hate filled, bulging eyed monster that, at a distance of ten feet, issued a shrill gurgling noise from her throat and then stumbled.

But she didn't fall. She managed to gather her superhuman strength for a final charge in the manner of homicidal maniacs determined to do one last murder before they joined their victims in the hereafter.

At six feet, she let out a gasp, released her grip on the crucifix and tottered a few more paces before finally collapsing. The earth around her shook as she landed. She lay still.

Crabbe had closed his eyes in anticipation of receiving his deathblow. He both heard and felt the thud and risked opening his left eye, where he saw, to his great relief that his adversary had been laid low.

Had the devil given up the fight? Had God's goodness come to his aid in his hour of need?

No. Neither. She had swallowed her whistle.

Crabbe had noticed the dangling string in the corner of her mouth but decided now wasn't the time to mention it.

She lay on her back, making no noise. A refreshing change.

The girls, now understanding the seriousness of the situation, came around the end of the net and knelt beside her, taking a hand each and patting it. Crabbe bent over the body. *What a way to go*, he thought. But she hadn't gone.

He grasped the string and pulled, and the whistle came out clean, as whistles are supposed to, but teeth followed. Not just one or two, but the whole top set.

Sister Rosemary was resilient, if nothing else. An ordinary human, upon discovering they were still alive, would have come round slowly, fluttering their eyelids, moaning softly and asking where they were.

None of this happened. No feminine affectations, no request for smelling salts. She just sat bolt upright and snatched her hands away from the girls. Then picked up Crabbe's racket and began to batter him about the head.

Naturally, he put his hands up to protect himself as best he could and it was then she noticed he was holding the string, with her teeth and her whistle attached. She stopped the racket mid backhand to berate him again, although he couldn't understand the actual words she used as they flew out her mouth covered in spittle, he got the drift.

Eventually, the haranguing ceased, and she snatched back the string and whistle and the teeth and replaced them. Then she raised herself to her feet using Crabbe as a support and with her weight pressing down on him, they changed places.

She gave him a final poke in the ribs that winded him, so he was unable to hear what she said next to the girls. But when he was unceremoniously hauled to his feet, once again, he understood that Sister Rosemary no longer wished to partner him.

A normal human being would have given up. Would have wanted to go somewhere quiet to recover. But Crabbe had worked out that there was nothing remotely normal about Sister Rosemary, therefore, he was not that surprised that the game was set to continue. Indeed, she didn't seem to have suffered any permanent damage, although with a face like hers it was difficult to be certain. At least, it had returned to its usual beetroot hue.

She took the whistle and gave it a powerful blow. The pea had gummed up so no sound could come out. Picking up her racket she pointed it to the other side of the net, indicating that Crabbe should now partner Koshkai.

He mouthed a 'Yes, Sister. Sorry, Sister,' at her, picked up his own racket and went to join Koshkai. They exchanged bows, and Koshkai pointed her racket to show him where he should stand. It wasn't necessary, he could see the area for himself, where the grass had been flattened by Cassandra's prowling feet. But being the gentleman he was, he bowed again and smilingly nodded his thanks and took up his position.

146

Once there, he thought it would look as if he knew what he was doing if he prowled a little too. He looked down to make sure his feet were the correct side of the baseline. What he saw filled him with embarrassment and horror. His underpants' legs, both of them now, were visible and flapping free in the breeze. He straightened up aghast, which was his mistake.

Had he stayed where he was, head bowed and gaping stupidly at his underpants, Sister Rosemary's service ball would have passed right over him. As it was, his world exploded.

12: THE PINK PRISON

Once more Crabbe felt as if he'd been hit between the eyes with a hammer and collapsed in an undignified, sprawling heap.

His forehead was numb, and he was aware of a drum being played somewhere in his head. Not the wake-up drum, so presumably, his eardrum. He would ask Mr. Davis.

Despite the force of the ball, he was only stunned if somewhat shocked. But head injuries of this nature are never to be taken lightly, unless you are a nun capable of shrugging them off. But Crabbe, when he had the strength to rise, found he couldn't. Within moments he was surrounded by teenaged girls who were determined to practice their nursing skills. Such skills consisted of holding him down and pushing his head back whenever he tried to lift it.

Sister Rosemary was outraged. She blew her whistle, the pea having dried out, and gave vent to her fury when she realised that for the girls to have got there so quickly, they must have ignored her instructions and been watching through the hedge.

Watching a boy!

The boy in question lay at her feet and despite the gradual worsening of the throbbing in his head, was content to not, for once, be the focus of her anger. He

148

looked up at the sky and realised with a shock that there was something wrong with his eyes. It was summer, and there should have been larks or something flitting above, but there were none, or if there were, he couldn't see them.

All he *could* see were the out-of-focus forms of girls, still kneeling around him even whilst being screamed at. He wondered why they were out-of-focus. He was very short-sighted, true, but could see perfectly well with his wire-framed spectacles. Crabbe was unaware that the tennis ball had struck him right between the eyes so hard it had divided his glasses. Each half now hung uselessly from either ear.

He recognised one face, a beautiful anxious face, and then he saw a pumpkin, then Cassandra. Gradually the blue sky darkened as it was filled with the faces of those who had been paying attention to the pumpkin's lecture and had, now it was over, turned their attention back to him. Soon the area above him was almost completely dark as more and more faces filled it and even if his glasses hadn't been divided, he couldn't have seen a lark had there been one, flitting or otherwise.

Many hands reached out to help him to feet, and he stood unsteadily. The drummer in his head began beating a bass drum, slowly and in a rhythm that reminded Crabbe of a funeral march.

And indeed, a march akin to this now took place, with Crabbe playing the part of the corpse, and the Upper

Crabbe in all Innocence

Fourth acting as very serious pallbearers. As they raised him, reverently, carefully and horizontally, the two halves of his glasses fell unnoticed from his ears and were ground to dust by thirty pairs of tennis shoes and whatever Sister Rosemary used to hide her cloven feet.

He felt the mortally wounded hero, being borne from the field of battle by his loyal band of knights. He could see the sky from up there, the sun and the clouds. Soft yellow clouds with yellow skin and narrow eyes. The clouds bowed. He tried to bow back, but as he raised his head, Cassandra put her face close to his and dabbed his forehead with her hanky. A kindly act, and in all probability, the first in her life.

Crabbe gave a sort of pained groan which he thought fitted in well with the proceedings. He realised that, although hurt, and although the drummer in his head wouldn't stop, he was rather enjoying being the centre of attention. He abruptly stopped the pained groaning and turned it into a shriek when Cassandra took her hanky away and he saw part of his head sticking to it. A shiny red and probably very important part.

It was a partially sucked boiled sweet, to be finished after games and kept till then tucked in her... Well, somewhere private, but Crabbe didn't know and groaned in horror, almost passing out.

They carried him back to their school, a converted Victorian mansion that had been greatly altered and added to over the years so that now, it looked nothing like a Victorian mansion.

Chris Hare

The procession passed solemnly beneath an arch, through double doors, into the hall and then, with even greater care, up a flight of stairs to the first floor where he was taken into a pink, almost circular room, like the inside of a tinted igloo, and laid on a bed.

Lying quite still and oblivious to the chatter around him, Crabbe was able to take stock of his injuries. His ribs were sore where he'd been jabbed, his arms ached through wielding that awful racket and his head throbbed where the drum soloist was still at it. He couldn't see very well and thought someone must have removed his glasses. He made up his mind to escape as soon as possible…if not *immediately*. He was about to be stripped. *By girls!*

He forgot his injuries and sat bolt upright, ignoring protestations and brushing away female hands from his upper body as he did so. He was horrified! His togs were in disarray, buttons undone, and tie removed from his waist. To escape, he would first have to stand and… Well, it didn't bear thinking about!

Deeply affronted at this unwarranted intrusion on his modesty, his hands leapt to all the parts of his body that were within reach, unsure which parts to guard next. He was yelping like a puppy, which was silly because they were *only* girls. But there were so many of them, giggling, chattering and grabbing.

A blast came from a whistle. A sound Crabbe was delighted to hear. It was like an old friend coming to the rescue even if it also meant the return of an old enemy but at least, with Sister Rosemary in the room there would be no more touching. Somehow his brain didn't transfer this information to his hands, which ignored the whistle and continued darting around his body like two butterflies before coming to rest on his chest.

Sister Rosemary forced her way through the now silent girls.

'Sister Juliet will be here to attend to you directly and I have telephoned your Headmaster to apprise him of the situation. I understand your first name is Lancelot.'

Roars of laughter instantly silenced by a shrill blast. 'You will probably remain here tonight under the care of Sister Juliet, who is Senior Matron and a qualified nurse. You are not to move without her permission,' she concluded.

'But Sister, thank you for your concern and kind offer of hospitality, but I really want to go.'

'Probably shock. Lydia, bedpan! The rest of you, change and then cookery class.' Yet another blast and the girls filed out.

Crabbe thought he was losing the battle, but wouldn't give in just yet, 'No Sister, I mean I want to go away from here. Back to my own school.'

'That's what I want as well. And the sooner the better. But as your injury occurred within the boundaries of St. Margaret's, and although it was caused entirely by your own inattention, we have a responsibility, even to you. You are a very disruptive influence and have been the cause of a great deal of trouble here today. Thanks to you, I have suffered a … Well, I'm not sure what the medical term for my injury is.'

Lydia came in with the bedpan.

'A pain in the neck?' suggested Crabbe, though quite innocently.

Lydia dropped the bedpan and was ordered to join the others.

No sooner had she gone than Matron arrived. She was the clone of Sister Rosemary, perhaps slightly taller. But to Crabbe's short-sighted eyes they appeared twin sisters. Were all nuns built like pugilists? He screwed up his eyes, to make things a little clearer. The two nuns were whispering, but Crabbe couldn't hear what they were saying.

He bunched his fists and held them up to his eyes like binoculars and stared hard. He tried to remember his Greek mythology. Was there one Gorgon or two? Were they sister-Gorgons? Were these two sisters in real life, or just Sisters in the 'nun' sense?

'*Nonsense*,' he joked to himself and gave a little laugh.

The two nuns stopped whispering and crossed to his bed.

'There's nothing to laugh at. I'm Sister Juliet, Senior Matron of St. Margaret's,' announced the new Gorgon.

Crabbe attempted to shake hands and received a slap on the wrist, which confirmed to him that they *were* sisters.

'Tongue.' He stuck out his tongue.

'Say 'ahh'.

'Yaahrgh.'

'Put your tongue away and say 'ahh', you fool.'

And so, Crabbe's examination continued: temperature, pulse, blood pressure, follow fat finger from side to side, gouge each eye with thumb.

Eventually, 'No lasting damage. In fact, he seems to be almost normal.'

'Huh!' exclaimed Sister Rosemary, as if she didn't believe it.

'But, better safe than sorry. You never really know with heads. We'll keep him here tonight and I'll have another look in the morning. Possibly we'll have to get the doctor in. Final decision to be made tomorrow after breakfast.'

Crabbe was worried and began to panic. If Matron took his blood pressure again now, she'd have found it dangerously high.

'I'm really not feeling too bad, Sister Matron,' he squeaked, 'If it's all the same to you, I'd rather…' He got no further as his agitated hand was slapped again and his head pushed down on the pillow.

'You stay in bed unless you wish to make use of the necessary, which is over there.' She indicated a pink-painted door. 'It is obviously a ladies' necessary, so *concentrate.*'

'Have we any suitable night clothes, Sister? asked Sister Rosemary.

Matron opened a cupboard and brought out a white cardboard box labelled 'First Emergency, ages 12 to 16'. Crabbe fell within the age group, but this was by no means his *first* emergency. He had been in emergencies before, though none had been as embarrassing or as terrifying as this.

'I believe he may be fed, Sister, so perhaps you would be good enough to arrange some supper for our patient? The Upper Fourth will have today's efforts available in an hour or so, thereby preserving those of us at the Staff table for another day.'

Sister Rosemary actually smiled.

She glanced at Crabbe. 'Indeed Sister. 'Blessed are the cracked, for they shall let in the light'.'

It was the first time Crabbe had seen her with any expression other than anger. It was also the first time he'd seen her teeth in situ, as opposed to dangling from a piece of string on the tennis court. It hadn't occurred to him that nuns were capable of smiling, and she even allowed herself a chuckle as she said, 'An excellent suggestion, Sister. I will arrange it immediately.'

She left and Crabbe thought he actually heard her humming!

'The staff has to test it, do you see?' He didn't see, but thought it better to nod, and give a weak smile.

Crabbe in all Innocence

She put the box on the end of his bed and removed the lid.

'You'll find everything you need in here, toothbrush and paste, carbolic and flannel, nightclothes. Go and wash, change and be back in bed in five minutes. I'll return to check you have washed behind your ears.'

She too, was fitted with a whistle and gave it a shrill blast to indicate the five minutes had started.

Crabbe waited until the door closed behind her.

Alone in the bathroom, he wondered what he should do. But he didn't wonder for long: he knew from painful experience just what they were capable of when crossed. He didn't think he could take much more.

As he splashed water on his face, scrubbed his ears and brushed his teeth, he could think only of escape. But how? He stripped off his shirt, shorts, plimsolls and socks, looking around the bathroom with myopic eyes. There were no windows. Why not? The bathrooms at his school were stuffed with them. Fresh air was considered vitally important at Chantry, especially in the bathrooms.

He dried himself with a towel from the Emergency Box. He wasn't the least bit surprised it was pink. Why do girls have this passion for pink? It was such an insipid colour, not at all manly. He pulled a pink nightie from the box.

'Oh glory,' he said out loud. He delved in again. There were no pyjamas, not even pink ones. All that was left was a little booklet and a few other bits and pieces.

'Oh glory!' he repeated as with bitter disappointment he realised he had been defeated: he couldn't escape wearing shorts – they belonged to the brown locker and that would be stealing. And he couldn't escape wearing his underpants. That was bound to be against hundreds of laws.

His underpants! The nightie was far too short – there were girls around – they might see! He took his school tie from the pocket of the shorts where it had, until recently, been employed as a substitute belt, and before that, a garrotte. He lifted the nightie's hem and knotted the tie round his waist over the elastic of his underpants. It would serve as a second line of defence should the army of the Upper Fourth launch another attack.

Crabbe climbed into bed and pulled up the covers. He sat up straight, a smug expression on his face as if anticipating a sweetie as a reward when Matron returned.

Matron returned, marching in without knocking.

'Very good Lancelot. You appear to be learning. Wipe that stupid look off your face. Hands.'

Crabbe clapped his hands.

'Fool! Show me your hands.'

Crabbe understood and held his hands out for inspection, palms upwards.

'Good. Turn.'

Crabbe in all Innocence

Crabbe misunderstood and twisted round on the bed so she could inspect the backs of his ears. He received a stinging slap on the left one.

'Fool!'

Having already discovered that Sister Rosemary's favourite word was 'silence' he now concluded that 'fool' was Sister Juliet's confirmed choice. Crabbe's was 'freedom', but it was more of a hope than a probability. It was all getting too much. He would have willingly swapped a double Latin period with Mr. Shapiro for this.

Sister Juliet grabbed his shoulders and screwed him back to face her. 'Fool! Turn your *hands* over.'

He did, and she peered at his knuckles (scrubbed) and his nails (clean but bitten).

'Turn,' she ordered again.

Crabbe was becoming institutionalised. Without thinking, he turned his hands back over, expecting a slap on the other ear. He was wrong.

He got a slap on the same ear. He knew what she would say next. She did.

'Fool! Turn *round*.'

Why she hadn't inspected the backs of his ears a moment ago was beyond him. Female logic, he supposed. He heard that nuns were supposed to punish themselves with bunches of twigs if they did something wrong, but this one, and Sister Rosemary, come to that, seemed to enjoy hurting people for doing what were they told. Were they angry at having been born too late to join in the Spanish Inquisition with Rasputin? They would have fitted in well, he thought.

Briskly, she rubbed her hands together as if they'd been hurt when slapping him. He hoped it was so.

'Very well. There is hope for you. Never forget that cleanliness is next to Godliness. Mickey Mouse suits you,' she said, indicating the embroidery on the front of his nightie. 'Supper is on its way. The Upper Fourth is deciding which of their offerings with which to entice you. Although games of chance are a mortal sin, the staff feels that although we did not take part, we have still won. Don't gape.'

This last was in response to the dropping of Crabbe's lower jaw and not having a clue what she was talking about.

'Now. Hospital corners.' She bustled around tidying the bed and bending him in half to deliver a punch to the pillow that would have finished off Joe Louis. Then she unbent him and told him to sit up straight and not to fidget.

Finally, she wheeled a trolley from the opposite side of the room and fitted it over the bed. 'This will serve as your Round Table, Sir Lancelot. Upper Fourth will be bringing your supper up directly. Try not to do the same.' With this admonishment, she departed.

Crabbe, having accepted defeat, considered his position. On the good side, he was going to get some food. And one of the nuns was bound to be there to make sure he got his fair share. On the other side of coin, he was incarcerated here until tomorrow morning at the earliest.

He thought further about his position, this time in the literal sense. He decided he would look his best when Upper Fourth came in if he were to be found in a 'nonchalant' pose – relaxed, in full control, thumbing through a magazine.

He wished he had a cigarette in a long holder. And a smoking jacket with a velvet collar like Noel Coward wears all the time. But he only had a pink nightie with Mickey Mouse embroidered on the front. Not even a magazine. He looked around: nothing but plain pink walls, doors and ceiling, and a white cardboard box.

What was a First Emergency anyway?

He reached for the box and took out the booklet. In letters large enough for him to see was printed, 'WHAT HAS HAPPENED TO YOU TODAY IS PERFECTLY NATURAL. THERE IS NO NEED TO BE ASHAMED.'

Crabbe questioned this.

Was it 'perfectly natural' for a boy to have to play tennis at a girls' school? To be tortured, stabbed at with a crucifix, half strangled and knocked unconscious by St. Margaret's heavyweight champion? Then to be stripped naked, or nearly so, by those same girls before being closely examined by Attila the Nun? Was all this 'natural'? Was it manly? *And why should he be ashamed?*

160

Chris Hare

He turned the first page. The first four words, 'THIS IS NATURE'S WAY,' were legible to him, but then whoever had printed it had changed to smaller type, and Crabbe could read no more. Just as well. He would have probably passed out again. He looked in the box, but all that he saw were a few cottonwool bandages.

He looked around the room. There was one other bed, empty, and beyond that a door giving on to a balcony. Could he escape that way? Tie some bed sheets together and climb down to freedom? It was the sort of thing they did in films. But then he remembered the problem of his clothes, and once again, he gave up and awaited his fate.

His fate appeared a few moments later in the guise of twelve or so girls from the Upper Fourth, led by Cassandra and, he was pleased to see, Koshkai, following closely behind. She bowed and smiled with a smile so wide it made her eyes disappear altogether. Each of the girls carried a china plate with an aluminium cover.

Crabbe adjusted his nightie and looked forward to some nourishment. He was hungry. It had been a long difficult day, and it felt as if several weeks had passed since the Head announced that he was to play tennis at St. Margaret's. The awful words had in fact only been uttered that very morning.

Sister Rosemary entered and blew on her whistle.

'Mr. Crabbe,' she said formally, 'the girls were unable to decide amongst themselves which of these dishes would tempt your appetite. The staff, who incidentally, are extremely grateful that you are here, feel it would be wrong to influence the choice, and therefore suggest you eat it all.'

'Thank you, Sister, but I don't believe I will be able to eat the whole banquet. Perhaps I might try a little from each dish?'

'That would be the most sensible way. Remember that these girls have been playing tennis for years and are consequently far stronger than you. It wouldn't be wise to upset one of them with a refusal. I'll leave you. I wish you *bon appetite* and *bon chance*, and despite what you have done to me, I will pray for you.'

She closed the door behind her, leaving Crabbe worried and feeling strangely alone. Although he hated her, he was sorry she'd gone. For a reason he couldn't quite put his finger on, he felt threatened. Perhaps it was the thought of his being left alone with all these girls, or the notion that if he found one of their dishes not to his taste, his expression would give him away and he'd be beaten up.

He decided he would cheerfully and smilingly enjoy everything and put on an expression of joyful anticipation. An expression that vanished as Cassandra loomed before him. She banged her plate down on the table. What little courage Crabbe had left deserted him, and he wriggled his way down between the bed covers.

Cassandra took hold of his shoulders and heaved him back. He smiled a painful smile, and explained, 'Just getting myself comfy.'

Cassandra proudly sported a Form captain's badge pinned to her blouse. With the absence of Sister Rosemary's protection, Crabbe decided to get Cassandra on his side, 'Ahh, Cassandra, I see you are Captain of this ship, err, Form. What would you advise?'

'I'd advise you stay alive.'

'Sound advice. And how would you suggest I accomplish that?'

'By eating mine first.' She lifted the aluminium cover from her plate and Crabbe saw what looked like a dreadful accident.

'Looks lovely,' he lied. 'What do you call it?'

'It's a cheese soufflé. What's it look like?'

It really wasn't a question. More of a threat. Crabbe didn't want to fall foul of her so smacked his lips in awful anticipation and said, 'My absolute favourite. And if I may ask, how did you get the red colouring? Double Gloucester perhaps?

'No. We ran out of cheese, so I used baked beans.'

'The very thing. An ideal substitute. My, my.' He risked a quick appreciative smile up to her. Something other than baked beans had produced this blood–coloured concoction. *Ah well,* he thought, *it can only get better.*

Crabbe in all Innocence

How wrong could he be? He asked for the knife and fork she was holding. She passed him the fork, 'You don't need a knife. It's a soufflé. Cuts like butter.'

She held the knife pointed towards him and Crabbe took the hint and scooped up a mouthful. He couldn't think why she had bothered to cover it since it was stone cold. To keep flies off? No, even flies wouldn't risk eating this. He put down his fork and sat back as if he'd just enjoyed a gourmet meal at the Ritz, not the disgusting mess wobbling in front of him.

'Wonderful. Delicious. Many congratulations.'

'What rubbish,' came a new voice.

It belonged to the very muscular Hockey Captain. 'You don't want that French muck. You're ill. You need light healthy food. This is a salad,' she concluded as she removed Cassandra's dish and replaced it with her own.

'I love salad – fresh and crisp. What sort of salad is it? Ham perhaps, or cheese?'

'Baked bean.'

'How original. Baked bean salad. You should have the recipe published. I'm sure you'd start a fashion.'

When the cover was removed, it revealed something even more disgusting than Cassandra's, if that was possible. Crabbe was sure there were at least two dead rats in there, beneath a single limp leaf of unknown origin.

In went the fork again and he transferred a tiny amount to his mouth. He closed his eyes as if in heaven, which is where he thought he would be if had to endure much more of this.

'Mmm,' he noised in insincere appreciation. He was relieved to find it tasted just like Cassandra's, so no rats. Unless, he thought with a shudder, she had included one with the soufflé. He wouldn't put anything past this lot. Except for Koshkai, who was so sweet she would never try to poison anyone.

Whilst musing, the salad vanished and was replaced with a soup.

'Soup first.' This was the offering of the Senior Librarian, who looked as if she could reach the top shelf of books without the need of a ladder.

'Indeed. First things first. Oh, look. It moves.'

'Of course, it moves. It's wet.'

Being wet was as near to soup as it got. It claimed to be *vichyssoise.*

Crabbe didn't know what vichyssoise was made of, but he pretty certain it wasn't crushed baked beans in milk, as this clearly was.

He cast his eyes in the direction of the 'necessary'. He would have an urgent need of it before too long.

One gulp and it was whipped away and replaced by another. And then another. And yet another. The 'necessary' became a 'vital' and then an 'absolute necessity'. Crabbe was on the verge of having his own *First Emergency* when Koshkai's dish appeared. And with it, a bottle of wine, perhaps *sake*, he thought. Whatever it was, Crabbe had never been so glad to see a cork. She bowed as she put down the plate and handed him a pair of short wooden chopsticks.

'Oh, you've been busy. Is this a national dish?'

She spoke very softly with a strange but charming accent, not looking at him directly but with her eyes lowered respectfully.

'Yes, Rancerot. Rive Lorm with Blean and Clumb Dlessing'. Popruar in Japan. Enjoy.'

Another little bow, and she took a pace backwards, still with her eyes lowered.

'I'm sure I most certainly will enjoy it. Thank you, Koshkai.'

He had never used chopsticks before, and soon found that stabbing at the food was not the way. He tried putting them both in his right hand, as he had seen Charlie Chan do on cinema nights, and tried again, with more success, although quite a lot went down his front and mingled with Mickey Mouse.

But it was worth it, the food was quite delicious. Cold, but for all he knew that was how it was eaten in Japan. What had she called it? Something with a *blean and clumb* dressing. By now he thought he must have tasted every way of cooking baked beans known to man, but this was different, somehow smoother and meatier.

He smiled at Koshkai, 'This is absolutely splendid. The dressing is *blean and clumb*?

'Collect, Rancerot. Good and tasty.'

166

'Certainly is. I can translate 'blean' but what is 'clumb'?

'Oh, you know. *Clumb. Bled clumb.*'

He understood. 'Oh, you mean breadcrumbs. Of course! And did you grate them from a loaf yourself?'

'No, no. Blird table. Sister Cook make sandwiches and put *clumb* out at night. Like early blird, I get up early and I take.'

As Crabbe chewed, the bell in his head started to ring, softly at first but gradually gathering its momentum. He continued chewing, despite his growing suspicion.

'I see,' he said, trying to smile, 'and the other ingredient?'

'Rive lorm,' she repeated.

'Just so. And er, forgive me, but what exactly is 'rive lorm'?'

'Ahh, you joke with me. Is saying about early blird.'

'Oh, I see. You mean 'the early bird catches the worm'?'

'Yes. Blird catch lorm. But lorm must be rive. Not good dead. So yesterday was rain, lorm come out and I catch.'

Crabbe stopped chewing.

She continued, 'Early blird catch lorm. But I more early and catch lorm first. You like more?'

The path to the 'necessary' was blocked by the Upper Fourth, and the French windows to the balcony were closed.

But for Crabbe, there was no choice.

167

Crabbe in all Innocence

Tick tock.

Chris Hare

13: CORRUPTION

'Not yet, not yet,' The Fates whispered as they looked down. 'Why are you in such a hurry to die? You have much more to suffer before your tapestry is complete. You must ascend higher, much higher, before you begin your final, painful decline. It is we, not you, who choose your time.'

As is ever the way with miracles, what followed was inexplicable. Had anyone else jumped through a set of French windows they would have been lacerated by shards of flying glass. Arteries would have been severed, flesh cut to ribbons, their life blood draining away in seconds, and they would depart this life, with a red, pulsating and agonising final breath. Crabbe was not *meant* to die just yet, so he didn't.

But he certainly looked the part.

Once through the windows and ignoring flying glass, his feet scrabbled for purchase on the balcony tiles, such was his frenzy to get away.

It was an attractive balcony before he got there. Built in the Spanish style, with low stone balustrades set between graceful, feminine lines of Spanish arches. There were vines in pots standing on the tiles, growing upwards, reaching for the spans on top of the arches where baskets of flowers hung, the blooms tumbling over the edges in a welter of colour. It was the pride and joy of the Little Sisters.

Was, because much of it was ruined by Crabbe as he blundered around in unseeing panic: it was dark, he'd lost his glasses and anyway, at that precise moment he didn't give two hoots about his surroundings. He just wanted to escape.

Nothing would stop him.

What stopped him was the stone arch he crashed into. It also stopped him from flying over the balustrade and landing on the concrete path, thirty feet below.

Had W-P been completely honest with himself when composing his lists, the most likely candidate for the prime position on the 'Not Such Good Points' inventory would have been 'diplomacy' for diplomatic he certainly wasn't. But now, as he approached the sanatorium, he knew, at the very least, he had to make an attempt. He would have to be sensitive, tactful and subtle. A complete reversal of his natural character, but he could see no other way.

The Head was Crabbe's first visitor, in fact, his *only* visitor as all contact with anyone else had been banned, other than Miss Griggs and the local doctor who injected a large amount of sedative into Crabbe's bottom. He also removed most of the bandages, where he found, apart from those on his feet, Crabbe's cuts and bruises were superficial.

Word got round. Rumours flourished. You can't have an ambulance drive up the school, even in the dead of night, without several pairs of eyes looking out of dormitory windows to watch a stretcher carrying a body swathed from head to toe in white bandages being borne into school by ambulance men.

Somehow, they knew it was Crabbe, and somehow, they knew he had contracted one of the ten plagues of Egypt (one of Russell's more excruciatingly awful readings at Assembly), which explained why his body was dressed as a mummy.

That rumour was permitted to circulate to give W-P time to plot and plan. He knew that no *thinking* adult would believe such a tale invented by imaginative schoolboys. And he knew that it wouldn't be possible to put the blame on Mr. Pinder. He crossed the quad to the sanatorium to begin his diplomatic mission.

Crabbe was sitting up in bed eating boiled egg and soldiers. He was still drowsy from the effects of the sedative and was searching his memory.

He remembered the tennis match, and Miss Griggs had told him that during a few lucid moments, he had mumbled something about worms, pink Gorgons and Mickey Mouse before retreating into his own private, unconscious world.

The Head sat by Crabbe's bed.

'I understand your school fellows know you as Elsie. Is that correct?'

Crabbe in all Innocence

'Yes, sir and thank you for coming to visit me.'

'Not at all. It's the least I can do. I've been keeping my eye on you. You show great promise.'

This was a complete lie. The Head knew practically nothing about Crabbe, apart from his being far too thin and consequently, his disastrous expedition to St. Margaret's.

'Tell me in your own words, erm, Elsie, what do you remember? It's important, *vital*, that I know the whole story.'

And it was.

He could be held responsible. It was all his idea. Crabbe was in his care. He should have sent a master to oversee, but he hadn't. He could be sued for dereliction of duty by Crabbe's parents. He would be pilloried. Summoned to appear before the Board of Governors. Harriet would kill him.

Crabbe was speaking. He could recall in clear detail, the tennis match, Koshkai and Cassandra. He could remember Sister Rosemary, her teeth and her crucifix.

But then there was a gulf of blackness, a void. Crabbe had no memory of what had happened after the match. His subconscious had blotted out St. Margaret's sanatorium and all that had happened to him there. He couldn't remember the Upper Fourth's attempts to poison him, nor his failed attempted escape from the dreadful place.

He assumed the injuries he had sustained were when being battered by Sister Rosemary, whom he remembered again with a shudder. His mind just wouldn't let the beast go. He fully considered her to be the most brutal woman on Earth, (but at this time, he didn't really know Mrs. Wilkes-Passmore).

Crabbe finished his story, or at least, the parts he could remember. 'I'm so sorry, sir, but no matter how hard I try, the last thing I recall is Sister Rosemary serving the ball to me. Then nothing. Sorry, sir.'

The Head's eyes lit up – here was salvation!

'Excellent, Elsie. Excellent.'

'I'm afraid I don't follow, sir.'

'It matters not. You have suffered a traumatic experience and you are not *meant* to remember. Therefore, my advice to you is to stop trying. In fact, I insist. Don't talk about it. Don't even think about it. It is never a good thing to dwell on the past. Nature has blotted out most of the episode from your mind, and you must respect that. You mustn't break any of nature's rules. It goes against nature.'

'If you say so, sir. I wouldn't want to break any rules.'

'Quite right. Do you understand what I'm saying?'

'No, sir.'

The Head's eyes rolled upwards.

He tried again, speaking very slowly as if speaking to a halfwit.

'Banish the whole incident from your mind. Put it behind you. And should you ever suddenly recall an odd detail, forget that too. It would only cause trouble.

Best not write home about it. You understand now? Do
I have your word?'

'Yes, sir. If you say so.'

'I do say so, I do. And as a reward for your
understanding, next year I will promote you to House
Prefect of Keyes. Would you like that?'

'Oh indeed, sir. If you think I would be equal to the
task. I would be honoured, and my parents will be so
proud.'

'Well done. You are excused lessons until you are
fully recovered, not that you can walk at present. Do
your injuries make you cry?'

'Oh no, sir! We don't cry at Chantry.'

Of course, it didn't cross Crabbe's mind that he'd just
been offered, and accepted, a bribe.

On his way back to his office to telephone his
opposite number at St. Margaret's to agree a figure of
compensation, W-P bore a smug, self-satisfied
expression. It changed as questioning furrows appeared
on his forehead. He had just abused his position of
Headmaster by colluding, threatening, bribing and
lying to a schoolboy.

Why had he joined the Army on leaving the church?
Why on earth hadn't he considered becoming a
politician? Clearly, he was well suited for the role.

Where men and boys were concerned, he knew his
devious and practised mind would get him out of any

difficult situation, as had just been evidenced by his handling of Crabbe.

But with women, he was out of his depth. To him, they had no sense of logic: their minds and the way they dealt with problems was a complete mystery. The telephone conversation he held with Reverend Mother Claire didn't go at all as he had expected.

He had been quite willing to pay for the damage caused by Crabbe – and from his *personal* account. That way he wouldn't have to answer any awkward questions that would have surely been asked had he used school funds. He couldn't risk that. The whole matter had to be closed – permanently. And the sooner the better.

He'd put off phoning Reverend Mother Claire while he considered how he should best go about bribing a nun.

But there was no inspiration. No ideas. For once, he was at a complete loss. It was whilst sitting at his desk, deep in thought, that his telephone rang.

It was Reverend Mother Claire!

His heart sank.

He burbled, 'Good morning, Reverend Mother. I, erm, I expect you're calling about yesterday?'

'Indeed I am. I cannot apologise enough.'

'Pardon?'

W-P's jaw dropped.

Crabbe in all Innocence

'I am so sorry. That one of your boys should have been so treated whilst in our care is unpardonable. How is the young man this morning?'

'Ah, oh. He's, erm…I've just been to see him. He's, err, very well, all things considered.'

'Praise be. What a blessing. Dr Wilkes-Passmore, I don't wish to sound indelicate, but please forgive me if I bring up the subject of compensation.'

'Of course, of course. Compensation. I was just about to telephone you, Reverend Mother, to discuss that very thing.'

'I'm sure you'll understand that the incident could cause severe damage to the reputation of St. Margaret's should the story be spread abroad. Perhaps we could agree to keep it to ourselves? We will, of course, pay for a new of pair spectacles for the boy, and any medical expenses. And perhaps, with your permission, we could send him something. A gift, perhaps?'

'Ah, oh. I'm sure such a thing would buy his silence,' replied W-P, it suddenly dawned on him that Reverend mother had turned the tables on herself.

'It is not a question of *buying* his silence,' she said sharply, 'people in our position never stoop to bribery.'

'No, indeed. Certainly not. Not a bribe, more a gesture of goodwill, perhaps?'

'Indeed. A gesture.'

They finished the conversation and W-P replaced the receiver with a broad grin on his normally unsmiling face.

He was still congratulating himself when, in late morning. Koshkai and Cassandra arrived at the school bearing gifts. They were shown up to his office.

W-P wouldn't let them visit Crabbe. He thought their presence might rekindle some hidden memory. He explained that at present, Crabbe was too unwell to have visitors.

Koshkai bowed, 'Crite unnerstand, Sister Headmaster. Prease to give him this.' She put the package on the desk and bowed again.

'And this is for you, sir,' said Cassandra. 'It's from the Reverend Mother.'

Repeating his thanks, he showed them out. 'I will have Crabbe's night apparel cleaned and repaired and returned to St. Margaret's by one of the masters. After yesterday, I can't risk a boy.'

They went, and W-P returned hurriedly to his desk like a small child on his birthday, anxious and excited to see what the packages contained. Crabbe had been sent a 35-millimetre camera and three rolls of film, which was a most acceptable and generous gift. (As ordained by *The Fates*, of course.)

Even more acceptable, was his own present. A bottle of ten-year-old single malt whiskey.

He had been bribed.

Shocking!

14: DRAMA

'The ghost that was reported as haunting St. Margaret's was *not* a ghost but an escaped lunatic who has now been recaptured and is being held securely in custody. There is no danger, and it won't be necessary for you to mention the incident in your letters home. Therefore, from this moment, there will be no further discussion on the matter.'

The Headmaster paused and cast his eyes along the massed ranks of Chantovians in Hall daring any one of them to gainsay him. Of course, no one did, although almost every single person present, schoolboy and teacher, knew W-P had just told a *whopper*.

The single exception was Mr. Finney, whose mind was elsewhere. He had taken Crabbe's nightie to St. Margaret's where he met Sister Rosemary, and the two of them had got on like a house on fire. Sister Rosemary, like all nuns, lead a chaste life, but she nevertheless harboured the thought that, had she not chosen to become a Bride of Christ, she would have married Mr. Finney as he clearly needed mothering and looking after.

That apart, they discovered they had something more practical and realistic in common. She, like Mr. Finney at Chantry, ran the Photographic Society at St. Margaret's. Over a convivial cup of tea, they discussed

178

ways of cooperating, perhaps even combining forces on a joint exercise.

Mr. Finney's thoughts returned to the present as the Head pressed on.

'Now, the School Play. I have decided, with advice from Mr. Pinder, that the Fourth-Year production in November will be *Macbeth* by William Shakespeare.'

Mr. Pinder would have preferred a comedy, and had suggested *A Midsummer Night's Dream*, but he was overruled by the Head who insisted it should be a play with at least one army in it so the boys completely devoid of acting talent could be non-speaking soldiers, thus giving their parents, those that bothered to attend, some slight value for their three hundred guineas a year.

'All boys currently in 4A and 4B will take part. Backstage duties will be undertaken by boys in the Fifth and Sixth forms. Readings will be held during English classes and the play will be cast at the end of term. Those boys with speaking parts will learn their lines during the Summer Holidays and will be excused *some* holiday homework, depending on the size of the part they are to play. Mr. Pinder will direct the main body of the play, and I, myself, will direct the battle scenes, drawing on my experience in the armed services. That is all.'

Speculation within the Fourth Year now centred on *Macbeth*, on who would play what part, who'd got the best Scottish accent, and which of them had the best legs to go with a kilt.

Crabbe stayed silent and looked down at his feet.

He'd been instructed to wear carpet slippers until his cuts were fully healed. Though now well enough to attend lessons, he was excused gym and sports, for which he was grateful. He honestly believed the only reason for taking so much exercise was that you died healthier.

Anyway, he was fully aware that his thin legs would look more at home on a sparrow, and he couldn't do an accent to save his life. He *knew* he would be cast as a non-speaking soldier, and the realisation filled him with dread as the Head would be directing the scenes. But, on the other hand, there was Mr. Pinder. He was one of the most popular masters in the school.

Mr. Pinder was one of those people, a rare breed, who seemed to have time for everyone. Whilst other teachers concentrated their efforts on the brighter boys, leaving the others to more or less find their own way, Mr. Pinder took an interest in all.

He was strict but fair, kindly and understanding and with a sense of humour that he sometimes found difficult to control. He was one of the youngest teachers at Chantry, but as one of the four Housemasters, was also one of the most senior. He was passionate about the subjects he taught, English Language and Literature, but his *overriding passion* were the works of Shakespeare.

Chris Hare

If a pupil showed interest in the bard, Mr. Pinder did all he could to further that interest. But if, as with the majority of pupils, the whole subject of Shakespeare and his interminable writings were regarded as nothing more than a huge yawn, Mr. Pinder took the trouble to find something from within the *Complete Works*, perhaps a character in a play or even a line from a sonnet through which he could draw a parallel to one of the pupil's existing hobbies, thereby stimulating interest.

It was often difficult but not impossible, and he always found something, however small, to start a discussion that would lead to a genuine and broader understanding. Few left Chantry without, at least, an *appreciation* of Shakespeare.

One who had *no* understanding of the plays, was the Headmaster.

For someone who was very well read, the Head showed a total lack of respect or understanding for any of the great man's works. He considered the famous speeches as merely filling in the time between battles and murders, which were the only parts of a Shakespeare play that really mattered to him. Possibly, Mrs. Wilkes-Passmore had had some effect on his thinking in this regard.

For all that, he felt that being Head of Chantry gave him the right to *adjust* parts of plays where Shakespeare had erred.

Crabbe in all Innocence

For the previous years' production of *Julius Caesar*, he had 'helped' to direct, not only the battle scenes, but also the assassination of Caesar. The Head determined that the conqueror of the known world wouldn't have just stood there waiting to be murdered. He would have put up a fight.

The plan backfired at the first rehearsal of this revised version. It was chaotic, with the conspirators all plunging their daggers in and Caesar plunging a few daggers back. At the end of the scene, Caesar was the only one left standing.

Thorpe-Bailey, playing the part of Mark Anthony, then took it upon himself to alter his 'I come to bury Caesar, not to praise him' speech by announcing that he had 'come to bury Brutus, Cassius, Casca, Metellus Cimber, Ligarius…' He had come to bury everyone who was still supposed to be alive, but *not* Caesar who was supposed to be a bloodied and mutilated corpse.

With considerable difficulty, Mr. Pinder persuaded the Head that they should 'stick to the script' for *Macbeth* and attempt to offer a performance as Shakespeare had intended. Mr. Pinder was determined not to allow a repeat of the *Caesar* fracas.

He really didn't want W-P involved in anything to do with the production. He didn't even want him to come and see it. But the Head was the Head, and so to a considerable extent, his hands were tied.

He put the future problems out of his mind as much as he could and concentrated on the current problem: teaching a set of Fourth Years how to act.

Mr. Pinder had no favourites, which was unusual among the staff at Chantry or, indeed, at any school. But it was a foregone conclusion as to who would be cast in the lead parts: Macbeth would be played by Hopkins Major whose father was a professional actor who had appeared in the West End with Noel Coward. Barnaby Gordon, the only boy in the Fourth Year whose voice hadn't yet broken, would be Lady Macbeth.

All the other characters, from Banquo downwards, would be played by whoever suited them best.

'A key point to make from the outset,' said Mr. Pinder, 'is that for a successful production, everyone involved must work together as a team. Whether you are on stage, waiting in the wings for your entrance, or undertaking a backstage task such as helping to move scenery, you must be as one unit, *working together*.'

There was a chorus of 'Yes sirs' from the boys, who were ranged around Mr. Pinder in a semi-circle.

'And,' he continued, 'I assure you that despite all the preparation, all the rehearsals and learning of lines and moves, something unexpected will most definitely occur during the performance, and we must be ready for it.'

His mind went back to the un-dead Caesar disaster of last year, but he refrained from mentioning it. Instead, he said, 'Possibly there will be a distraction backstage, and one of you might miss his cue to come on. Perhaps, there's an unexpected reaction from the audience, something we've not foreseen in our planning, and it causes an actor to forget his lines.' The boys listened attentively.

'Should this happen, and it most certainly will, what will we do?'

Silence greeted the question.

'Anybody?'

He glanced round at the rather bewildered faces, which stared back blankly.

'Very well, I will tell you. *We will improvise*. Rather than just standing there hoping something will happen while the audience yawn and look at their watches, *we will make something happen*. We invent, we *ad lib*. We move on!'

'But sir,' a boy called, raising his arm, 'will we not have a prompt?' This was from Hopkins Major, who knew about these things.

'Most certainly, there will be a prompt. Mrs. Wilkes-Passmore has undertaken to do that for us, but I would rather she was not called upon during the performance.'

The boys took this to mean it would be letting the side down to forget their lines, which it would be, of course. But Mr. Pinder's reason for not wanting Mrs.

W-P to be heard was that her voice was so booming, it would probably be heard at St. Margaret's.

'You will understand what I mean if we do some improvisation, rather than just talk about it. You will all have an opportunity to show what you can do. Indeed, *improvisation* will form a major part of Drama lessons over the next few weeks. Only after we have seen how successful you are, or otherwise, will we read and cast the play. Now, I want six volunteers.'

Twenty or so hands were raised, but they were all ignored.

'You six.' Mr. Pinder indicated the boys on one end of the row. They rose and approached him. Mr. Pinder noted that Crabbe was among them and that he was obviously holding back, not wanting to be involved in something he had totally failed to understand. He was already blushing dreadfully.

'Right, let's see how we get on. There are six of you. I want you to get together for five minutes and invent a play for six characters. It can be about anything you like. Decide how it will start and finish, and then act it out, making up the words as you go along. Five minutes.'

Mr. Pinder wasn't expecting too much but was surprised at how well they took to it. The inventiveness of boys never ceased to amaze him.

He was not amazed at their subject matter however, which was a murder. Nor at where the murder happened, which was in the library at a Country House.

Crabbe in all Innocence

Nor even at the boy chosen to play the victim, which was Crabbe.

The characters in the improvisation consisted of the usual suspects: the victim, who had been shot in the dark so no-one could see who pulled the trigger, a butler, the Lady of the Manor, her aunt who was deaf, a police inspector and his stupid sergeant who just stood there bending his knees in the time-honoured manner of stupid sergeants, licking the point of his imaginary pencil before making imaginary notes in his imaginary notebook.

The play ended in less time than it had taken to invent it. And the boys, of their own volition, lined up when it was over and bowed, acknowledging genuine applause.

'Excellent, top marks for enthusiasm,' Mr. Pinder complimented as they returned to their seats. 'A couple of points. Firstly, who did it? And why? What was their motivation?'

'Who did what, sir?'

'Who killed Crabbe? It was, was it not, a murder mystery? Complete with police inspector and stupid sergeant – well done, by the way Cartwright. Very inventive.'

Carters was, until a few moments ago, the stupid sergeant and smiled shyly as he received nudges and pats on the back.

'But who actually did it? Who fired the fatal shot? And for what reason? The whole point of a murder mystery is that at the end, the audience finds out who the killer is. What was the surprise ending? You just sort of stopped. Two more minutes I think, whilst the next six come forward. Try to find a reason for the murder, with a twist at the end.'

Crabbe didn't bother to join the hurried discussion. The others were whispering loudly to each other without listening, and Crabbe knew that any contribution from him would be ignored anyway.

Cartwright, who felt he had been awarded an Oscar by being complimented for his performance and was therefore qualified to speak for them all, raised his hand.

'Sir, we've worked out a surprise ending.'

Mr. Pinder paused in his instruction to the next six boys and turned.

'Well?'

The surprise ending came as much as a surprise to Crabbe as to anyone else.

'He committed suicide. Because he couldn't be murdered because there weren't any actors left over to play the murderer, if you please, sir.'

Such was the logic of schoolboys, and Mr. Pinder hid a smile behind his hand. 'Well thought out, but surely that should have been made clear to your audience. And why was Crabbe killed right at the beginning?

'We thought it would be kinder, sir.'

'Most considerate. But that gave you one less actor to help develop the plot.'

187

Crabbe in all Innocence

The discussion continued, with gradually, all the boys coming to understand what was needed in an improvisation.

Even so, whilst the characterisations improved, the remaining groups all did a murder in a Country house, with a butler, a deaf aunt *et al*.

At the end of the lesson, Mr. Pinder stood, 'A good beginning, a promising start. Next week we will do the same again, with each of you playing the same parts. But between then and now, I want you to think about your roles and see how you can pad them out. How you can give more life to them. It will help you respond quickly should and when, something goes wrong with the performance of *Macbeth*.'

It was a relieved and altogether happier Crabbe who went to bed that night, sure that yellow worms and pink nuns were relegated to history and would play no further part in his dreams. As he drifted off to sleep, he wondered how he could give 'more life' to a corpse.

During the weekly English/drama classes, and before going to sleep each night, he thought of a way: not exactly a way to give life to a murdered body, but to bring his actual death to life.

Mr. Pinder a great lover of the theatre *as a whole,* not just of Shakespeare, was very enthusiastic, and was delighted to see his enthusiasm rub off on his pupils. Crabbe especially, used the sessions to come out of his shell, and Mr. Pinder was full of praise for his, and all the boys' progress.

With patience and repetition, encouragement and constructive criticism, they were able to lengthen their dramatizations to all of ten minutes, and they gradually understood what it was that was required to mount a believable, entertaining and original performance.

Slightly less original, was the title that each of the eight groups gave their pieces, which was '*Murder at the Country House*'. Mr. Pinder pointed out that the use of the word 'Murder' in the title rather ruled out the notion that Crabbe, and the bodies from the other seven groups, had committed suicide.

He hoped by this that the start of each play would *not* therefore, begin with the discovery of the body on stage, and that the victim would at least be around for a few minutes to take a more active part in the improvisations before being murdered.

He was, however, frustrated in his hope. The point of *suicide* not being *murder*, was accepted.

And so, rather than having the victim kill himself within moments of the play starting, he was, for the sake of accuracy, *murdered* at the beginning instead.

And to bring variety to the death during the following weeks, they took turns at being the murderer, and each was allowed to choose the way in which the killing would be carried out.

Crabbe consequently suffered the indignity of being shot in the head, stabbed through the heart, being poisoned by the butler who told him it was a glass of very rare vintage port when it was, in fact, an inkwell of navy-blue ink that stained his teeth and ruined his shirt.

Thereafter, he was beaten to death with a poker (a rolled-up newspaper) and strangled with his own school tie, which brought a smile to Mr. Pinder's face and a painful memory to Crabbe. But however ghastly the manner of the murder was he, and the victims of the other murders, spent the remaining eight or nine minutes lying lifeless on the stage, being dead. And whilst Crabbe found his portrayal of the corpse was in itself a satisfying central role to play, it did preclude him from taking any further part in the improvisation.

He recalled Mr. Pinder's entreaty to 'pad out their roles' and give more *life*.

Lying there, while the action continued around him, and trying to put aside the frightening whisper from Cartwright that they were considering how to behead him, he was struck with an idea. It took hold, and each night, he developed the thought in his mind.

The following week, instead of just dropping dead, (it was knife through the heart week), he staggered round the stage, uttering a blood curdling scream and clutching at his mortal wound, before dying in unbearable agony, centre stage.

His 'padding' was well received. He repeated it next week and added dying with his eyes open and staring unseeing (he got the idea from the brass eagle lectern), and with his tongue hanging out (Sister Rosemary).

But despite his progress, he still had to die early on and consequently take no further part, until, during the final improvisation before the readings of *Macbeth* began, he had another idea – his masterstroke he called it.

He had died by swallowing a poison dart from Darkest Africa, fired by the maid through a blowpipe at the Lady of the Manor, aged ninety-three, the intended victim, who had dropped to the floor at the vital moment. Quite an athletic move for the old girl, commented Mr. Pinder. Crabbe came in with his mouth open to say, 'Dinner is served' and swallowed the dart, his hands flying to his throat and then following its passage down to his thigh, where, apparently, it proved fatal. After doing his, by now famous death scene complete with dreadful screams, staring eyes and lolling tongue, he suddenly sat up and joined in with the improvisation. The cast reacted badly. Gloves even kicked him.

'Sir, sir! Crabbe mustn't speak, he's dead. He should go to the mortuary where he belongs. Tell him, sir!'

But Crabbe was prepared.

'Well Crabbe? Why have you suddenly come to life? We are most eager to know.'

'Sir, it is not I, George, who speaks.' The murder victim was normally called 'George', sometimes 'poor George'. 'It is the *ghost* of George come to haunt those

191

who wronged him. As such, he is surely entitled to join in. Wouldn't you agree, sir?'

Smiling broadly behind his hand, Mr. Pinder said, 'I do agree. Indeed, I do. And of course, you'd know all about ghosts, wouldn't you Crabbe?'

Crabbe turned bright scarlet. Did Mr. Pinder know? Had he guessed?

In fact, the episode at St. Margaret's and Crabbe's part in it was the talk of the staff room until the Head had put a stop to it by, with heavy sarcasm, telling his staff that when he'd instructed *all boys* to cease discussing the episode, he wasn't *only* referring to the pupils.

'But, well done,' Mr. Pinder said with a nod of praise to Crabbe. 'A neat variation.'

Crabbe blushed to an even deeper shade. He smiled broadly as he stammered his thanks. He was very, very, proud. But pride comes before a fall, and he fell into a deep despair when *Macbeth* was cast. Kirby, Cartwright and Glover were non-speaking soldiers. And so was he.

Chris Hare

15: THE SWORD FIGHT

Mrs. Wilkes-Passmore had no official duties at Chantry, but that didn't stop her getting involved whenever and wherever she felt the school would benefit from her expertise. Such interventions were never welcomed by the staff, but as she was bigger than most of them *and* the Head's wife, her interference had to be tolerated.

Mrs. W-P had once appeared on stage in her Girl Guide troop's first ever pantomime as Giant Blunderbore in '*Jack and the Beanstalk*'. It was also the troop's last ever pantomime as, following her solo dance, the structure supporting the stage was discovered to be severely weakened and there were no funds available for repairs and reinforcements.

Nevertheless, she felt the experience entitled her to become involved in school productions, so that was that.

The Head himself, had never had any desire to tread the boards. He felt his talents in the world of drama lay more in writing, and because of his military experience, in directing battle scenes.

From the outset it was clear to Mr. Pinder that having the Head directing any part of the production was a bad idea. It wouldn't work. But it was the Head's idea, so it *had* to. Mr. Pinder had been allowed to cast the play as he had wished without interference. That was the limit of his freedom. Thereafter, he was plagued with suggestions, advice, notes and, when they didn't produce a response to satisfy the Head, *demands*.

One such was how they should rewrite large parts of *Macbeth* as Shakespeare had, in the opinion of both Dr and Mrs. Wilkes-Passmore, got the *balance* wrong: there was far too much talking and not enough blood.

Mr. Pinder did his best to ignore the Head's wishes by adopting delaying tactics, 'What a splendid idea, Headmaster. I'll be sure to fit it in when we reach that scene in rehearsal.'

The actual rehearsals proved rather a problem. Mr. Pinder wanted to use his lessons to coach the cast in the art of speaking blank verse and discussing motivation and characterisation. The Head insisted that the time would be better spent teaching them how to fight staged battles.

A compromise was reached: Wednesday afternoons, acting, Thursday evenings after prep, fighting, although to an outsider, it would appear that preparations for *Macbeth* dominated most days at Chantry.

Although principally renowned for its academic and sporting achievements, practical subjects were taught too; carpentry and metal work were included, and these classes now were given over almost entirely to making scenery and props.

In metal work, the boys were given the task of hammering out the bumps in the school's set of tin

Chris Hare

armour that had been lent to St. Margaret's for their production of '*The Romans in Judea*'.

The carpenter's shop was a buzz of activity with soldiers making wooden swords and spears. The Head had ordered that each boy make their own arms early on so that he got used to carrying them at rehearsals.

He insisted that all swords were to be exactly one yard in length. No more and no less. 'You will see why when we demonstrate a sword fight. Having measured out your sword using a yard-rule, you will then cut an additional piece of wood eight inches long that you affix six inches from one end of the sword to act as a guard to protect your hand. You will cover the blade with silver paper. You will not put an edge on your sword, nor sharpen it to a point. No one is to be injured. Is that clear?'

Fifteen soldiers replied as one, 'Yes, sir!'

There should have been sixteen, but Bunting was confined to the sanatorium with suspected mumps.

They made their swords and presented them to the Headmaster for an inspection to ensure each of his instructions had been obeyed. He checked the edges and ends, unsharpened and un-pointed, and therefore, hopefully harmless. He ran his fingers down each blade to make sure no one had hidden any protruding nails under the silver paper. No one had, because no one had thought of it.

He made a rare mistake; he didn't check that all the swords were exactly three feet long. Had he done so he would have discovered that Crabbe's sword was a little more than three inches longer because he'd used a metre rule by mistake. But he didn't check, and he didn't notice. No one did: they all saw what they expected to see.

Similarly, after the Head instructed the boys to make their spears three times the length of their swords, no one noticed that Crabbe's spear was around ten inches longer than any of the others.

The boys were full of the excited chatter of anticipation as they made their way to Hall for their first 'fighting' rehearsal. Mr. Pinder came for revenge on the Head who had turned up at both 'speaking parts' rehearsals to give unhelpful and uninvited advice.

'Pay attention,' said the Reverend Doctor, leaning against the brass eagle lectern on the stage. 'The whole point of the stage fight in which people get killed, is that no one actually *dies*. Bear that in mind and *do not try to kill or even injure someone*. I will be extremely displeased if anyone disobeys me. Now, you will be put into pairs of boys of a similar height, you will be in opposing armies, and you will have sword fights with your partner. One of you, I will tell you which in due course, will *appear* to die. The victor will then go off stage giving the impression that he is going to another part of the battlefield to kill someone else. He will not – I repeat, *NOT* seek out another enemy among the living on the stage. Is that clear?'

'Yes, sir!'

'Very well. Now, everyone stand up so that you may be sorted into pairs according to height.'

They did as they were told and were duly put into twos by the Headmaster.

Crabbe was left over, standing alone, and blushing.

'We seem to have an odd boy here, Mr. Pinder.'

Chortles from the other boys.

Crabbe blushed deeper.

'Yes, Headmaster. Bunting is in the sanatorium. Though not as tall as Crabbe, he is the only boy available.'

'Very well, Crabbe. Bunting will be your opposite number when he recovers. Now, we will *demonstrate* a sword fight rather than talking about how it is done. Crabbe come up here.'

It was the first time he had ever been on the stage in Hall in the presence of the Head, and he became even more embarrassed and started to sweat. But he climbed up reluctantly and gave the eagle a terrified smile.

It was unfortunate that Monsieur le Becq, head of middle-school French and universally disliked by every pupil apart from Crabbe who didn't really have an opinion, had chosen to spend his free period watching the rehearsal. That is to say, it was unfortunate for Monsieur le Becq.

He was quite unique at Chantry. The only Frenchman on the staff, he wore his hair long in a supposed 'arty' fashion, and he had a full bushy beard. He was in his early twenties, and those in authority hoped he would grow out of his French ways and realise in time, how much better it was to look English.

'Monsieur, would you kindly act as Crabbe's partner?'

Monsieur le Becq began regretting coming to the rehearsal, but did as he was told, muttering an unconvincing, '*Delighted, 'Eadmaster.*'

'Now, soldiers, you will understand why I insisted your swords be of equal length. Crabbe, I see you have yours. Monsieur le Becq, please borrow one and stand one sword length from Crabbe and hold it just in front his face.'

They did as they were instructed and Monsieur le Becq raised his borrowed sword to within half an inch of Crabbe's embarrassed nose.

'Take note, soldiers, that Monsieur's sword does not quite reach Crabbe's face. Nor will it, unless one of them moves closer. Therefore, when you have your sword fight, you will *not* move your feet. You will at all times remember you are pupils at Chantry. You are *not* effeminate actors dancing around in tights on a Hollywood film set. So, having first ensured that you are the correct distance apart, you may swing your swords at each other, and no one will be hurt, but it will look to the audience as if you are actually trying to kill each other.

Monsieur le Becq, be so kind as to strike a blow at Crabbe's head. Crabbe, do not raise your own sword to parry. Just stand quite still and allow Monsieur to attempt to cut your head off.'

Crabbe, with sweat now freely running down his crimson face, glanced round for a last image of earth that he could take with him to heaven. He saw the brass eagle and quickly looked away. He looked to the front where he saw the other boys gaping up at him. He also saw the Headmaster, who had limped off the stage to get a better view.

He wished his parents were here to witness his final moment. Crabbe stood still, and awaited execution as Monsieur le Becq swung his sword.

Crabbe heard the swishing sound.

'There, do you see?' It was the Head's voice.

'Yes, sir, incredible…brilliant…' came the voices of the combined soldiers of the Fourth Year.

From their viewpoint, below stage level, it appeared that they were about to see Crabbe's head skidding and bouncing in front of them, neck bloodied red with bits of bone trailing severed veins and pulsating arteries throbbing out his lifeblood.

But they didn't.

His head was still where it had been, still wearing glasses, still bright red and still on his shoulders.

'Excellent. Thank you, Monsieur. Did you all see that? Did you understand?'

'Yes, sir.'

'And you Crabbe. Do you understand?'

'I understand the theory sir, but I didn't see it.'

Crabbe in all Innocence

'Of course. You couldn't see because of your close proximity to Monsieur le Becq.'

'No, sir, with respect, sir. I couldn't see because I had my eyes shut.'

'Naturally, dear boy. Of course, you did.' The Head, delighted at the way his first rehearsal was going, almost smiled.

Monsieur le Becq gaped. The soldiers couldn't believe their ears. Crabbe was dumbstruck. The eagle just stared.

No one had ever heard the Headmaster refer to a pupil as a 'dear boy'.

'A natural reaction. But, with practice, comes confidence. Now, you take a swing at Monsieur, Crabbe.'

'Oh glory.'

'Crabbe, it is a natural reaction for you to hold back when instructed to assault a master, but this is acting. You must not regard Monsieur le Becq as your superior, but an enemy on the battlefield. Someone you must kill. Is that not so, Monsieur?'

'Indeed, 'Eadmaster. Crabbe, you know zat no 'arm will be done. I will not blink. I will not even move a muscle. I won't be injured but I might just give a grunt for ze sake of realism. Strike, Crabbe.'

Reluctantly, Crabbe struck.

High above *The Fates* looked down. *This was the moment.*

It was now that everyone noticed Crabbe's sword was the wrong length.

No, not *quite* everyone. Monsieur le Becq couldn't see anything.

Crabbe saw the Monsieur blink and move all his muscles in a spasm just before he collapsed. He didn't grunt though. He screamed. And as for the not being injured, Crabbe thought he'd never stop bleeding.

It was as Crabbe smashed Monsieur round the head that he realised his sword was longer: only by a matter of inches, it's true. But when the blow struck with great speed and determination under the eyes of the Head, the eagle lectern, and the Fourth Year, those inches proved almost fatal. It was assumed by those watching that the only reason Monsieur stopped screaming was because, when reeling backwards, he head butted the eagle lectern and he knocked himself out.

The Fates smiled their grim smiles. It had started.
Tick tock. Tick tock.

16: THE ROYAL MESSENGER

Crabbe visited Monsieur le Becq and Mr. Pinder (who couldn't stand the sight of blood and had fainted) in the sanatorium the following morning and was greatly relieved to find Mr. Pinder asleep and Monsieur le Becq, his head heavily bandaged, alive and kicking.

He kept kicking his bedclothes off and insisting to the nurse that he didn't want to spend another minute in the same room as Bunting with what *he'd* got. Roger Bunting was in the bed opposite, propped up on pillows and reading the most recent edition of Hotspur.

The nurse would not relent and pressed down on Monsieur le Becq's chest whilst Crabbe replaced the bedsheets.

'Don't worry, Monsieur. Bunting has slightly swollen glands, not mumps. He is not at all infectious and will return to class in a day or two. He has said he will leave you his comic if you behave. Isn't that kind of him? Say 'thank you' to Bunting, there's a good boy.'

'Nurse! If you please! I am not a 'good boy', I am a *master*. Please remember that, and also zat zese boys are my *pupils*. I would appreciate your addressing me wiz more respect.'

'Now, now, whose got a sore head then? No bedtime story if you speak to Nursey like that. We don't have crosspatches here.'

Chris Hare

The boys were amazed to see Monsieur stick his tongue out when her back was turned.

But they were more amazed when he returned to take classes next day, his head still swathed in bandages. They assumed it was his particular French desire to behave as he thought an Englishman would: keenness, stiff upper lip, being a good example, and not allowing a small thing like a two-inch gash in his skull keep him from his duties.

Mr. Pinder, although a true Englishman, was perfectly happy to rest and recover in the sanatorium, even under the patronising eyes of the nurse but then he received a visit from the Headmaster who told him that he would take over the direction of the boys with speaking parts until Mr. Pinder fully recovered.

He also mentioned that he was going to rewrite the ending of Macbeth as he'd discovered Shakespeare hadn't left enough time for Russell to change the set for the last act.

It was this last that made Mr. Pinder leap out of bed as soon as the Head had gone, and rush past the nurse who was carrying in his breakfast tray of weak tea and scrambled eggs on toast.

He found the army to be in a state of mutiny.

Nobody wanted to go on stage with Crabbe, let alone fight with him. On the one hand, he was lauded for striking the hated Frenchman, but on the other, he was a Jonah. Mr. Pinder saw a way out. A solution to suit all parties.

Crabbe in all Innocence

'Crabbe, I understand your disappointment at being thrown out of the army, at not having a part to play in Macbeth. Doctor Wilkes-Passmore and I have discussed the matter and have found a compromise – something that will suit the Head's desire to rewrite Shakespeare whilst at the same time including you in the play and demonstrating your talents.'

Crabbe cheered up. 'Really, sir? What talents?'

'*Your acting talents*, Crabbe. In the murder plays you presented last term you undertook the role of 'Poor George', and died most convincingly. Towards the end of Macbeth a Royal Messenger will come on stage with news. It is a very minor part that could be undertaken by any of the soldiers. The Head is enlarging the role, and you will play it. You will have a short scene with Macbeth, who will kill you.'

'Will I have any lines to speak, sir?'

'You will. Just a few. To tell you the truth Crabbe, you will be there to pad it out to give Russell and his crew more time to remove a castle from behind the curtains, which will be closed, and set a few rocks and trees for the final battle scene. I should emphasise, to save you from further disappointment, that it is not an important role in itself and no matter how good you are, I doubt that it will be remembered but it is still important within the context of the smooth running of the production. Learn your lines and your moves, and just do your best. Incidentally, Royal Messengers wore trews, not kilts.'

Chris Hare

Whether or not this was true, Mr. Pinder had no idea. He had arranged with St Margaret's for the loan of their summer uniform plaid skirts for the boys to wear as kilts, but the Head had refused to allow Crabbe's thin legs to appear naked on stage, hence the trews (which were in any event, a pair of the groundsman's long john's, dyed red).

'But what will Bunting do sir? He won't have a partner to fight without me.'

Mr. Pinder smiled; he was pleased. Any of the other boys would have thought only of themselves. It was typical of Crabbe to think of others.

'No, the Headmaster has foreseen that and has made Bunting a palace guard. He will stand around at the back of the stage during various scenes and guard things. You won't be required on Thursday evenings anymore. Instead, you will attend the 'speaking' sessions on Wednesdays, in Hall. Did you correct the length of your sword Crabbe?'

'Well, actually, I burnt it sir. I felt so terrible at the thought of my injuring Monsieur. I was going to make another one.'

'No need, Crabbe. You won't carry a sword, just a spear. You'll have to climb over a wall and a sword would get in your way. I take it your spear is of the correct length?'

'Yes sir. Three times the length of my sword.'

It may be thought unbelievable that these few words failed to ring a warning bell in Mr. Pinder's brain.

Crabbe in all Innocence

Perhaps he was still feeling unwell. Possibly, it was the strain of dealing with the Headmaster's constant interference.

Whatever the reason, no warning bell rang.

And of course, nothing crossed Crabbe's innocent mind.

That is, until *The Night*.

Crabbe felt very much the 'new boy' at his first *speaking* rehearsal and sat at the back of the semi-circle ranged round the stage, doing his best not to be noticed. And in the main, he was successful, Mr. Pinder concentrating on Hopkins Major, who as expected, was playing the lead, and Barnaby Gordon, he whose voice hadn't broken.

At least, it hadn't broken when he was cast in the role of Lady Macbeth but started to break the following day. It now seemed unable to make up its mind whether it wanted to be a soprano or a baritone. He was able to cover both extremes in one sentence, sometimes going from squeak to gravel and back again during the course of a single word.

Such is the way with boys, and Mr. Pinder took it all in his stride. 'It is the least of my worries,' he said, 'As long as Gordon *looks* like Lady Macbeth and *moves* with a feminine gait he will be accepted in the part by the audience. Not *all* ladies squeak.

'Mrs Wilkes-Passmore certainly doesn't,' came a voice from the back. Mr. Pinder affected not to hear the comment and raised the back of his hand to his mouth to hide a grin.

When he felt himself able to speak without laughing, the rehearsal got under way. Crabbe was intrigued to see how actors learned to be in the right part of the stage at the right time. It was called *blocking*.

Mr. Pinder handed him a duplicated sheet of paper with squares drawn on it to represent the dimensions of the stage. Across the top the squares were numbered 1 to 8, and down the left side A to H.

The others had been given their sheets of paper two weeks before when Crabbe was still in the army, so whilst Barnaby Gordon was croaking his way through a soliloquy on stage, Mr. Pinder came and sat beside Crabbe to explain how it worked.

'When you get your lines, which the Headmaster has promised by Friday, I will give you the stage directions and you will note them on this grid. So, if I say, 'Royal Messenger, enter at *7-D*, then you will come to the stage here.' He tapped the sheet of paper in the appropriate square.

Neither of them noticed that when he said *7-D* several boys whispered 'hit'.

Mr. Pinder continued: 'And if I tell you to drop dead at *8-B*, you will die here.' He tapped the paper again.

'*Near miss.*'

He heard this and bellowed, 'Are you boys playing *Battleships* again? And Gordon, I told you to cut that word. Do not say 'damned'. It may give offence.'

207

Crabbe in all Innocence

He got up and went to the front, seemingly intent on correcting Lady Macbeth's line of 'out damned spot'. He instantly forgot about Crabbe, and about all the other boys who were, as he suspected, playing *Battleships* instead of concentrating on the rehearsal.

Gordon repeated the line without the offending word, 'Out spot.' And then he said 'walkies', which brought uproar.

'Silence!'

'Sir. Couldn't I say another word instead?'

'Such as?'

'Well, what about 'blasted' sir?'

'Certainly not. That is equally rude.'

'But sir,' Gordon replied, 'you let Macbeth say it when he goes on about the *blasted* heath. You didn't say it was rude.'

'It isn't rude in *that* context. It has a different meaning. It means the heath has been blasted by strong winds and gales.'

'Why couldn't it mean blasted by a bomb sir?'

'Because they didn't have bombs in those days, silly boy.'

Mr. Pinder, although rehearsal was due to last for an hour, had had enough after twenty minutes.

'That will suffice for today. You may all go except Macbeth and the Royal Messenger. We will rehearse your scene, which won't be easy as Raspu…that is, Doctor Wilkes-Passmore, hasn't yet written it.'

The rest of the cast trooped off, leaving Hopkins, Crabbe and Mr. Pinder alone in the Hall.

Without an audience of bored schoolboys there to disrupt proceedings by laughing too loudly at anything that went wrong, they got on very well.

'We don't know the words yet, but they are *secondary* to the action. When the curtains close on the Dunsinane scene, we have to remove the cardboard castle in the background and replace it with a background of trees and rocks where Macduff kills Macbeth. Now, this short scene is to give some extra time for the stage crew to make the changes of scenery.

You Crabbe, will make your entrance down left at *F-8,* you will climb over the ruins of the wall, cross the stage to *H-1*, knock on the door which will be opened by you, Hopkins. Crabbe will hand you a message, you read it, don't like what you see, so shoot Crabbe with a bow and arrow when his back is turned. Crabbe, are you feeling quite well?'

Crabbe's face had turned deathly white at the thought of being shot with an arrow.

'Yes, thank you sir. It's just that...'

'Don't worry. It will be a stage illusion. You will appear to have been shot. I then want you to stagger around dreadfully injured, giving one of your screams as you did when you were Poor George and then die at *D-7*. Now, we don't know how long it will take to change the scenery. Something unexpected is bound to happen, so I will get one of the boys to stand behind the

209

curtain and whisper when all is ready. You will then stop staggering and screaming and drop dead.

'At *D-7*.'

'Just so. Most of the lights will go out, Russell or someone will sneak on in the semi-darkness and drag your lifeless body into the wings, the curtains will open, the lights will go on and we'll continue with the final scene. Do you foresee any problems?'

'No sir. None at all,' replied the boys in unison.

In their dormitories that night, the two of them were thinking over their parts in the new scene. Crabbe had complete faith in Mr. Pinder's ability to produce an illusion to make him look as if he's been shot with an arrow and drifted off to sleep considering ways in which he might improve his stagger.

17: DRESS

Hopkins was rather disappointed when he learned he was not allowed to shoot Crabbe. He had practiced night after night with his bow and arrow, and now considered himself an expert every bit as good as Errol Flynn.

It had crossed his mind that as there would be one Dress Rehearsal, then a free day, and then the one and only performance of *Macbeth*, he could deliberately miss Crabbe at the Dress, but still get him for real on the night. During the school holidays Hopkins tended to watch far too many American gangster films at his local cinema.

The Head and Mr. Pinder between them had made a contraption from string and a broken balsa wood arrow that would make it look as if Crabbe had been shot clean through. It would be operated by Crabbe pulling a string threaded through his cloak and armour so that at the correct moment, the two broken ends would suddenly flip up into view. The one in front was daubed in red paint to look like blood and the one at the back had the feathery bit sticking out like they always did in American cowboy films, according to Hopkins.

Such was the theory.

And, indeed, such was the practice. It worked perfectly!

Crabbe in all Innocence

They rehearsed the scene time and time again under the watchful eye of Mr. Pinder and the menacing glare of the Head, who seemed to be *daring* them to get *his* lines wrong, although he never said so in so many words.

No one, other than these four, were allowed to attend these rehearsals. It was, according to the Head, another of his secret weapons to be visited upon an unsuspecting audience. He wanted to gauge reaction.

In the event, Crabbe's scene was about the only part of the Dress rehearsal that *did* work. Nothing else went as planned. It was as if weeks of rehearsals, discussions and the learning of lines simply had not occurred.

Hopkins Major as Macbeth had the largest part, but the booming voice of Mrs. Wilkes-Passmore as prompt was heard more often than his. And far louder.

When the curtain opened on Act One, the witches were revealed wearing their pointed hats and tattered cloaks and completely oblivious to the fact the play had started, were playing hick, hack, hock.

Lady Macbeth, on the other side of the stage and fourteen pages before she was due to make her first entrance, was steadying a stepladder at the top of which could be seen the lower limbs of Banquo trying to fix a broken spotlight.

The Headmaster was backstage, organising things that didn't need organising, and was probably, thought Mr. Pinder, responsible for starting the Dress without bothering to tell the actors.

Chris Hare

From his chair halfway down Hall, he called out, 'Stop. Where is Browne?'

Digby Browne put his head innocently round a cardboard tree. 'Here. Yes sir?'

'Ah, Browne. Was it you who opened the curtains?'

'Yes, sir. The Head said. As Stage Manager it is part of my duties.'

Indeed, it is, Browne. But so is ensuring the actors are ready, and that the lights work. One other thing, did we not plan to play some music as an overture? If I remember correctly, it was to stop as the dialogue started. Do you remember that, Browne?'

'I do, sir. Indeed, I remember it very clearly.'

'Then what happened to the record?'

'I forgot it, sir. It must still be in my dorm.'

'Then go and get it while Banquo works on the spotlight.'

Half an hour after they should have started, they started again. It was a bad beginning, but it got much worse. The broken spotlight and missing music were minor when compared to the actors coming on at the wrong times, the missing props and forgotten lines. To Crabbe, sitting in the auditorium with assorted soldiers who were not required on stage, it appeared that Mrs. Wilkes-Passmore was reading the whole play out loud on her own with just occasional mumbled interruptions from the actors. Not only was she doing the prompt's job, she was also calling out, 'You should have gone off stage then, boy.'

213

Crabbe in all Innocence

Mrs. W-P actually came *on stage* herself during the critical soliloquy of Act Two. She called to Mr. Pinder that she was getting cramped stuck in her small corner wedged in by scenery and thrones, and needed a cup of tea, and some cake.

Crabbe, with his kindly heart, felt sorry for Mr. Pinder. He had worked non-stop to ensure the success of this production, and it was all going wrong. He just sat in his seat *tut-tutting and no-noing* at every calamity and writing furiously in the margins of his script. During one pause, caused by a banner falling on Gloves, Crabbe tried to cheer Mr. Pinder up by saying, 'Never mind, sir. It can't get any worse.'

'You haven't done your scene yet, have you Elsie?'

The sarcasm was lost on Crabbe, who replied, 'No sir. But I shall do my best.'

'I'm sure you will. But that is what everyone is doing. *Their best*. And it's a disaster. Twenty-four hours from now Hall will be packed with parents, the Mayor, the Head, who will not be backstage tomorrow, thank goodn…the vicar from St. Anselm's and a reporter from the local paper…I need a large glass of, err, aspirin.'

'Have you got a headache, sir?'

'Not yet.'

A backdrop shot suddenly skywards revealing Lady Macbeth and the ghost of Banquo playing snap, and Mr. Pinder returned to writing his notes. Crabbe resumed his seat. He sat through two and half acts, watching the play as it lurched painfully along.

It was nearly time! He went backstage.

The victorious soldiers in the final battle before Crabbe's entrance trooped off as the lights dimmed and the curtains closed to a desultory applause. The dead soldiers got up and went after them to watch Crabbe's scene, followed by the Headmaster.

Crabbe felt terribly alone.

He looked round the corner of the ruins of the wall he was to climb. In the gloom he could just make out the vast shape of Mrs. Wilkes-Passmore through Macbeth's open castle door, and beside her Macbeth himself.

He could see them! That door should be closed!

The first sign of terror appeared: a nerve in his left cheek started to twitch.

From somewhere behind the curtain he heard nails being withdrawn noisily from the struts holding up Dunsinane. At least, Russell and his crew were there.

Was Irvine?

He noticed his spear was wobbling in his nerve-torn grip.

A whispered voice: Irvine's.

'Okay, Elsie. Give us one more minute. When you see the footlights come on, throw your spear and climb over the wall.

Relief! Irvine was there, and ready!

Despite the reassuring voice, Crabbe realised he was terribly nervous. His mouth was bone dry.

Crabbe in all Innocence

The door!

He looked again. It had been closed.

Entirely alone now, for the umpteenth time, he checked his costume and that the hidden strings were in place. He could feel they were. He put his glasses in his sporran and ensured the message was still safely tucked into the waistband of his red trews.

The waiting was awful. Doubts flooded his mind. What was he doing up here? He was a schoolboy, not an actor. Would he remember his lines? Why couldn't he have used a yard-rule like everyone else?

Never again.

Never, ever again.

He could see the footlights brightening. His moment had come.

He raised his head above the crumbled battlements and stared round the deserted stage. He sensed the eyes of the school on him. They were staring at him. He could *feel* them.

They were expecting him to do something wrong.

Aitkin whispered, 'Only a matter of time.' The ripple of giggles was instantly silenced by a glare from the Head.

Mr. Pinder was biting his nails.

On stage, Crabbe dropped his spear over the wall. It landed with a clatter in exactly the right place.

The hammering backstage stopped. All he could hear now was the hammering of his own heart. Out front on the other side of the footlights, there was only silence.

Everyone was waiting!

With great care, he climbed over the ruined battlements. Slowly and deliberately, feeling each stone with his foot before putting his weight on it. He reached the safety of the stage and picked up his spear.

He risked a quick look round. In the gap between the curtain and Macbeth's door, he saw that Digby Browne had somehow got into the tiny space of Mrs. W-P's prompt corner where she was tightly clutching his hand. His face was screwed up with the pain.

Mouth still bone dry, heart still thumping, Crabbe moved across the front of the stage towards the door.

Would he be able to speak? Your mouth needs a little spit to form words and Crabbe's had never been so dry.

He knocked at the door. The knocker didn't come away in his hand.

The door opened and Hopkins Major stood there. He had the first line.

'Aye?'

'Art thou my Lord Macbeth?' Crabbe said.

His mouth worked! Mrs. W-P and Browne smiled happily and squeezed hands even tighter. Browne didn't seem to notice the extra agony. From the front he heard a huge collective sigh being breathed out.

Macbeth replied, and Crabbe delivered his next line. And the next. It was going splendidly! He was no longer afraid – he was enjoying himself!

Macbeth said, *'Hand me the message, varlet.'*

Crabbe in all Innocence

He took out the piece of rolled up greaseproof paper from his waistband and handed it to Macbeth, bowing as he did so.

'Be gone.'

This was the most difficult part: having given the scroll to Macbeth, Crabbe had to walk slowly away towards the other side of the stage to the crumbling wall. Behind him Macbeth would unroll the scroll as he turned to go back inside the castle then briefly reappeared at the door with a bow and arrow and delivered the line: *'I'd prayed 'twas news of a battle won!'* before stepping back slightly to make it look as if he was firing the arrow.

They hadn't been able to work out a way for Crabbe to know when Macbeth had released the arrow with his back to him. Hopkins suggested he might say, *'Take that, you sidewinder!'* but that's the sort of thing Hopkins *would* suggest.

The Headmaster said that he would consider the problem in the chapel after lunch. The result of his thinking was brilliant, and yet so simple, he wondered why Shakespeare hadn't thought of it himself. He'd forgotten Shakespeare didn't know anything about this scene.

'Very well,' said W-P, 'this is what you will do: when Macbeth delivers the line ending *'battle won,'* you take the word 'won' as being the figure 'one'. You will then count to eight silently to yourselves. On seven, Hopkins will appear to fire his arrow, and on eight, Crabbe will pull his string.'

It was, as the Headmaster kept saying, 'ingenious!' They practiced counting at the same speed out loud, and then did it in silence. Before long, they were in perfect but noiseless harmony.

He bowed and turned and heard Macbeth say, *'I'd prayed 'twas news of a battle won.'*
Two, three, four, they both mouthed silently. On *eight* Crabbe pulled the string and before he could begin his death wail, he heard a gasp from the audience. *What had gone wrong?* In panic, he looked down to see the bloodied balsa wood arrow sticking straight out through his heart. *Nothing had.* The gasp had been one of shock, of horror. It had worked perfectly. All he had to do now was die when Browne said.

He staggered round, then up centre to *B5* clutching and wailing and listening for Browne. *'Okay Elsie – all ready back here. You can die when you're ready.'* He gave a final lurch forward and dropped dead precisely on square *D7*, eyes wide open and tongue lolling out.

Browne let go of Mrs. W-P's hand and dimmed the lights to minimum.

There was silence.

Absolute silence for about five seconds.

Then, thunderous applause.

Without the glare of the footlights and without glasses, Crabbe could see little. But he was aware that when Irvine came to drag his corpse away, he was clapping wildly and only stopped to take hold of Crabbe's body. As he was being pulled off stage, Irvine whispered that Mrs. Wilkes-Passmore had got hold of Hopkins Major in a headlock and was kissing him!

From the darkness of the wings, Crabbe heard the applause peter out to a stop, to be replaced instantly, by the sound of twenty-five pairs of feet rushing from Hall to take their places for the final act.

Crabbe, his moment of glory at an end, got out of the way and went to sit alone in the science lab dressing room. All he had to do now was stand at the end of the line of soldiers and take his bow.

The play ended, and the actors lined up and bowed.

With the whole cast and crew on stage, Mr. Pinder said, 'I have made notes. Copious notes. But it would take too long to go through them all now. You *know* where you went wrong, the lines you forgot and the cues you missed. There is little more I can do for the production now. It's up to you, the actors and the stage crew. Actors, you may go. Try to get a good night's sleep and try not to be downhearted – you know you can do it. Remember the old theatrical saying, *'Bad dress, good show.'*

Browne and your crew kindly remain behind for a while. I have a few ideas that may help speed up the set changes between scenes. Finally, I will say this. You have all just seen what is possible. You've seen the benchmark. Now it is up to you – each of you, to reach it.'

Twenty minutes earlier Crabbe thought he would die of fear. Now he thought he might possibly die of pride.

'Die? Not yet. Not for some time,' said Atropos, looking down. *'Come sisters, let us speed up our work, for soon we go to the Play!'* She gave a maniacal laugh and returned to her loom.

18: PERFORMANCE

Crabbe was disappointed. He had received a telegram from his parents saying they were really sorry, but they wouldn't be able to get up to Chantry as his father had been summoned to Head Office. They sent their best wishes for *Macbeth* and said they would be thinking of him.

It wasn't too bad, he thought, after all they had made the trip on every other Parents' Day which couldn't be said for any other boy in the entire school.

Yesterday, Mr. Pinder had called everyone together in Hall.

'The reason the cast and crew have a free day between the Dress Rehearsal and the Performance is to give everyone time to reflect on their parts – either their acting part in the play or the part they play backstage. I won't dwell on last night. There is no real point. You must know what you did wrong, and it is up to *you* to put it right. I will not be backstage tomorrow night to guide you.

Keep up the pace, pick up your cues, and keep the action moving. In some scenes you were too slow. I thought the scenery was moving faster than the actors.

You were excellent in the last act, and you don't need me to tell you why. But I *will* tell you – it was because a light was lit from a totally unexpected quarter and it showed you the way.'

Chris Hare

Crabbe felt himself going pink, and when Hopkins Major patted him on the back and whispered, 'Well done, Elsie,' he blushed crimson.

Mr. Pinder continued, 'The time for experimenting is long past. You have developed your characters, and you relate well to each other within the context of the play. Just keep everything going, try to show more thought when delivering the soliloquies, and tidy up the climaxes – give urgency.

That is all. Be in the dressing room tomorrow fully made up and costumed by seven. Good luck to you all.'

Crabbe had had a little trouble getting to sleep after the Dress. He was very excited, and his imagination ran riot. Was a career on stage to be his future? He had no idea what he wanted to do after he'd left school.

West End theatres and his name in lights? Contracts and agents fighting to sign him up? People crowding around Stage Doors begging for his autograph. Film offers?

A stage name - should he have one? Or should he stick to Lancelot Crabbe? He started thinking of catchy names. Nothing memorable came to mind, or if it did, he didn't remember it when he woke up the following morning.

Breakfast for the cast and crew was in the gym. It was a quiet, sober affair. Crabbe seemed to be the only one who wanted to talk. Most of the cast had their heads buried in their scripts, mouthing their lines between large bits of doorstep, occasionally whispering across the table to each other with ideas to improve the action in certain scenes.

A thought struck Crabbe. Could *his* performance be improved? He had done well at Dress, everyone said. But had he *really*? Could it be that he had been told he had done well simply because everyone expected him to do badly? And instead of being congratulated on getting it right, the real reason for praising him was that he hadn't got it *wrong*! The thought worried him, and he decided that after breakfast, he would go to Hall and run through his part a few times.

He would be alone. He could concentrate.

Everyone else had the same idea.

The place was cluttered with soldiers marching and fighting, with props, scenery being hoisted and lowered again. Lines that were meant to be asides to the audience, were being screamed to try to drown out the sounds of hammering.

Everyone was deadly serious. There was no levity, no jokes and no idle chatter. The atmosphere was infectious in a negative sort of way, and after being completely ignored, Crabbe decided to keep to himself.

Unfortunately, the crumbled battlements over which he was to climb were in bits, which meant he wouldn't be able to practice his entrance.

The door to Macbeth's castle wasn't there either.

Browne and Woods were using the entire length of the stage to drill small holes in cardboard blocks of stone through which to pass a long length of string.

224

Browne was concerned it was taking so long to change settings between scenes, and felt responsible, in part, for the slow pace of the play. He explained that by pulling the string, his team would be able to drag the battlements in or out of position and save valuable time by not having to rebuild it all stone by stone.

'It was you who gave me the idea, Elsie, or rather it was you pulling the string on your fake arrow. We should be able to set or strike it in a few seconds. At the Dress it took five minutes.'

'Glad to be of help,' he said quietly, aware that without his crumbling battlements or Macbeth's front door, and with the stage covered in cardboard stones, there was nowhere for him to go through his moves.

The morning passed slowly.

He felt a strange mixture of emotions. A little excitement, perhaps at the thought of the performance, but mainly a strange feeling of anti-climax because soon it would all be over. Weeks and weeks of hard work. In just a few short hours it would all become a thing of the past. Part of his memories. Was it all worth it?

His mood was apparently shared by a few others, for it was a sombre group of boys who, after lunch, made their way to the playing fields to watch rugby against Gayton High.

Chantry won, thirteen points to eight, but hardly managed to raise a cheer. What was the point of it all?

Glory, fame, recognition.

225

Crabbe in all Innocence

That was the point. As the evening neared, the mood brightened with nervous anticipation. The cast chattered excitedly in the science lab/dressing room. They joked, wished each other *good luck*, and most strangely of all, apologised to each other for past wrongs. It was as if they were real soldiers, about to go 'over the top' and knew some of them wouldn't return so it was important to make peace with one another now before it was too late.

The Hall started to fill up as the audience arrived, and although the cast were not allowed out front in their costumes, they were unable to resist peeking through the curtains, totally ignoring the pleas from Browne to clear the stage.

Mr. Pinder came backstage ten minutes before curtain up to give them a final pep talk. Then they heard the strains of *William Tell* – the quick bit in the middle, drifting through the open window of the science lab. Time to go.

With a final glance in the mirror to check make-up, a final slap on the back to anyone whose back was within slapping reach, everyone in the first act went.

Which meant Crabbe was on his own. They were all on at the beginning or soon after curtain up, and everyone not immediately required was unwelcome in the wings, which were already crowded with sceneshifters and props, the huge presence of Mrs. Wilkes-Passmore, and actors waiting to go on.

226

All alone, he went through his lines for the thousandth time. It was not at all necessary, he knew them backwards and could probably say them in his sleep. But it was comforting to know that if anything were to go wrong tonight, it would not be his fault for forgetting his lines.

It wasn't. He didn't forget any of them.

He didn't speak any of them either, after the first one.

The forces of good that had combined at the Dress to help him give a performance of note now dissipated and were replaced by the forces of *Heroic Failuredom*. It appeared to be nobody's fault, in the main. Just bad luck.

Actually, the performance he gave was very well received. Although what happened was a far cry from what Dr Wilkes-Passmore or Shakespeare had intended. Crabbe was glad, naturally, to be complimented after the play, but in all honesty, it was like winning a race because all the other runners had fallen and broken a leg.

The first half had gone well.

The boys were full of it when they returned to the dressing room during the main interval. Everyone had made his entrance on cue, and in the right costume. Mrs. W-P's voice had hardly been heard, no one was injured, and the scenery had been raised and lowered smoothly and at the correct times.

All that was to change.

Crabbe in all Innocence

Crabbe had been nervous last night, and now he wondered why. Tonight was far more frightening. Hall was packed with people he didn't know.

Strangers.

His lips went dry again, his tongue feeling far too big for his mouth. He noticed his twitch was back, and that suddenly his feet had turned to lead.

He dragged himself reluctantly backstage and waited, listening in the wings – permitted now, as he was due on stage in just a few seconds. He wished it was over. He shared none of the enthusiasm apparent in the rest of the cast.

The chaps *were* doing extremely well, he thought, as he heard the familiar lines being delivered. He took off his glasses and put them in his sporran, at the same time, checking the message for Macbeth was safely in place.

A page before his entrance, he readied himself.

The footlights dimmed, and he reached up to drop his spear over. The wall had grown.

It's the wrong wall!

He couldn't climb it without a ladder. The battlements were at least a yard higher than they were at the Dress. *Oh glory! What to do now?! And why hadn't someone said something?*

But the show *must* go on.

He reached up with his spear and dropped it over the top. He heard it land, then he heard it rolling. There was a bang and a flash that briefly lit up everything around him. As his eyes returned to normal, he saw that the stage, lit only dimly by footlights, was now even dimmer.

It was now and only now, that those additional few inches on the length of his spear made their mark.

Given Crabbe's history and form, a betting man might lay odds on that extra ten inches being inserted in someone's unsuspecting rear or, had the blade been sharp, cutting through an overhead rope tied to something heavy. Not so. The spear stopped rolling nine inches in front of the left-hand set of footlights. It was the very last inch that touched something vital, and the duly speared bank of lights died as it exploded.

As quick as a flash, in the wings opposite just as the sudden burst of light lit up Crabbe's face, Hopkins Major whispered to Russell, 'Oh, look! It's the genie,' and Russell mouthed back, 'Oh no its not. It's Mister Chad. And cripes, we've set the wrong wall!'

He froze. As he had many times at Assembly when arriving at one of those overly complicated biblical names.

Crabbe's feet scrambled, desperately trying to find a foothold. He was unaware that Wood, having seen his predicament came to help by acting as a mounting block for Crabbe to stand on. Crabbe repaid Wood's kindness with an unknowing kick in the face.

Russell pointed, jerking his hand in the direction of the flat to the right of the stranded Crabbe.

Crabbe in all Innocence

He glanced up, and saw a rope looped round a hook. Crabbe immediately understood what Russell meant. He was to take hold of the rope and use it to pull himself up and over the wall.

What Russell didn't intend was that Crabbe should unhook the rope, which he did, sailing skywards as the counterweight on the other end, the solid brass eagle from the lectern, came down and struck Hopkins Major, rendering him senseless.

Crabbe, therefore made his entrance, not as a Genie and not as Mr. Chad, but airborne as Peter Pan.

He landed astride the battlements firmly and it doesn't need to be said that when landed on by a chap, painted egg boxes filled with plaster can cause untold agony.

Another round of applause and also a few giggles.

He used the clapping to cover his undignified descent from the battlements and on his way down heard a 'twang' as a button flew off the back of his braces and rolled its way into the broken set of footlights. As he made his painful way to Macbeth's door watching the button rolling and wondering if anything else could go wrong, it occurred to him that he had probably taken more time making his entrance tonight than he had for the whole of his scene during the Dress.

Despite the loss of one bank of foots, there was still enough light from the remaining three. Feeling as if a horse had just kicked him, he knocked at the door. The knocker came off in his hand. He'd been expecting this and put it down.

Lady Macbeth opened the door. *Lady…?* She was supposed to be dead.

Something was wrong.

'Aye?'

'Art thou my Lord Macbeth?'

'Do I look like a man, thou stinking varlet?'

That wasn't the line, and this isn't the actor. Gordon was standing in for Macbeth and they'd have to *ad lib*!

'Err, well, erm. Er. No, now you mention it.'

'Then why sayest thou it, thou dung beetle. I art the ghost of Lady Macbeth, worm.'

'I say! Steady on!' said Crabbe, forgetting for a moment who he was. He was confused. What was he doing here? What was Barnaby Gordon doing *there*?

'What are you doing here?' Gordon asked, as if he could read his mind.

Gordon started to twitch an eye and give little jerks with his face. Crabbe got the impression the answer to all this was behind him, but it was far too dark to see.

He said, 'Errmm'.

'What wanteth thou, oh ugly one?' That was rich, coming from the largest ears in the Fourth Year.

'I've forgotten.'

'Vile knave! Could it be thou hast come hither with a message, verily?'

'Brilliant. Yes, that's it. Well done. A message for my Lord Macbeth. Is he in?'

'Would that he were but he's out.' Barnaby started twitching again.

Something's gone terribly wrong. Better carry on improvising, but IN character.

'Gone for a drink, has he?'

'He's been injured by a flying eagle. Givest me the message, oh stupid one.'

'Right you art,' Crabbe said, getting the general idea. He put his hand in his waistband for the scroll of greaseproof paper. *It wasn't there!*

It was there before he came on. He'd checked.

'Ermm,' he said, to fill in as he patted around his long johns, searching.

'What is that, fool? Thy lunch?'

He looked down at his long johns to where Barnaby Gordon was pointing. There was a huge bulge by his left kneecap. Somehow, the scroll had worked itself all the way down there.

'Aargh!' he said with relief.

'Thou are not as stupid as thou lookest. Tis a safe enough hiding place.'

Gordon held out his hand for the scroll.

Crabbe lifted his kilt and plunged a hand into the opening of his long johns and down the leg.

The audience giggled.

'Fool,' said Gordon, taking it between finger and thumb as if it were infected.

Crabbe felt Gordon was rather overdoing it with the insults. He was the Royal Messenger, not the village idiot. Still, Gordon was standing in for the absent Macbeth, and between them they had at least managed to keep the play going without any help from Mrs. W-P.

Did he know what to do next? Better give him a hint, just in case.

'I'll be off, then.' Crabbe said, winking with his upstage eye and indicating his chest with his thumb.

'Aye. Get thee hence. They face offends me. That is, it offends *ONE*.'

Gordon knew! *Good old Gordie.* It was obvious he knew what to do next, and to make sure Crabbe understood, he mouthed '*two*' at him as he turned to pick up the bow.

Crabbe bowed on a silent '*three*' and turned. *Four, five, six, seven, EIGHT.*

He pulled the string and was relieved when the pointed end of the arrow came out through his heart. He clutched it and paused a moment to allow the dramatic effect to dawn on the audience.

He awaited their gasp, but he only heard their laughter.

Gales of it.

What had gone wrong now?

Stunned for a moment, he wondered if the feathered end had come up at the back. Clutching his chest with his right hand, he staggered a bit and felt behind him with his left.

Nothing!

233

He ran his hand up and down his back. He couldn't feel the other end under his costume. *It must have worked. So where was the bit with the feathers?*

The laughter was still at its height and here and there people clapped. Through all the noise he heard someone call out from backstage, 'Lower'. He lowered his hand and found the missing part of the arrow sticking out of his bottom.

His bottom!

The sweat that had started when he flew upwards from the battlements and got far worse during his ad-libbed scene with Gordon, now poured off him. *Off him* as, mortally wounded, he bent over and dripped on the footlights to the left of the ones that had already gone out. These lights sizzled a bit before exploding.

As only the left half of the stage was now properly lit, he decided to not die at D7 but somewhere around H6 where he'd be seen.

Screaming in a mixture of agony at being murdered and embarrassment at having a feathery shaft sticking out of his rear, he moved upstage and between shrieks whispered through the curtain.

'You ready, Brownie?'

'Hours ago!'

He died, as planned, with eyes open and tongue hanging out. But he died, *unplanned* at H6. There was tremendous applause at his death, and even some cheering.

As Crabbe lay there. He hoped the clapping was for the manner in which he had met his end, but as it had all gone so dreadfully wrong, he thought the audience might be applauding because he *was* dead and would take no further part in the play. Thank goodness my parents aren't here to witness my ignominy, he thought.

From a distance of about a yard, the footlights were incredibly hot. He'd died much closer to them than he had at the Dress. Did a corpse normally keep sweating? This one did.

He didn't stop blinking either. Why were those lights so bright?

Oh glory! He'd died far too close to the front. He could see the people in the front row clearly. The Head glaring, the vicar asleep.

Could he give a final gasp and turn over? *No. Corpses didn't do that.*

They didn't sneeze either, but he couldn't help it. There was so much dust down there. Anyway, it saved his eyes from the glare of the footlights since the sneeze landed on and extinguished the third lot. *Only one bank of footlights to go.*

The stage was not for Crabbe, he decided. As he lay there, he wondered about many things, but he didn't wonder why Russell hadn't come on to drag his corpse away. He'd forgotten that bit. Russell had come on but finding D7 empty, had gone straight off again.

Why had the arrow trick gone wrong? It had worked so well before – perfectly. With a shudder he hoped wasn't seen, he remembered his braces twanging. Of course! The unexpected flight and landing astride the ruined wall had dislodged the back part of the arrow. Ah well, too late to worry about it now. *Water under the bridge*. His part in *Macbeth* was over.

If only it was.

He was still on stage when he shouldn't be, and the last act was happening around him! The chaps rallied, as real troopers do.

The last act, after Macbeth's beheading, is all about peace and harmony, the wickedness of man's ambition and the futility of war. Macduff and his generals, with a few prisoners from Macbeth's army were on stage casting about after the battle and going on about 'senseless carnage' and 'Brave Scot killing Scot'.

At this point Macduff noticed Crabbe's prone body and, in a brilliant piece of improvisation, he decided to use it as a prop in his final speech. Instead of delivering his lines directly to the audience, he spoke them at Crabbe, emphasising the important bits with a kick at Crabbe's corpse.

The others quickly saw what Macduff was up to and joined in.

Possibly, they felt they could make their point more obviously by moving Crabbe from his position behind the set of dead footlights. Crabbe assumed that when Macduff took hold of his ankles and started to drag him along, it was to pull him into the wings thus putting an end to his torment. But no, when he got to the last remaining set of working footlights, he let go.

'Look thee at yon poor ignorant but valiant soul,' said Macduff, 'slain this day to satisfy man's ambition. You, you men of Macbeth's defeated army, do you not see the shame you have brought to these glens, these isles, thy clans, by siding with the monster?'

Crabbe realised his kilt had ridden up exposing his private region, which was still, thankfully, bruised but intact within his long johns. Not to remain so for long as Bunting came to the front and tried to drag him back again. He was not as big as Macduff, and only succeeded in moving him an inch or two, so he beckoned for a couple of fellows to help him out and together they got Crabbe back into the gloom of the second set of fused floodlights and Bunting gave his 'He died. He's dead. He is forgotten' speech and kicked Crabbe again to prove his point.

This was getting beyond a joke.

Crabbe was being dragged back and forth, from bright lights to dim, any moment expecting to be speared by a lethal splinter and kicked and all when he wasn't even supposed to be on the stage.

Macduff spoke the final line: '*Let us take a dram together for these noble fellow's sacrifices,*' – *noble fellow* was better than *dolt*, Crabbe thought – '*and drink to peace, and never more to war.*'

The remaining lights went out and the curtain closed.

Crabbe in all Innocence

The audience applauded wildly and called out *Bravo!* and *Well done!* He could hear the vicar's wife saying, 'Wasn't that good, Gerald? So funny. Do wake up, Gerald!'

Crabbe could hear her so well because he was on the wrong side of the curtain but it was dark, he thought he could creep along the front of the stage unseen, slip behind the curtain and take his place for the final bow.

He had a second thought. No. It wasn't right to join the others in the line-up after he had just given the worst performance in the long list of plays the school had witnessed in its entire history.

No. He wouldn't bow. It *would* be wrong. Like asking for a medal for helping to launch a lifeboat on the *Titanic* after admitting you were the lookout who didn't shout 'look out' loudly enough.

He fished in his sporran and pulled out his spectacles, got up and *very carefully* made his way unseen in the darkness across the front of the stage. He would squeeze through to the prompt corner, slip out the side door, change in the dressing room, go to the dorm and await years of ribbing and sarcasm. Perhaps he would be ostracized, *ignored.* He would certainly be summoned to the Head's study after Assembly on Monday. He might even be expelled!

Such were his dismal thoughts as he slowly made his way towards Mrs. Wilkes-Passmore's corner ignoring the thunderous applause and cheering.

238

Chris Hare

He didn't get there. He moved too slowly for fear of crowning his personal disaster by falling off the stage. He had got precisely as far as the place where the curtains met when they closed, when they opened, and every light that still worked suddenly blazed into life.

The leads, Macbeth, (now recovered from the attack by the brass eagle), Lady Macbeth, Macduff, King Duncan and the Three Witches were at the back of the stage preparing to march to the front to receive their applause. Crabbe noticed one or two actor's feet take the first step before they suddenly stopped. They froze at the sight of him.

Louder cheering and applause came from the audience.

The decision about what to do next was taken from them as the rest of the company forced their way on stage, anxious for their share of recognition. The eight leads were shoved to the front and, with Crabbe now with them, the nine of them bowed in unison, with shy smiles acknowledging the frantic clapping and cheering.

In the middle of the front row, the Head joined in with the applause heartily. Then he paused for a moment and turned to Mr. Pinder on his left and pointed at Crabbe. They were clearly discussing his fate. Such is the price of fame.

He wasn't ostracized or beaten up, and Hopkins Major didn't even seem to mind that Crabbe had pinched his place in the centre of the line-up. Dr Wilkes-Passmore came to the dressing room to congratulate them and said that as a reward for their hard work he had instructed the kitchen staff to prepare a special high tea in Hall the following afternoon, after they had cleared away all the props and scenery.

It was, thought Crabbe, probably the idea of hot buttered crumpets and scones with unlimited jam and cream that saved him from a certain death.

Mr. Pinder rushed in and told Hopkins and Barnaby Gordon to hurry back to the stage in full costume as the reporter from the local paper wanted to take their photograph to print with his review. Then he made his way across to Crabbe, who sat quietly with his back to him waiting for the axe to fall.

But he said, 'And Crabbe, he wants you in the picture as well. Then go to the back of Hall. Your family were able to come and watch after all, and they're all still clapping.'

Chris Hare

19: FLIGHT

Of the many customs that made up life at Chantry, none was believed to be older or more obscure in origin than that concerning the portrait of Old Mother Sharkey.

No one knew who she was, or why her portrait hung on the back wall of Hall, or what, if any, her connection to Chantry was. No one knew how long she had been hanging there and it was completely unknown why she was called 'Old Mother Sharkey'.

For all that, she had a purpose. As the Head had remarked on numerous occasions during Assembly, especially after a disastrous result on the cricket field, 'None of us is entirely useless. We can all, in failure, serve as a horrible example to others.'

And the portrait did that.

A horrible example. Her role was to gather dust for 364 days of the year whilst glaring down at the stage or at whoever was reading the Lesson, at plays being struggled through, and above all, at the Shells.

The only thing that was actually *known* about Old Mother Sharkey was what she looked like. If there was a prize for ugliness, Old Mother Sharkey would win it by a distance.

'Ugly' in her case, is really a too kind-a-word to use. It fails to provoke the imagination sufficiently to conjure the heights or the *depths,* of her hideousness:

the yellowing wizened face that was deeply lined and wart encrusted and that awful, doleful expression.

Her head was perched on a filthy Elizabethan ruff-encased neck at a slightly impossible angle, as if the painting had been made just after she was cut down from the gallows. The nose must have cost the artist a small fortune in paint, such was the size of it. Wisps of grey hair stuck out from beneath her black bonnet, as did the ears, only slightly less revolting than her nose. She had no teeth, or if she did, they were probably blackened with rot concealed behind her thin, cruel lips. The whole effect was nothing short of loathsome. Nevertheless, the lady filled an important role.

Her image was evoked by prefects at the beginning of each school year on new boys who were lonely, homesick and scared stiff.

'If you don't stop that noise and go to sleep, I'll get Old Mother Sharkey to pay you a visit.' Without fail, this had the immediate effect of silencing the youngster, whilst at the same time, guaranteeing that sleep would evade the boy for several nights in a row until sheer exhaustion took over.

For the prefects, this and many of the customs and traditions at Chantry, had a wider element to them that ranged from being a little unfair, to the other end of the scale where they consisted of mental and physical barbarity. But they worked. They had the desired effect. The ends justified the means however tortuous.

Chris Hare

The Headmaster, and by his example, most of the staff, used different tactics. They would create enough fear, and then offer salvation. Or sometimes, the same thing but reversed, the promise of reward, and then the suggestion that it might be withheld.

These methods were not unique to Chantry. They were the backbone strategy in almost every English public school. The accepted way to instil discipline, gain instant obedience and keep control.

Founders' Day was the one day of the year that Old Mother Sharkey didn't glower down on anyone. On this day, again no one knew why, she was taken down by the School Prefects and given a much-needed dusting before being rehung, with all due ceremony, at Assembly the following morning.

'My congratulations,' said the Head when Old Mother Sharkey was back where she belonged, and he was standing on the top of his steps. 'Your general behaviour during yesterday's celebrations to mark our Founding was exemplary. I have received no reports of misdemeanours from any of your masters, and it appears there has been no damage to the fabric of the school buildings.

As you are aware, the distinguished Old Chantovian, His Grace the Duke of Chandos in his address to the school yesterday followed tradition by asking me to grant you a half-holiday, which I do now – next Wednesday afternoon.'

A round of grateful applause from the boys.

'Except', he continued, 'for the boys of Forms 4A and 4B.'

Very muted murmurings from the Fourth Year, instantly silenced by severe glances from the teaching staff.

'Your excellent performance of *Macbeth* last term, your hard work and dedication, minds me to think of a greater reward.'

100% attention from Fourth Year.

'I am considering the possibility of your spending a weekend away from school. It is by no means definite. There are difficulties to be faced and overcome, and arrangements for your accommodation to be made. I will say nothing more at present. Give me no reason for displeasure. I will have no compunction in abandoning the plan, should you give me cause.'

The time-honoured method of acquiring obedience in the English public-school system was thus employed ensuring success, by a master of the art.

Speculation as to where they were going ran rife. Everywhere, from Aberystwyth to Windsor were identified *definitely,* as *the destination.*

The answer came from an unlikely source. Messrs. Wildman, Elames-Turner and Bond Minor. They of frequent appearances in the Head's study, had, whilst waiting for himself to arrive and administer their latest beating, taken the opportunity of being alone for a few minutes to have a poke around the Head's desk.

'Little place, about eighty miles north of Paris,' announced Wildman to the gathered boys.

'Really? France?' asked Aiken, excitedly.

'Hastings,' replied Elames-Turner.

'The seaside town?' asked Crabbe.

'Be a bit late for the battle,' said Bond Minor.

The Head was rather surprised at the lack of surprise when he made the announcement.

'You will depart by train on Saturday morning. Mr. Pinder and M. le Becq will accompany and supervise you.'

Mr. Pinder had been 'invited' to lead the group because he was popular and would therefore be unlikely to have to deal with any major misdemeanours because the boys wouldn't let him down. Monsieur had been *told* to go for no other reason than that W-P didn't like him, and anyway, it would be a reminder of the last battle the French had actually *won*.

'On the first afternoon,' the Head continued, 'you will be taken on a conducted tour of the battlefield, and you will visit the Abbey. You will each write a five-page essay on the battle that I will mark as I have a comprehensive knowledge of the subject. Do you know why?'

Kirby whispered, 'Because he was there.'

Mr. Pinder heard the comment, but ignored it, suppressing a smile.

'Because I have read a great deal about it. As I told you, *'he who ignores the past is blind to the future'*.

Crabbe in all Innocence

This means, gentlemen, that you must remember what has gone before so you will be able to recognise the signs should the same thing happen again. In other words, don't make the same mistake twice.'

Crabbe wondered if the Head was warning them that the Norman Conquest was about to happen again.

In a way, it was, although not this time by the Normans, but by the combined forces of the Fourth Year.

The train journey was uneventful, the Abbey uninspiring, and the battlefield boring. But that didn't matter to the boys. They were away from school for a whole weekend with money in their pockets *and they were free*!

Some, those of the *Hopkins* party, went to the cinema to see the latest Alan Ladd western. Others, the athletic types, went on a cross country run, but the majority made a tour of the town's numerous cafés where they happily gorged themselves on fresh cream cakes. M. le Becq, being French, went to church, whilst the whereabouts of Mr. Pinder went unnoticed and unknown. That left Crabbe, Tobes, Gloves and Carters. They decided they would go to the funfair at the end of the pier.

They paid their tuppence entrance charge and made for the penny arcade where they spent a carefree hour shooting tins off a shelf for a prize of chewing gum, throwing wooden balls at coconuts, and winning bars of stale chocolate from a glass encased slot machine that had a small crane in it.

Crabbe, not a good shot and without a strong throwing arm, and having a dislike for stale chocolate, was happy to join in and give the few bars he won to the others to share out.

He was not at all happy though, when a ride on the Big Dipper was proposed. There was a viewing platform halfway round where people could stand to see the cars whizzing by, and Crabbe decided he would prefer to stand there and watch and, seeing as he had his camera with him, he could take a photograph of the others as *they* enjoyed the ride. He couldn't understand how, or why, people would offer themselves up to be hurled along narrow rails at incredible speeds, to be thrown around within the confines of an extremely uncomfortable wooden car on wheels, and turned upside down, screaming, knuckles gripping a totally insufficient 'safety' bar, their stomachs moving around inside them for several minutes until their battered, tormented bodies came to a brutal, jerking stop.

He knew all this because he did it. The others dared him. And he had paid thruppence – *thruppence* – for the pleasure.

After five of the most uncomfortable, unnerving, terrifying minutes he had ever spent, the car shuddered to a halt and Messrs. Glover, Cartwright and Kirby leapt out and rushed to the pier rail. They had discovered that chewing gum, coconut and stale chocolate did not go well with being thrown around at upwards of thirty miles an hour. They were most unwell and having their own problems failed to notice Crabbe's predicament. He couldn't get out of the car. Total paralysis had set in, apart from that nervous twitch that first appeared during *Macbeth*.

That aside, he couldn't move.

And though now stationary, and safe, he was finding it impossible to let go of the safety bar. His eyes stared ahead as he relived every inch of that awful journey.

The conductor, if that was his title, came along the row of cars to collect his next batch of thruppennies from his new passengers. There were none. Those few holidaymakers who had been tempted to take the ride changed their minds when they saw the effects on Crabbe's classmates.

He recognised Crabbe and said, 'Staying on for another trip, sonny? Only tuppence then.'

He mistook the meaning of Crabbe's twitch, assuming it an indication to help himself to a tuppence from Crabbe's blazer breast pocket where he could hear loose change being jangled around by Crabbe's rapidly beating heart.

'You've got a much better constitution than your friends. Never seen people be so ill. Give me your camera, no point in tempting fate twice. I'll give it to one of your friends when they come up for air. Enjoy your trip.'

Chris Hare

Crabbe, although desperate to get out and never go near one of these contraptions ever again, tried to stutter, 'Oh glory, thank you,' as the conductor returned to the engine room. Crabbe managed a petrified scream as the cars moved off again. The conductor, as is the case with all fairground people, decided he must drum up more business, and he did this by calling out at the top of his voice that he was sending the cars around twice for the price of a single trip. News that did not endear him to Crabbe. In the event, he only went round a further one and a third times before getting off.

The first part of the journey was upwards. This bit wasn't too bad, and Crabbe managed it with his eyes open. Then the cars veered sharply to the left and sped downwards towards the sea. He travelled this part with his mouth open.

But it was on the slow journey up towards the viewing platform that he noticed he was being waved at. By Cassandra and Koshkai. *What were they doing here?*

Crabbe was shocked out of his terror and managed a sort of grimace. The girls smiled back and waved again.

Crabbe wondered how he looked in the gathering gloom of early evening dusk. He was sure he'd turned green. He managed to release one hand from the safety bar and gave a limp wave.

Why was he like this? Why did he always manage to look foolish in front of girls? Why couldn't he enjoy the

249

ride like the others? It was unmanly. He WOULD enjoy it!

He hated it. If anything, it was even worse than the first time. It seemed to go even faster, and he knew that even if he survived, he'd have no choice but to embark on a third circuit.

Why he did what he did next, he'd never work out.

It was probably bravado. It was certainly stupid.

On the revolting bit that shoots the cars round at break-neck speed at an almost impossible angle, he made a ridiculous decision. He decided that if Cassandra and Koshkai were still on the viewing platform, he would take both hands off the safety bar and wave.

They were and he did but had he taken even a moment to think about it, he would have realised he was alone on the ride and would be the only one waving. They would know it was him. There was absolutely no need to stand up to show yourself. But he didn't take a moment to think at all. He stood and held his hands up high above his head.

Just an inch or two lower and he would have passed under the stout metal struts that were holding the ride together. But, as it was, he inadvertently gripped a strut firmly with both hands. Consequently, he left the car very quickly. The metal strengthening bar now acted as a spindle round which he was revolving. Slowly at first, but as the empty cars rushed by beneath him, he spun and picked up speed.

250

Chris Hare

His brain was obviously affected because instead of wondering what he should do next, he found himself formulating a question to ask Mr. Davis at the next science lesson: *Could he please explain about centrifugal force?*

Koshkai and Cassandra failed to notice his exit and had left the viewing platform to obey a shrill whistle from below. Crabbe was left to continue his aerobatics, spinning faster and faster, gaining momentum as the impetus of his rotating body spun and spun. He had no choice but to let go.

He let go and became a human cannonball, shooting skywards and off out to sea, somersaulting through the air as though nothing could stop him.

Suddenly, it all slowed down, and Crabbe thought he had paused, to rest on a cloud perhaps. Doubtless, Mr. Davis would say the forces of gravity were getting involved.

He looked down at the world: *his world. And he wanted to go back!* So, he started the return journey.

It was a strange sensation. He knew he was falling to earth but somehow, the earth was coming up to meet him. Whichever, he thought, same result. Flattened on a piece of Hastings or skewered on a spiky bit of the pier from which he had recently been propelled, or, if he missed both, a watery grave just off the South coast.

It was almost the third option that claimed him.

Almost, because whilst he landed *in* the sea, he landed *on* a large net that was floating before being hauled up on to the deck of an ancient fishing boat. He splashed around, kicking and yelling.

He was barely conscious when they dragged him aboard, fighting for space with herring, cod and a thing with tentacles that wriggled furiously in the icy water.

Chris Hare

20: AT SEA

Crabbe, with assorted fish and wooden barrels, was lowered in a series of jerks to a spot two feet above the deck of the fishing boat, where he lay helpless, unable to move. He stared up at the arm of the boat's derrick that held the net on a rusting hook.

Not that he could see the hook, and not only because it *couldn't* be seen against the black sky. He couldn't see it because the lenses of his glasses, which had miraculously survived the journey *in situ* were draped with seaweed.

He couldn't hear anything either, as his ears were filled with seawater. In fact, only one of his senses was still working: his sense of terror. A feeling obviously shared by the thing with tentacles, who sought comfort in its hour of need by wrapping one around Crabbe's neck.

After a couple of minutes, during which time much of the seawater drained from Crabbe and his newfound friends, a lever was released and they all fell to the deck, a jumble of arms, legs, fish, barrels and tentacles.

A beam from a torch lit up the scene.

The thing obviously didn't care for the light and it uncurled its tentacle from around Crabbe and slid along the deck until it was grabbed by a fisherman and thrown over the side.

253

Crabbe in all Innocence

Crabbe got unsteadily to his feet and stood violently shivering. A voice from the open wheelhouse door called out, 'Hello. What have we here? Neptune, is it?'

Activity around the net ceased as five or six fishermen saw Crabbe for the first time. The man who had called out emerged, hooking the door open so that the single bulb in the wheelhouse added a little more light to the proceedings.

'What have we here?' he said again, 'Jonah isn't it? Been regurgitated by the whale, is it?'

Crabbe was still unable to hear. Or see. Or speak, for that matter. But he could move, slightly, and picked off the larger strands of seaweed that were still clinging to his glasses. It left a thick layer of slime on the lenses.

'Come with me and we'll get you dried out, isn't it?'

He stepped over the edge of the net and took Crabbe by the elbow, leading him towards the wheelhouse. He said something to the gaping fishermen who immediately started picking up the floundering fish and throwing them back into the sea.

Had Crabbe been aware of his surroundings he may well have wondered what was going on. It would have crossed his mind that a fishing boat with a large net and several fishermen were actually fishing. The logical conclusion. But illogically, they were busy returning their catch to the deep.

He may have also wondered why the barrels that had accompanied him from the sea, and which were being stacked neatly on the deck, all had names painted on them, *The Greene Man*, *The Rose and Crown* and *The Royal Oak* among them.

Crabbe was not aware of his surroundings.

He was not really aware of anything and allowed himself to be guided to the wheelhouse and pushed down to sit on the top of yet another barrel, *The Coach and Horses*.

'Righto boyo. I'm Captain Prys Owen, master of this little tub. You dropped in at exactly the right moment as I've just made some cocoa, isn't it? Have a mug with a drop or two from *The Railway* and you'll soon feel better.'

Captain Owen took a tin mug from a hook above a barrel that had a small wooden tap fitted to the side. He filled it half full and topped it up with thick dark cocoa he poured from an ancient saucepan.

'There you are. Drink this. *The Railway* will never notice if they're a few measures short. Anyway, they didn't pay for last week's delivery.'

Crabbe, some of his senses slowly returning and able to see a little through his grease-streaked glasses, took the proffered mug in a shaking hand and put it unsteadily to his lips. He swallowed a large gulp unaware it was scalding hot.

When the boiling cocoa infused with half a mug full of liquid from The Railway's barrel hit Crabbe's stomach, he uttered the first real sound he had made since leaving the Big Dipper. Up until that moment his speech had consisted only of chattering. Not talk, but teeth.

'Wait here boyo. I'll get some togs from below. Then we'll have a little talk, isn't it?'

The captain took Crabbe's tin mug and filled it with more cocoa and even more liquid from The Railway's barrel. 'Back in a mo, don't go away.' When Crabbe took another gulp, more carefully this time, his ears suddenly *popped,* and he could hear again.

The crew on deck, having thrown every last fish back over the side, gathered around the wheelhouse and stared at Crabbe through the grimy windows. They pointed at him and spoke to each other, but not in a language Crabbe had heard before. Crabbe tried a pathetic smile, but he still wasn't in control of his mouth or teeth. The smile didn't work, so he gave a limp wave.

One or two of the mystified fishermen waved back. Captain Owen returned and the crew went back to their duties.

'Norwegian, they are. From Norway, isn't it? I'm Welsh,' he said unnecessarily. 'Dry yourself with these and put the clean togs on. Should fit,' he continued, passing Crabbe a rough blanket and towel, and putting a pile of clothes and sea boots on the chart table. 'Now then, young man. I've seen it all before. Not worth it. Just not worth it. Throwing yourself into the sea for the sake of a woman. You young chaps are always doing it. Bit of a tradition. That was it, wasn't it, isn't it?'

256

Crabbe tried to tell him he was wrong, that it had been an accident, but all that came out was frozen babble.

In any case, it wouldn't have made any difference and while he stripped and dried himself, he was treated to a discourse on the evils of womanhood. Every wicked woman from Delilah to the mistresses of Edward VII were known to the captain, as were all the dreadful things they'd done. During the sermon, Crabbe gradually recovered his power of speech but found it difficult to pronounce his consonants, particularly Ps, Bs and Ds.

As a result, he was unable to explain that he had been thrown from the Big Dipper on the pier. The captain, misunderstanding Crabbe, assumed he was Polish.

'From Moscow, are you?'

As is the way with Welshman when speaking to a foreigner who didn't understand, he gesticulated wildly and raised his voice, 'WHERE ARE YOU FROM?'

Crabbe pointed to the sky.

'FROM MARS?'

'N-n-n-n...'

'NIGERIA?'

'N-n-n-n...'

'No. You couldn't be. Too pale. FROM WHERE THEN?'

'N-n-n-n...'

'Never mind. I'LL PUT YOU ASHORE AS SOON AS I CAN. DON'T WANT TO BE CAUGHT IN

THESE WATERS IN DAYLIGHT.' He thought for a moment and then, by way of explanation added, 'TIDE'S SHIFTING.'

Crabbe nodded, having given up the attempt to communicate verbally. The captain refilled his mug with cocoa and another generous measure courtesy of *The Railway* and went below again. He returned a few moments later with a rucksack.

'PUT YOUR WET GEAR IN THE RUCKSACK. DON'T WANT ANY OF MY STUFF BACK. GIVE IT TO THE POOR WHEN YOU GET HOME TO CALCUTTA.'

The clothes probably did fit someone, but that someone wasn't Crabbe. The long johns and vest were huge, the legs covering his feet and the arms flapping over his hands. He looked like a semaphore station at ease.

The corduroy trousers had clearly belonged to a midget and the sweater, one of those thick white ones with a roll neck, was big enough to fit Mrs. Wilkes-Passmore. The boots were an average fit, one being a size 10 and the other size 8. Both Crabbe's feet were size 9. But they were the same length, so they covered his legs where the trousers finished at half-mast.

Completing his rig was the cap and Crabbe, by now, light-headed and feeling rather happy, (courtesy of *The Railway*), used the glass of the wheelhouse to set it at rather a rakish angle. He raised the mug and toasted himself. He fancied he looked rather like Errol Flynn in one of his pirate films. The rest of him looked like someone from a circus.

The captain turned to the wooden wheel and with his back to Crabbe, pulled some levers, pressed some buttons and uttered a few oaths.

From deep beneath them the ancient engine groaned and spluttered into life, Captain Owen moved the wheel and the boat slowly chugged towards the pier.

'DON'T WANT TO SOUND UNWELCOMING, BUT I'VE GOT TO BE IN CALAIS BEFORE DAWN TO REFILL...THAT IS, TO GET SOME PETROL. THAT'S WHAT THE BARRELS ARE FOR. IN CASE YOU'RE WONDERING. NOTHING TO DO WITH SMUGGLING SPIRITS, ISN'T IT. HAVE TO PUT YOU ASHORE AT THE END OF THE PIER. CLOSEST WE CAN GET TO LAND.'

Ten minutes later, a bedraggled but strangely happy Crabbe was helped over the side and onto a small landing stage. He turned and endeavoured to stutter his thanks.

'YOU'RE VERY WELCOME, I'M SURE. UP THE LADDER WITH YOU, ISN'T IT, AND MIND HOW YOU GO, OFFENDI,' screamed the captain as Crabbe looked up at the Big Dipper, now lit up against the darkness of the February sky.

He stopped climbing halfway and turned to his rescuers, who were all looking up at him. He waved his thanks, and thinking that might not be enough, blew them a kiss.

Crabbe in all Innocence

As the boat turned towards the open sea, belching smoke from its ancient funnel, the captain called out, 'MARK MY WORDS, COMRADE. DON'T END IT ALL BECAUSE OF ONE WICKED GIRL. THERE ARE PLENTY MORE FISH IN THE SEA.'

An unfortunate simile thought Crabbe.

The moon was out now, and with the light from the pier attractions Crabbe could see well enough to not fall in the sea again, but it wasn't sufficiently bright to show him exactly where he was.

He got off the top of the ladder without mishap and walked into a black wooden wall. What should he do now? What would the Head do?

He would take stock. He would consider what had gone right and what had gone wrong, then he would draw his conclusions and set himself a target.

Crabbe decided to follow suit.

He was safe. His life had been given back to him and he was light-headed, but safe. He knew where he was, roughly, at the end of the pier in Hastings. He knew what he wanted. He wanted to get off the pier, go to the hostel where they were staying, dry his clothes and have something to eat, followed by sleep.

Conclusion and First Target: get off the pier.

He walked into the wall again and belched in a most un-Chantrylike fashion.

'Beg pardon.'

Then he had a fairly sober thought: walls are there to keep people out, but they also have doors to let people in!

Find door.

Crabbe groped his way along the wall until he found the end. He couldn't see beyond it, but he could *hear* waves underneath.

Wrong way.

He inched back the way he had come, past the point where he'd started, and he found a door. A door with a handle!

A more heroic type would have thrown it open and marched through to freedom.

Crabbe knocked. Nothing.

Then he heard the unmistakeable sounds of a car riding over rails and he immediately knew where he was – at the base of the Big Dipper.

Throwing caution to wind, he tried the handle, the door was unlocked. He was about to be free! Tentatively, he moved forward and got stuck.

Some giant unseen claw had arrived from nowhere and taken hold of his shoulders in a vice-like grip. The rucksack on his back had wedged between the two uprights of the door frame. He realised what had happened and slipped his arms through the straps and let the rucksack fall to the decking. He'd find out exactly where he was and come back for it.

The door slammed behind him. It was dark inside. Total blackness.

Crabbe in all Innocence

He could hear the rumble of the Big Dipper and feel the wooden floor vibrating under his feet, but he could see nothing.

He must be careful. At any second one of those cars could come shooting round and kill him. *Where exactly was he?* He didn't remember any completely blacked out areas on his two-and-a-bit rides on the Big Dipper.

Unless, when he came through this part, he had his eyes closed. Yes, of course, that must be it!

He carefully put a foot forward, feeling for the rails. *Safe.* He stretched out his arms, touching only blackness and inched forward slowly.

He bumped into something, which moved away.

He lowered his hands, and whatever had moved away, moved back and hit him and he gave a little jump in fright, letting out a barely concealed squeal.

It moved away again. He raised his hands in case it came back.

It came back only this time he was ready and expecting it, and as it touched his hands, he could feel it had an outer covering of material encasing something solid. He gripped it to stop it moving and ran a free hand up the material. He felt a rope. The light dawned. That is, the light of realisation, he could still *see* absolutely nothing. It was a sack acting as a counterweight – part of the Big Dipper's workings. Of course, it was! Wasn't it?

The rumbling of the cars got louder and louder, then deafening, and all the lights went on as a car crashed into some double doors and shot through. People were in the car screaming.

But none as loudly as Crabbe because, during that short five seconds before the lights went out again, he glanced up at the sack. It was a body, dead and hanging by a rope now swinging gently. He dropped to the floor in shock. Apart from a diminishing rumbling sound, all around him was deathly silent.

Crabbe lay still, his mind distanced from this terrible scene by surprise and the drink from The Railway's barrel.

It might have been the realisation that there was something wrong with what he had witnessed or the lights coming back on again as another car of screaming people crashed through the doors and sped screeching round the track. Whatever it was, it was enough for him to open his eyes and glimpse a sign hanging around the dead man's neck. It read 'Dr. Crippen'.

It went dark again. The car went. The noise of it diminished too. It was like being on a deserted, haunted platform on the London Underground.

He rolled from his back onto his hands and knees and crawled back, he thought, to the door by which he had entered but by this time, he was disorientated and shaking but not from the cold, from the sheer cold terror.

263

Crabbe in all Innocence

Dr. Crippen was hanged years ago. What was he doing here?

The truth of his situation didn't dawn on Crabbe until after he'd bumped into Mary, Queen of Scots who was kneeling in prayer by the block before having her head chopped off.

It was actually her bottom he bumped into (head-first, naturally) while crawling away from the door he thought he was crawling towards. Not knowing what had got in his way this time, he paused and pawed the area in front of him without realising he was pawing at the royal buttocks. These felt like a large sack of potatoes. Each hand shaking, they crept up each side of her waist to under her arms and around the curve to the front where they each took firm hold of a royal bosom.

This was the moment the lights came back on. The double doors crashed open for another car, the mechanical queen lowered her head to the block and the executioner struck. Then Crabbe realised, at last, that he was in the Tunnel of the Black Museum ride and not the Big Dipper.

It was also then that he recognised the two screaming faces in the car, the one on the far side being large and red, the face nearest more a pale yellow with long black hair streaming behind. This was the stuff of nightmares for Crabbe but seeing Koshkai could have turned it into a dream.

But this was no dream because the couple in the next car were Mr. Pinder and Sister Rosemary. Both stared open mouthed as they saw Mary, Queen of Scots' body kneeling, her decapitated head lying bloodied in the basket, and the head of Lancelot Arthur Crabbe sported instead on her neck.

Crabbe's eyes followed the disappearing car that contained Koshkai – *his* Koshkai. Memories of worms and baked beans and jumping through closed French windows, together with the awful experiences of eating those dreadful meals came flooding back and were just as instantly banished.

In the darkness, he too stared open mouthed, thoroughly embarrassed that, yet again, the loveliest girl he had ever met had found him in a compromising situation.

Another car came, more people screamed and vanished out of sight through the double doors and on into the next room where they were torturing people and the lights went out.

But Crabbe didn't really notice it. He hadn't actually *seen* his Housemaster, or his greatest enemy sitting in the same car. And he didn't see the late queen's head when it sprung back to await a further decapitation for the entertainment of the next carload of joyriders.

It hit him squarely on the forehead, and he lay dazed and unaware that just above him was the bloodied edge of the executioner's axe.

Mr. Pinder and Sister Rosemary *thought* they had been seen by a Chantry boy, and that was enough –

more than enough, in Mr. Pinder's case, to send him frantic with worry.

In fact, it was all perfectly innocent. Cassandra had been anxious to show Koshkai this particular piece of English culture, and Sister Rosemary had given her permission, provided she came along as chaperone since she'd seen three undesirables being ill near the Big Dipper.

But she was rather afraid of going on the Tunnel of the Black Museum ride and seeing Mr. Pinder strolling and taking the air on the pier, had asked him to accompany them. And being the gentleman he was, he agreed.

All quite innocent, but he thought they had been seen by Crabbe, who would jump to the wrong conclusions, as Crabbe always did.

Meanwhile, Crabbe was coming to his senses. It was pitch black again, but he took a moment and gathered his thoughts. His first Conclusion and Target had been to get off the pier. Getting off the pier remained his Target, but his first Conclusion was replaced by the Second, to get out of this ghastly wax museum with its dreadful waxworks, terrifying noises and awful lights suddenly coming on and going off again without warning.

Leaving Queen Mary to her fate, he felt his way to the rails on hands and knees. Hopkins said Red Indians put their ears to rails to listen for the trains carrying General Custer and his troops who were coming to cull them. If he didn't want to emulate Mary, by having his head cut off he knew he had to hurry. The conductor of this ride might copy the Big Dipper man by offering a reduction if customers went round twice. He couldn't risk being seen by Koshkai in the act of assaulting Mary, Queen of Scots.

But she saw him in the next room anyway, where there was a tableau of the French Revolution. Marie Antoinette was there, strapped down on the guillotine and Crabbe was trying to climb over her. He hoped he would be taken for one of the executioners. A vain hope because they were wearing wigs and tricorn hats. He was wearing a huge fisherman's roll neck sweater, and glasses.

He was spotted by more people being one of Jack the Ripper's victims. Word got round about 'the ghost' – and a little later, just before he'd completed the circuit and arrived back at Mary, Queen of Scots, he was seen dying of the plague, eyes wide open and tongue lolling out, naturally.

21: CONSEQUENCES

Mr. Pinder was not himself.

For several evenings after their return from Hastings, he had absented himself from staff suppers and retired early. He was waiting for the sword of Damocles to fall. His colleagues could hardly fail to notice, but none felt they could approach him and raise the matter.

And so, being English, or in the case of Mr. Davis, Welsh (or M. le Becq, French, although being French he didn't count), they pretended there weren't any problems and ignored him, thus adopting the time-honoured British tradition that if you pretended there was nothing wrong, there *was* nothing wrong and it would all go away and everyone could carry on being happily British (except M. le Becq).

The reality was that it *did matter* to Mr. Pinder: a boy at his school, a boy *from his own House* had surely seen him in the company of a Catholic nun.

Nothing had been said, so far, at least not to him.

In truth, there really was nothing much to say. He had just rescued a damsel in distress, a fine figure of speech – there was nothing about Sister Rosemary that could possibly thought of as 'damselish'.

But, for all he knew, they all knew. Everyone went quiet suddenly when he walked into the staff room and he was sure he could hear them whispering and mocking him behind his back as he left.

At least it hadn't reached the Head's ears yet, which gave him some time to try and think of a solution to his dilemma. But he was forced to admit, he couldn't see a way out.

It was only a matter of time before W-P heard and he would be summoned to the Head's office, told his behaviour was utterly reprehensible. Told that he had let the school down, let the boys down and worst of all, let down himself and it would be better for everyone if he immediately resigned.

And then, as soon as he had walked through the school gates for the last time, civil war would break out. His erstwhile colleagues would begin vying with each other to see which of them would take over as Housemaster of Keyes, legitimately receiving another fifteen shillings a week, and a quarter share (tax free) of the Housemasters' unofficial earnings from their garden produce endeavour.

It would be dog eat dog until whichever of them succeeded in landing a sufficient number of low punches, of spreading the most groundless rumours about his colleagues, and of doing the best job of sucking up to the Head. He, the victor of this squalid mess, would then be appointed.

It was all very worrying, all very depressing for Mr. Pinder.

He had worked hard for his House and was justifiably proud of their achievements. He had done his best to transform his boys from being young, confused adolescents into smart, well-behaved gentlemen. And he had done this, not by threat, but by example.

Even after the shock of seeing, and being seen by Crabbe on the pier, he had characteristically behaved like a gentleman and had seen Sister Rosemary and her two charges safely on the train at Hastings Central. It was unfortunate that the three of them were only away on a day trip from St. Margaret's – some sort of reward or celebration at the two girls being promoted to prefect at the start of the next school year.

It was after he had seen them off that his behaviour became most uncharacteristic. He rarely drank – a sherry at Christmas to be sure, but that was his limit, hardly ever touching anything stronger than lemonade during the rest of the year, although during the preparations and performance of *Macbeth* he had been sorely tempted.

But now?

He was in a town where he was unknown, except by pure bad luck of having been chanced upon by Sister Rosemary, but she was long gone. The boys were out enjoying themselves, and M. le Becq was probably confessing his sins somewhere. Wherever he was, M. le Becq would never step inside an English public house. So why not? Mr. Pinder felt in need of a strong drink.

He forgot he had promised to be back at the hostel in the early evening to take charge and allow le Becq to go to church again by the time he found himself in the snug of the *Horse and Nosebag*.

He had half a bitter, then a pint and then another. Then a whiskey, neat.

He didn't remember going back to the hostel, didn't notice Monsieur was still at church leaving the boys unsupervised, didn't check that they were all asleep – they were, apart from Glover, Cartwright and Kirby who seemed anxious to not stray far from the bathroom and he didn't take note that Crabbe, who during Mr. Pinder's sojourn in the snug had become his nemesis, was nowhere in the building.

He spent the night sleeping the troubled sleep of the guilty. But in the morning, he felt much better, bright and carefree.

Perhaps, he thought, he had been mistaken in avoiding alcohol so acidulously. It was as if the guilt had been lifted off his shoulders. He smilingly glanced around the dining room where his party were taking breakfast. Monsieur was there, shriven and trying his French best to look righteous. Cartwright, Glover and Kirby, admittedly looking rather pale but nevertheless were there, so were all the others, and so was Crabbe. He looked very tired. Had he been up all night planning who to tell the awful truth to first?

I mustn't appear too friendly, Mr. Pinder thought. *I must be the picture of innocence. This boy could well be the ruin of me.*

A little too gruffly, he said, 'Morning Crabbe. You look as if you've been asleep in your school uniform. In

271

fact, you look as if you didn't get to bed until four this morning.'

Not really surprising, since Crabbe didn't get to bed until four that morning.

Mr. Pinder thought he might be sounding *too* unfriendly. He needed Crabbe on his side, though what he would do if he won him over, he didn't know. With a concerned note in his voice he said, 'Did you sleep at all, Crabbe?'

'Thank you, sir, like a top.'

In fact, having tottered around for what had seemed like days, visiting (and taking part in) scenes of every type of execution known to man, when he eventually got back to the Mary, Queen of Scots tableau, he was so relieved at knowing where he was it felt like calling in on an old friend.

He had thought of a *modus operandi* whilst in the Burning at the Stake Room, where, as yet another car shot through, he could be seen piling faggots under Joan of Arc, he realised that it was better to not look at the victim directly but instead in the direction the victim's latest carload of visitors was travelling. The lights stayed on long enough for him to plan and make his next move.

In the brief time thus afforded, he took note of the positions of the assistant faggot-pilers and wax spectators and mentally plotted a way round them towards the double doors.

It worked almost perfectly. In the darkness, he moved on.

In the American Execution Chamber, he slightly misjudged where he was and when the lights came on to admit the latest car, he found himself in no man's land and had to leap onto a wax model of the poor chap about to be electrocuted. In those brief few seconds of light, Crabbe looked like he was a ventriloquist's dummy.

As the mechanical arm of the executioner pulled the switch, sparks flew from the murderer's head a few inches from Crabbe's own, which gave him quite a start. But the effect so impressed him he forgot about his Second Conclusion for a few minutes and hid behind a wax warder for three cars worth to watch it again.

In his hiding place, as the fourth car came by, he looked at his watch – gone ten! The police would have been alerted and were probably out now, searching for his body. As soon as the car had gone and the lights went out, he groped his way to the next horror.

It was Vlad the Impaler, who was happily shoving wooden stakes into his victim's private parts.

Crabbe decided against taking an active role in this and hid behind a canvas backdrop of Castle Dracula. He plotted his next move as he peeped out at the cars going by.

Next were the Spanish Inquisition, the Black Hole of Calcutta, the Massacre of the Innocents and then to

Crabbe in all Innocence

Nero's Coliseum, where they were feeding Christians to the lions. Crabbe actually liked this one. He had always been very fond of animals and took time to pet a wax lion before moving on.

Eventually, by this circuitous route of blood, gore and untold suffering, he arrived back to witness the latest beheading of Mary, Queen of Scots.

Was this the end of the Second Conclusion?

Well, not really since he was back where he'd started. All that had happened was that time had moved on. He hadn't seen Koshkai and Cassandra again and he'd had a free tour of the most awful exhibition imaginable.

Other than that, he was still lost, still in the Tunnel of the Black Museum, and still on the inside when he should have been outside looking for his school clothes.

Oh glory!

Casting his mind back through what he had witnessed of centuries of man's inhumanity to man, he remembered which wall contained the door by which he had first entered. Lying prostrate, he waited for the next car to come and light his path to freedom.

Thus, he found the door, and outside on the decking, the rucksack full of his wet clothes where he'd left it.

The moon was full and bright by now, so he was able to see another door a few feet from him. He opened it cautiously and found himself underneath the Big Wheel.

He had never been on a Big Wheel and had no intention of going on this one. But the road to Hell is

274

paved with good intentions, (as already noted), and the good intention Crabbe had now, perhaps bizarrely, was to get his school clothes dry.

The cars were empty, the ride lit up, but not moving.

He hung his soaking clothes, garment by garment, on a car to dry. There was no one around, but he walked nonchalantly to the now closed coconut shy to make sure.

When he returned, the wheel was moving, and his clothes had gone. He looked up to heaven, seeking new guidance and saw his underpants rising slowly above him, followed in succession by his vest, trousers, shirt, tie, socks and shoes. He wasn't surprised. There was little else that could go against him that day.

Although what goes up, *must* come down.

He settled down to watch his pants flying proud for the whole of Hastings to see, or, at least, any member of the Hastings community still awake at this time of night. He wondered why they kept the vast wheel turning when there were no customers around wanting to take a ride.

Then he wished he hadn't been so quick to tempt providence. He had no sooner finished thinking it when the wheel stopped, and all the lights went out.

Oh glory! What now?

Cartwright's godmother had sent her godson a book of Bulldog Drummond stories for his birthday, and Crabbe had been one of many who'd borrowed it. All the boys in his year had spent a whole term being

Crabbe in all Innocence

Bulldog Drummond, mainly on the wall bars in the gym, until Cartwright's godmother sent him a copy of *A Study in Scarlet* for Easter, a book which introduced the Year to the adventures of Sherlock Holmes, and from that moment, Bulldog was forgotten and the boys spent their pocket money on magnifying glasses, and could be seen all over the school grounds examining things and looking for clues and saying 'Elementary, my dear Watson'.

Crabbe remembered his Bulldog days and accepted that he had no choice. He couldn't stay there until morning and wait for the pier to re-open and the Big Wheel to start up again so he could retrieve his washing.

He had managed to get all his togs hung out on the front of a single car, which was now rocking gently in the night breeze some thirty feet or so above him.

He climbed the nearest car with the intention of pulling himself up from there to the next one and so on to the fifth where his clothes were basking in the moonlight. As he reached up, convinced that with the sort of luck he'd 'enjoyed' so far that day, he would be spotted by a passing policeman and thrown in jail. Thankfully, no passing policeman passed his way, so he wasn't.

He was thrown from the car though, as he climbed onto the seat upsetting its balance causing it to rock back and forth.

He only pitched about six feet before hitting the ground and was quite unhurt. With Crabbe's record of *accidents*, six feet was a drop in the ocean.

He decided to accomplish his rescue mission without climbing from car to car but by traversing the outside of the wheel using all the struts and bars as hand and footholds. It was what Bulldog Drummond would have done, he told himself.

It took an age, but with extreme caution, he succeeded in climbing to the part of the wheel where the car bearing his clothes was parked.

With even greater care, he manoeuvred himself through the metal structure and onto the seat, where it tipped up.

He screamed but was able to grab the safety bar and hung on whilst his school uniform took off into the night.

He managed to climb down in the end and spent the next hour or so walking around the now deserted funfair retrieving articles of his clothing. He got it all and crept back to the familiarity of Mary, Queen of Scots' room and changed there.

He folded the borrowed seaman's rig neatly, as he had been brought up to do, and left them outside Mary, Queen of Scots' door, then he found his way off the pier, leaving tuppence on the turnstile in case there should be an exit charge and was back at the hostel by four in morning.

Crabbe in all Innocence

He climbed through an open ground floor window, found his bed and dropped into it completely exhausted but relieved to find his camera under the pillow.

On the train journey back, Mr. Pinder slept the sleep of the innocent, although occasionally troubled by thoughts of nuns. He was jerked awake when the train ran over a particularly tiresome set of points.

Opposite, dozing, was none other than Crabbe, who was taking every opportunity to catch up on his sleep. He stopped dozing when Mr. Pinder called out, 'Don't you dare say a word.'

Crabbe, who at that moment was dreaming of yellow tennis rackets, was instantly awake. 'I won't, sir. Not a word, sir,' he said convincingly but without understanding why he had said it and seeing that Mr. Pinder had dropped off to sleep again, followed suit.

Back at school that evening, Mr. Pinder felt himself in need of another drink. There was none in his room. In fact, as far as he knew, the only alcoholic drink in the whole of Chantry was a decanter of dry sherry on the Head's sideboard, kept for visiting dignitaries and the better class of parent.

There was a public house in the village. Two, if you counted the one by St. Margaret's, but he couldn't risk being seen taking a drink in a local public house. He was in enough trouble as it was. But he *could* buy some sherry there – for the Head, should anyone ask.

278

With that piece of deception, he started his descent on the slippery slope. *If only Crabbe hadn't seen him!*

But Mr. Pinder had seen Crabbe, looking like the sole survivor of the Marie Celeste, and had assumed, not unreasonably, that he had been seen too.

Seen by Crabbe! It would be all over the school. He must do something to stop Crabbe opening his mouth. But what? Murder him? Bribe him? A bribe would be the best way. What on earth could he use to bribe Crabbe into not revealing his awful secret?

He must act. He must have another drink. It helped.

Mr. Pinder missed Assembly. An unheard-of occurrence. He later claimed he had suffered a headache, which he had. The mother of all headaches. His head thumped, he couldn't see too well, and his mouth was as dry as old bone.

It was a dull morning, cloudy with no sign of the sun so it was not at all clear why Mr. Pinder entered the 4B classroom wearing sunglasses. He made several attempts at taking the single step up to the master's desk, and once there, had difficulty climbing into the swivel chair. But he made it eventually, and slumped down, the chair revolving as he did. He went round several times before he told everyone to keep still which to the boys was strange as they were standing to attention at their desks.

He stopped turning with his back to them. 'Sit,' he ordered the blackboard. The boys sat.

279

'Take out your Tennysons and read aloud from the *Idylls of the King,* starting with *The Coming of Arthur.* One verse each, starting with you, Richardson.'

Mr. Pinder pointed at the bottom left corner of the blackboard. There was only one Richardson, and he sat on the extreme right of the front row.

'Begin, Richardson.'

Richardson stood and opened his book, 'Leodogran, the King of Cam…'

'Quieter.'

'Beg pardon, sir?'

'There's no need to *yell*, Richardson.'

'No, sir. Sorry, sir. I'll start again. Leodogran, the K…'

'Too loud. Much too loud.'

'Yes, sir. Leodo…'

'You are deafening me, Richardson,' he said to the corner of the board.

'Sorry, sir. 'Leod…'

'Still far too much noise, Atkinson.' There wasn't an Atkinson in 4B. 'Read it in silence. Speak your verse silently, then the next boy will take up the poem, also in silence. And *keep still!*'

It was clear Mr. Pinder was unwell.

There was some confusion in the reading since it wasn't apparent when a boy had finished speaking the verse to himself but by common silent consent, they read their pieces sitting down so they didn't disobey the instruction to 'keep still' and cause Mr. Pinder further

280

distress and it was clear, even to insensitive teenagers that he *was* distressed. Something was obviously wrong, and they were concerned. Had it been M. le Becq or Mr. Shapiro, who was also hated by everybody, they would have given him a very bad time. Using all the old schoolboy tricks, they would pretend to be deaf, deliberately misunderstand instructions, have coughing fits and constantly ask to be excused for a few moments.

These were all tried and tested ways of provoking a master to red-faced fury.

But they would never dream of giving Mr. Pinder 'the treatment'. He was the most popular master in the whole school. Strict, certainly, but always fair. He never sent anyone to the Head for punishment and never gave out pointless lines.

Many of the masters, most of them in fact, in addition to their usual accoutrements of cap and gown, carried canes. They were permitted to lightly chastise the boys, although the term 'lightly' was often given a very liberal interpretation.

It worked. Masters were feared and generally, obeyed.

It was often said by people of that generation that 'it never did *us* any harm', but no one ever stopped to consider if it did them any *good*. Being beaten for forgetting your hymn book ensured one didn't forget one's hymn book a second time, so from that point of view harsh discipline worked. But it was not the only way. Mr. Pinder proved that.

He made use of detention, never the cane, as punishment. So did the other three Housemasters. Detentions were a great deterrent to crime, particularly when ordered to be worked at a time normally reserved for leisure.

With ordinary masters, as opposed to Housemasters, a detention consisted of having to write a three-page essay in Latin or working out a few pages of fractions or logarithms. Mr. Pinder and the other Housemasters though, when they took detention, gave the boys practical tasks that were of more benefit to their health than to their brains, digging over the Housemasters' vegetable gardens or weeding or harvesting the crops in Autumn.

And they produced some wonderful crops too. Large tomatoes, tons of potatoes, leeks, turnips, peppers, radishes, runner and broad beans, peas and so on. All in perfect condition and, by coincidence, on a par with those sold at the village grocery store opposite the school.

They felt that at the same time as they were being punished, they were also contributing to the well-being and comfort of the Housemasters, which, Mr. Pinder said, they were. More than they would ever know, he hoped. Why he hoped that was never disclosed.

4B carried on with *Idylls* and at the end of the verse the boy reading it gave the next fellow a nudge so he might know when to take up the poem.

Crabbe was last and delivered his verse from 'Merlin and Vivien' with silent gusto towards Mr. Pinder's back. When he'd finished, after a final sweeping gesture with his free hand, he looked up to the rostrum expecting to be told what to do next.

All he heard was a deep, resonating snore.

The boys looked around at each other, not knowing what they should do now. Hopkins Major, in his capacity of monitor, whispered that they should carry on with something else. He suggested, this time in his capacity as Macbeth, going through the play again.

This was not acceptable to those boys with non-speaking parts, and after a great deal more heated but barely audible whispering, they decided to do *The Charge of the Light Brigade* in the same silent manner as before. But as it was such a short poem, and wouldn't go round the whole class, they further elected to keep repeating it until they had all had a go.

It was one of Crabbe's favourite poems, full of stirring words and glory, and he thought it would add to the soundless reading if he climbed on his chair and gave a lot of dramatic gesticulations. He whispered his plan, which was accepted as an excellent idea.

They were so lost in what was probably the first ever silent-animated rendition of Tennyson's famous epic poem that they failed to react to the Headmaster's knock or entrance.

He was the most powerful person on earth, after God and Mrs. Wilkes-Passmore. Possibly even more powerful than God. His presence always commanded instant silent, rigid respect and sheer terror.

Except for today.

Even Glover, who was facing the door whilst miming out the bit about 'While horse and hero fell', failed to notice it open and admit the dread being.

'What is happening here?'

Instant silence.

Spiked cannons froze. Russian Cossacks ceased writhing in their death-throws. Boys stopped coming back from the mouth of Hell, and Glover even managed to stop in mid-tumble whilst being a hero shot from his trusty desk.

Nobody answered.

'Where is Mr. Pinder? He was unwell earlier. I have come to see if he is feeling better.'

As one, the boys looked at the chair on the rostrum.

The empty chair.

The boys never lied. It simply wasn't done. A chap's foremost duty was to ensure that one's reputation for being an honest chap was never impugned.

Equally important, a chap never snitched on a chap. One never ever 'told', no matter how often a chap said, 'Do that again and I'm telling'.

And now, these golden rules, these *tenets* of the schoolboy code of honour presented Crabbe with a major problem. For he, from his viewpoint on top of his chair, could see Mr. Pinder, or at least a significant part of him. And clearly, no one else, including the Head below him, could.

Mr. Pinder had slipped from the swivel chair and was lying on the floor in the space between the rostrum and the blackboard.

'If you please, sir,' Crabbe offered in a squeaking voice, 'Mr. Pinder was still feeling unwell, and is lying down for a few moments.' That at least, was true. He hadn't snitched on him and he hadn't lied, as such, even if he had misled the Head by not informing him that Mr. Pinder was actually lying down just a few feet from him. He prayed his subterfuge would not be discovered by another snore.

'I see,' said the Head. 'He is a fine example to us all. Most courageous despite being unwell. I trust you young gentlemen will heed him. Which of you was left in charge?'

Crabbe looked down at everyone else. Everyone else looked up at Crabbe. He could see he was outvoted.

'If you please, sir. I was.'

The Head strode towards him and held the horse's head handle of his stick in the region of Crabbe's groin.

'And your name is?' he asked, jabbing with his stick.

'Crabbe, sir.'

Crabbe in all Innocence

'Oh, yes. Crabbe – the Royal Messenger from *Macbeth*.'

'Yes, sir. Lancelot Crabbe, sir.'

'And what were you doing when I entered?'

'Sir, we were performing the actions to a silent reading of Tennyson's *The Charge of Light Brigade*, sir.'

'Is that what Mr. Pinder instructed you to do?'

'Well, no sir. He told us to do the *Idylls of the King.*

'Then why, Crabbe, were you not doing it?'

'With respect, sir, we *did* do it – all of it. Right up to 'Guinevere'. And because Mr. Pinder was unaware we had finished, owing to his indisposition, we decided to carry on with something else.'

Crabbe, still atop his chair, and staring unflinchingly down at the Head's bald pate as he was being questioned, was unaware that other more pleading eyes were also upon him. Not his classmates, who were all looking to the front, comfortable in the knowledge it was happening to Crabbe and not to them.

It's a strange phenomenon, nothing you can put your finger on, this being *aware* you're being watched. Crabbe allowed himself to unobtrusively scan the area in front whilst being interrogated, and he found the eyes that were the cause of that strange feeling. Well, not *eyes* exactly, more one complete eye, next to a half closed one.

Mr. Pinder had managed to raise his head above the level of the rostrum and was staring at Crabbe in a worried looking, pleading sort of way. Crabbe could *hear* the very thoughts emanating from Mr. Pinder's mind: *Tell the Head I'm here Crabbe, and I will kill you!*

One didn't snitch on a chap, as has been said. But a master? Presumably, the same rules applied, and so he raised his head slightly so Mr. Pinder was no longer in his line of sight.

The Head carried on relentlessly, 'And whose idea was it to go from *Idylls* to *Charge*?

The truth was it was no one's idea in particular. It was all of them. The Head had been known to lay into a whole class with a stick before now, but Crabbe couldn't let that happen. He couldn't snitch on the *whole* class.

'If you please, sir. It was mine,' he lied.

'It does please me. It does indeed.'

Crabbe's eyes widened in amazement and he risked a quick glance at his tormentor. He certainly *sounded* pleased, but still looked as grim as ever.

'Well done, Crabbe. You show leadership. Mr. Pinder would be justifiably pleased. You are in his House, are you not?'

It was obvious he was in Keyes because of the green braid around the school badge on his blazer.

'Yes, sir. I am a member of Mr. Pinder's House.'

'A House point for Keyes then. Well done.'

Crabbe was stammering his thanks when the bell went for break, 'Right, cut along,' said the Head.

287

Crabbe in all Innocence

Crabbe climbed down and they all filed out to the playground. He made sure he accompanied the Headmaster expressing his thanks ensuring he was on the opposite side of him to Mr. Pinder. It would never do for his Housemaster to be seen now, not after Crabbe's efforts to save him.

Mr. Pinder had learned his lesson.

He realised he had been on the brink of professional ruin and had been saved from falling into the abyss by a most unlikely knight in shining armour. He vowed he would never touch another drop, to put the incident of the Tunnel of the Black Museum behind him, and to reward Crabbe in some way.

But he had to find out how much of the story had leaked out, exactly what Crabbe had said.

Crabbe, of course, had said exactly nothing because Crabbe had seen nothing and therefore had nothing in fact, to say. He did everything he could to stop himself thinking about the pier. It had all been very embarrassing.

And so, when Mr. Pinder sought him out for a quiet word after prep that evening, neither of them knew what the other was talking about.

'Crabbe, I must first thank you for what you did in class this morning.'

'Not at all, sir. I could see you were unwell. Are you feeling better now, sir?'

'Thank you, yes. I believe you were the only one who could see me. And you didn't tell the Head that I had er…fainted in class?'

'Oh no, sir. Certainly not. I'd never snitch on a chap. Not even you.'

'You haven't told any of the other boys, have you? No? Are you sure?'

'Certainly not, sir. Not a word.'

'I am grateful for that, Crabbe. It would never do for it to be known that a master had been seen in that state, even though, as I'm sure you are aware, it was due to a combination of stress and overwork. But it places me in your debt, Crabbe, and that is an equally invidious position for a master to be in with a pupil. You understand?'

'No, sir.'

'Very well. We'll come back to that. Let us talk for a moment about the incident on the pier at Hastings.'

Mr. Pinder knew! How? Crabbe hadn't told a soul!

'Yes, sir. Very embarrassing, sir. I really wouldn't like the details of that episode to get out.'

'Neither would I, Crabbe. Neither would I. The consequences of rumours being spread around the school about what was witnessed on the pier are too just too dreadful imagine.'

How much did Mr. Pinder know? Did he know about Crabbe's assault on Mary, Queen of Scots? About Crabbe's underpants going round on the Big Wheel?

Crabbe blushed deeply.

'I feel the same, Crabbe. It could be taken as a shameful episode, and one that is best put behind us. Do you agree?'

'I do, sir. Absolutely. I hope it's never mentioned again.'

Mr. Pinder felt himself going a little pink.

'I believe I'm guilty of misjudging you, Crabbe. You are proving very loyal, and you are showing that you have a sense of honour, which is all too rare these days.'

'Thank you, sir.'

He, the groper of a royal waxwork, the public displayer of underwear, had a sense of honour? Was Mr. Pinder still unwell?

'No. Thank *you*, Crabbe. Let us come to the point. Through your prompt actions this morning, you saved me from a potentially very embarrassing situation with the Head. And for agreeing to say nothing about the incident on the pier.'

Ah! That was it. If it got out what Crabbe had done at Hastings, Mr. Pinder was worried that it would damage the reputation of the school!

'I owe you for those kindnesses, Crabbe. I am, as I say, in your debt. But I must discharge that debt. I must repay you so we are *all square*. I cannot maintain my impartiality among the boys if I feel beholden to one particular boy. Now do you understand?'

'No, sir,' replied Crabbe, still completely misunderstanding Mr. Pinder.

'Right, then let me try this. At the end of term, the Head will name next year's School and House Prefects, as recommended by the Housemasters. If I name you as my choice for House Prefect of Keyes will you give me your word you will never mention either incident again?'

22: PREFECT

Crabbe developed a swagger.

His elevation to the elite of Keyes House meant he was allowed to wear an embroidered waistcoat and carry his own silver topped ebony cane.

He was not allowed to hit anyone with it, not that he would have anyway. The cane and waistcoat were badges of office, together with an *official* silver badge edged with Keyes green, to be worn only on Sundays, parents' days or when he was away from school.

He was inducted into the Prefect's Club. A very secret society that met once a week on Sunday evenings, while the masters and the rest of the school were in Chapel. The prefects were in the Chapel as well although more correctly, they were under it, in the crypt, enjoying their weekly Prefects' Feast.

The Feast consisted of whatever they managed to liberate from the school's pantries and stores. To feed the hundreds of hungry mouths at Chantry there was always so much food available that a few dozen eggs, rashers of bacon, pies and pasties and anything else that could be easily cooked in a stone sarcophagus, were never missed. Pork chops were a favourite, as was liver and onions.

There was never any danger of discovery by the authorities either because on Sunday evenings the Prefects *were* the authorities, tasked with patrolling the school buildings and dormitories whilst the usual occupants were in Chapel, praying and singing their hearts out and wondering where that delicious smell was coming from.

Crabbe was proud of his silver badge and polished it almost every day before wrapping it carefully in tissue paper and replacing it in its box in the bottom of his school trunk with his other treasures, Mr. Red Ted, a much-shrivelled conker, something that resembled a dried out, long dead worm, two cameras and his letters from home.

At Mr. Finney's Photographic Society, he had his portrait taken wearing his waistcoat and badge and holding his ebony cane. He printed it himself and sent it to his very proud parents who had it nicely framed and placed in the centre of their living room mantelpiece where it was admired by almost everyone in Felbridge Avenue – and beyond.

Crabbe's duties as House Prefect were in fact few. It was more of an honour than very much else. He wasn't included in the band of prefects who showed Shells and their parents around since his sense of direction was well known as akin to that of his father.

Someone else took over banging the Keyes Drum after Russell was promoted to School Prefect, and among other benefits, this should have also meant that he wouldn't be required to read from the Bible at Assembly anymore, but the Head decided he needed revenge and declared that Russell should continue. W-P thus earned Russell's everlasting hatred, which bothered W-P *not one jot.*

Crabbe was expected to help keep order and discipline, tour Keyes dorms after lights out and report anything amiss to a School Prefect who would decide whether to deal with the wrongdoer by punching him or referring him to Old Mother Sharkey or to Mr. Pinder.

He was also expected to keep an eye on the younger boys during break times so their boisterous games didn't result in too much bloodshed.

Other than that, he just paraded around feeling powerful, proud, and important. And happy.

He had done well in the school exams – better than expected, and he had donned the mantle of Stage Manager for the Fourth Year's production of *Henry V* very successfully and without any of the mishaps that occurred in *Macbeth*. James Russell had taken the trouble to come backstage and compliment him.

Mr. Pinder was pleased with him and had never mentioned Hastings again. Crabbe often blushed with the thought of it, but each time he went over those dreadful events in his mind, Mr. Pinder went up in his estimation. How he'd found out about Crabbe's misdeeds, he didn't know. But Mr. Pinder did know and had put the valuable reputation of the school before everything. He was Crabbe's hero.

Also, the Head was pleased with him and readily agreed with Mr. Pinder's proposal to promote Crabbe to Keyes House Prefect, commenting that he intended to put Crabbe's name forward himself. This was true, although Mr. Pinder didn't believe him.

M. le Becq was not at all pleased with him and as he was being strapped down onto the stretcher, he had threatened him. His exact words were, "You weel never leave zis school alive, Crabbe."

Crabbe didn't take the threat seriously, although he did feel dreadful about being the instrument of M. le Becq's downfall, again. Crabbe put the threat down to a mixture of the pain killing injection given by the ambulancemen and the master's being French that would cause him to say such a thing, and in front of dozens of witnesses too.

Crabbe had never understood why people chose to collect bird's eggs as a hobby although, in M. le Becq's case, it wasn't so much a hobby as a curriculum requirement since he ran Natural History as his extra-curricular class. He wanted to show the boys what a blackbird's egg looked like. He could have drawn one, or found a photograph, but no, for him, it had to be the real thing, which was why he borrowed Ernie's ladder. He intended to use it to climb to a nest in the thirty-foot elm tree standing in the junior playground.

It was an unfortunate coincidence that Crabbe happened to swagger by as a particular wild kick from one of the juniors landed their football on the flat roof of the art room.

Always willing to help, especially the juniors who looked up to him with ill-concealed awe, Crabbe also borrowed the caretaker's ladder from where it was left, propped up against an elm tree.

He was almost at its top on his rescue mission to retrieve the ball when he saw M. le Becq begin his descent.

Crabbe wasn't able to translate any of the words used by the Monsieur as he shot by, but the stream of French stopped abruptly when he hit the hard asphalt below.

The fortunate thing was that the leg suffered a clean break and there were no complications. As the Head told the school at Assembly the following morning, 'Monsieur le Becq will be back with us after the half term. It was an accident, nothing more and there will no need to mention it in your letters home.'

So, Crabbe was not punished, but instead his standing in certain quarters rose even higher, and he was congratulated on ridding the school of *that revolting Frenchman* for a few weeks by several juniors. The Head's intense dislike of the French, it seems, had filtered its way right down the school to the youngsters to the First Year.

This heroic status resulted in Crabbe being requested to take playground duty at least four times a week. He thought it was because the juniors happened to like him, but it was because the youngsters were hoping he would rid them of several more hated masters. Mr. Shapiro being top of their list.

It was whilst attending to one of the boys, a seven-year-old who had tripped and scraped his knee, but wasn't crying because one didn't at Chantry, that Crabbe was jolted out of his happy state.

'And what are you going to do when you grow up?' asked Crabbe kindly, dabbing at the knee with his handkerchief.

'Diplomatic Corps, like my father. What are you?'

'What am I what?'

'What are you going to do when you grow up? When you leave here?'

Crabbe stammered out a reply, 'Ah, well, erm. Not quite decided yet. Plenty of irons in the fire.'

'Well, you'd better make your mind up. You haven't got that long, you know.'

Having shared his advice, the lad went skipping away, his scraped knee completely forgotten, leaving Crabbe somewhat perplexed.

He didn't know. He hadn't got a clue what he'd do when he left Chantry. Oh, he had thought about it often enough, but hadn't been able to arrive at a workable conclusion. There were no irons in the fire because there was no fire. As far as he could see, he had no 'real options', just as Dr Wilkes-Passmore had said all those years ago.

Some of his Year, the brightest ones from wealthier families, would stay on in the Sixth Form for a further year before going to a good university. Their number included the doctors and lawyers of the future, plus Kirby, Cartwright and Glover.

Crabbe in all Innocence

It couldn't include Crabbe. Colonel McBeattie's generous bequest of scholarships didn't extend beyond the Fifth Year. And the Reverend Wilkes-Passmore wouldn't for one moment entertain the idea of altering the Colonel's instructions, even if he could. The cost would affect the W-P pocket.

Doctors and lawyers...No, the very idea of messing about with all those revolting bits in the insides of people, all slimy and covered in blood upset Crabbe.

As for the law, well he *had* considered it, but there was the basic requirement of being able to argue a case in front of a judge, and Crabbe was not good at arguing. He could definitely be relied on to think of a counterargument, come up with a witty retort or defend a position, but not until several days afterwards, by which time the moment had passed.

He was aware that he lagged behind others in this field and set himself a Target: he would take steps to improve.

He joined the Debating Society. He thought the cut and thrust of argument and counterargument would hasten his brain cells into action and so bring convincing words to his mouth, but it never did.

When called upon to speak, nothing would come out. At least, not that week. He would 'erm' a few times, look up at the ceiling, raise a forefinger and go 'ahh', all as if about to expose the flaw in the proposition or deliver a brilliant riposte. Instead, there would be nothing but an awkward embarrassing silence.

But with the best will in the world, it was all he could ever manage, and eventually, he had to accept the situation. The *law* was not for him.

This inability to speak in public also precluded him from politics. Not that he knew anything about politics or even had the least shred of interest. He just decided *The Right Honourable Lancelot Arthur Crabbe, MP* sounded rather well. But that was as far as his political ambitions got to.

So then, not Parliament, not the medical profession, and not law.

What then?

The military? Teaching? The stage? After his success in *Macbeth*, he had thought briefly he might like to be a professional actor but gave up on the idea almost immediately once he admitted his nerves would never stand it.

He decided to ask some boys what they intended to do when they left Chantry.

'A train driver.'

'A train driver too.'

'A train driver, me too.'

He asked some older boys. Everyone he spoke to had their lives planned, mapped out ready before them: Hopkins Major would be going to RADA, Barnaby Gordon would be joining his family's coffee importing business. Bunting was going into forestry. His dormers had plans. In fact, everyone knew exactly what he'd be doing after he'd left the school.

Crabbe in all Innocence

Everyone, except Crabbe. He wrote to his father, seeking advice. The reply he got didn't help – 'It's your life. Your future. You decide. And don't forget, we're always here for you.'

'Ah, well,' he thought, 'as Mr. Micawber always said, something is bound to turn up.'

What actually turned up surprised him.

He didn't know Mr. Finney had been seeing Sister Rosemary. He didn't know Sister Rosemary ran the St. Margaret's Photographic Society, and he didn't know that the leaders of both Societies were swapping ideas.

'Last year,' Mr. Finny explained, 'my boys took photographs of our school chapel. The best of them, as chosen by the Head, was taken at night by our mutual friend, Lancelot Crabbe, and used as Chantry's Christmas card. I'm pleased to say, it was very well received.'

Sister Rosemary said, 'Yes, Mr. Finney, I remember it well although as I'm sure you understand, we didn't display it with the others as the photograph depicted a Protestant establishment. Nevertheless, it was an excellent idea. One that, with your permission and the agreement of Reverend Mother Claire, we might copy.'

'Indeed, why not. And if it helps, I'll ask if any boys would be willing to pop along to offer suggestions based on the experience of last year.' Reverend Mother Claire agreed, providing the visiting boys from Chantry didn't include Crabbe among their number.

23: HARROW

Harrow certainly wasn't the last place on earth that Crabbe would wish to visit. That distinction belonged to St. Margaret's. Therefore, when he was told he had been excluded from the party of boys visiting St. Margaret's for a joint 'photographic outing' he was delighted. In fact, to use words which he felt might be appropriate both to the news and to his reaction on receiving it, he was *absolutely* delighted at being cast out. A leper, an untouchable, exiled! He'd been excommunicated, although he wasn't sure that was the correct term.

It didn't matter. He wasn't going to St. Margaret's.

But he was going to Harrow, as part of Chantry's second eleven – not to *play* cricket, of course, since he was still pretty useless at anything involving a ball. He was going in his capacity as House Prefect to keep discipline among the Chantovians, and as the trip to Harrow included staying overnight there would be plenty of opportunities for the boys to get to up to some mischief or other.

Truth to tell, he was also pretty useless in regard to discipline, but all the youngsters liked him and wouldn't dream of doing anything wrong which, if discovered, would reflect badly on Crabbe. They, therefore, ensured their rule breaking deeds were

301

carried out privately and only with the certain knowledge that Crabbe was elsewhere.

Currently, the cricketers were in the third-class carriage, puffing away on illicit cigarettes, whilst Mr. Pinder and Crabbe, as 'officials' were travelling first class. Mr. Pinder was dozing. It had been an early start and he used most of the three-hour journey to catch up on his sleep.

Crabbe, on the other hand, was wide awake. He was sitting opposite Mr. Pinder checking his photographic equipment, which didn't need checking because he'd checked it with Mr. Finney the previous evening.

Crabbe's photography had greatly improved. At every opportunity he went out in the school grounds or the village, a familiar figure recording anything and everything for posterity.

The Head asked to view his work to see if there was anything of particular interest that could be included in the School's quarterly newspaper, as by tradition the only news The Chantovian carried were lists of sporting results and a chronicle of former pupils who had recently breathed their last. The latter proved particularly useful for Mrs. Pearl who could update their records of former *living* pupils, thus making a saving on the unnecessary expense of sending invitations to school reunions to the dead ones. (W-P had been the one to think of this.)

Crabbe was encouraged in his photographic endeavours by Mr. Finney who criticised or praised

Crabbe's efforts accordingly and gave limitless help and advice which Crabbe happily accepted and put into practice. Such enthusiasm impressed the master who soon came to regard Crabbe as his Photographic Society's star pupil.

He often advised Crabbe on the purchasing of new equipment, although Crabbe didn't need to buy anything apart from rolls of film, because Mr. Finney was quite happy to lend Crabbe anything he required. Thus, Crabbe was able to experiment, taking photographs from early morning with the sun just coming up to late at night, when time exposures were needed.

He began to wonder whether it was possible, and viable, to take up the profession of photographer. The idea certainly appealed, and the more he thought about it, the more he liked it.

His main problem, one shared by every schoolboy throughout the kingdom, was financial. He was always short of cash.

Then, quite suddenly one morning at the end of last term, Crabbe woke up with an idea from somewhere.

Somewhere?

It was a way of raising some money. He had his birthday and Christmas money in his school account, safely in the hands of the bursar, but the costs of processing and printing his photographs left little for anything else.

Crabbe in all Innocence

He put his idea to Mr. Finney, who passed it on to Mr. Pinder who asked the Head for his opinion. All agreed. It was so simple it was incredible that no one had thought of it before.

A tradition at Chantry (yes, another one) was that when a boy left, so that friends could keep in touch, they would go around handing out printed visiting cards with their future address printed on it. Crabbe's idea was to replace the visiting card with a photograph of the boy with his name and new address printed on the reverse.

The photographs would be taken by Crabbe as it was his idea. They would be called 'Leavers' and sold at cost plus a shilling for Crabbe as photographer, and a little extra to generate funds so he could buy his own equipment. After all, he thought, he couldn't go on borrowing cameras and lenses from Mr. Finney *ad infinitum*.

With Mr. Finney, he negotiated a discount from the chemist to have the Leavers photographs printed and then arranged with the printer of The Chantovian to have the backs of the photographs printed with the subject's contact details.

Everyone benefited. Everyone was pleased. Everyone earned money, including the school as the Head decreed that, in line with the wishes of the School Charter as drawn up by *Ye Ten Goode Men*, and translated, in this instance by Dr. Walter Wilkes-Passmore himself, a levy on sales was to be made, a tariff raised for the benefit of... erm, something or other.

Recalling the disaster of that awful McBeattie scholarship business, W-P had his solicitor draw up a contract which all parties, including Crabbe, were required to sign. He ensured that the terms included a clause clearly stating an expiry date which would end the agreement exactly twenty years to the day after it was signed.

Additionally, the cost of the Leavers photographs was not to be met from the boys' school accounts but added to their final account when they left. This way, reasoned W-P, cash would be left in their school account and available for spends at the tuck shop, from which the school took a small commission.

The idea of Leavers photographs wasn't an instant success because Englishmen, even the younger ones, are by nature averse to change. That said, they are also given to vanity, by far the stronger force of these two attributes and, as a consequence, Crabbe's balance in the bursary also greatly improved.

Crabbe, the chemist and the printer were always kept busy towards the end of term, but no one minded.

Having checked his equipment and put the case up on the luggage rack, Crabbe checked the contents of his rucksack. Items had been added over the months. Just things he found useful when out on his photographic adventures, including a raincoat, primus stove and paraffin, and the necessities for making a pot of tea, matches, cheese sandwiches, a bottle of tomato ketchup and a tin of plasters.

Bathed in the bright sunshine of early October, the train chugged across the English countryside belching thick black smoke. Crabbe was reminded of the journey with his parents so many years before, on his way to begin his new life at Chantry. Long, long ago, he thought. Almost a lifetime. Crabbe didn't realise how close to the truth that thought was.

Back then, he was just a schoolboy, apprehensive at the thought of what that future held. He remembered Mr. Pinder welcoming him, the Shells' Run, his introduction to the Keyes morning drum, *Macbeth*. So many memories that, helped by the passage of time, were remembered as being happy. Even the sadder ones. He gave the House Prefect badge on his lapel a quick polish with his sleeve and let out a quiet sigh.

The train chugged into Harrow Station and the Chantry party were greeted by Mr. Bourne, Harrow's cricket coach, and Samuel Gibbins, captain of the second eleven, and that usually ever-present ingredient for a game of English cricket, very heavy rain.

Also there, fortunately, was Harrow's version of Ernie – complete with handcart for transporting Chantry's cricket equipment and overnight needs. Luckily, he had a tarpaulin to keep everything dry.

By the time they'd walked up the hill to the school, the rain had stopped. Mr. Pinder and Mr. Bourne followed Gibbins as he led the visitor's team to the cricket pitch where they decided they would abandon play for the day because of the very wet state of the ground.

A note in the score book read, 'Heavy rain having adversely affected the pitch, Messrs. Milne and Gibbins (the two captains), decided it would be imprudent to attempt the game today. Consequently, they agreed the toss would be at 11am tomorrow morning, with play due to start at 11.30am, weather permitting.'

The team decided to get some practice in the indoor nets. Mr. Pinder and Mr. Bourne went off in search of tea and Crabbe, left alone, went off to explore.

He wondered up behind the Harrow School Speech Rooms where he climbed on his camera case and peered in through a window, but it was too dark. He couldn't see anything, not even a brass eagle lectern, if there was one. All he could see was his own reflection and that of St. Mary's church behind him.

He had never visited this church before, even though it was famous and close to Stanmore where his family lived. He knew there were a few noteworthy graves though – the first man killed by a train was buried there, so was the first man killed in a car accident. He'd heard the first man to be killed by a hot air balloon exploding was here somewhere too. Some of him. The rest being in Watford, apparently. And there was a flat gravestone that Byron or Wordsworth or someone, used as a table to pen some poetry.

Crabbe in all Innocence

Crabbe stood under the lichgate and gazed up at the magnificent Norman church. A plaque attached to the roof above him informed the visitor that St. Anselm had consecrated the church in 1094 and that Charles II had been there.

'What a sight,' he was thinking and, 'Now, this is what I call a church.' As he gazed, out of the blue, a brand-new train of thought arrived: *'A photograph, LC. Take a photograph – but not now. Wait for darkness, moonlight. Dramatic cloud effects.'*

'I could take a photograph of this. When it gets dark, with the moon somewhere, and clouds. Maybe some bats. Far more dramatic than in the daylight.'

He smiled contentedly, saying to himself, 'I won't forget today in a hurry.'

'That's true. And neither will anyone else,' agreed unheard voices from above.

24: TOMB

A strange feeling came over Crabbe as he walked from the deep shadow of the lichgate to the brightness of the sunshine on the other side.

He'd had strange feelings before, particularly in his teenage years, but never anything like this. It was like being born again, but born into a world free of conflict, free of hatred, free of Sister Rosemary.

It was so peaceful here, and so beautiful. Leaves in autumn shades blowing gently along the path, delicate pastel-coloured flowers nestling against gravestones. Crabbe wasn't in the least bit surprised that whoever it was came here to write his poetry.

As he looked up at St. Mary's he was again filled with the desire, *the need*, to take a photograph of the church. The feeling was inexplicable, but so insistent, so intent. He *had* to – *as if his life depended on it*. Even if it was the last thing he'd ever get to do on earth.

He knew he was being over dramatic and really not thinking all that logically. But he couldn't escape the feeling that *something*, perhaps an unknown power, was commanding him to create something beautiful here.

Photographs could be beautiful, just like paintings, music and poetry. Nature was filled with beauty. At least, it was for those who cared to pause and take it all in. Right now, Crabbe took a deep breath of fresh

Crabbe in all Innocence

English country air. It smelled clean after the rain. Bracing and pure.

It was perfect.

What could possibly go wrong?

That's the exact line spoken by the hero in several of the who-dunnit books sent to Carters by his godmother. And no sooner had the hero said it, than something would go dreadfully wrong. Heroes could read, so they must know what would happen if they said it. So why did they say it?

Crabbe didn't think about any of that before he said it. He just said it anyway. And what went wrong? Well, where to begin?

Crabbe started by scouting around for a suitable position to take his photograph from. His *work of art.* Mr. Finney had always impressed on him the advantages of being elevated when taking architectural photography. A higher viewpoint, he'd said, presents a far more pleasing aspect of any building.

Around Crabbe, there were graves everywhere. He looked round at hundreds, probably thousands of headstones, most leaning away from one another as if those buried there didn't quite get on. There were memorials of every shape and size, from simple crosses to great slabs of marble with epitaphs intricately carved, each word extolling the virtue of whoever lay at rest beneath. Many graves had wrought iron railings around the edges marking out the plot for eternity and keeping the occupant safe from Burke and Hare.

Chris Hare

Crabbe wondered if it really mattered. The dead were dead, so did they care? Some graves, a very few, were obviously tended and well-cared for with fresh flowers placed in small urns. So perhaps it didn't matter to the dead, but did it matter that much to the living?

He was in danger of losing that carefree frame of mind that had embraced him only few minutes before. He pulled himself together and carried on looking.

His jaw dropped.

How he hadn't noticed it before, he had no idea – it was big enough, and had a statue of an angel on top. Perfect! A broad smile lit up Crabbe's face and he gave a little skip of joy then he stood still and gazed in awe at the tomb. It was a huge marble monument which might have been the entrance to a mausoleum, one of those underground crypts where generations of a single family were interred piled on top of one another. It was about halfway between the church and the lichgate. Perfect!

Without intending any disrespect to the departed, it didn't matter to Crabbe whether the tomb belonged to a whole family or a single, fat tall person. It was the height of a tomb not the corpse that was the important thing. Luck was going his way. Could he climb up there?

He wondered what it would look like to anyone who happened along. How would he explain being up there grinning like an idiot on top of a tomb? What would he say?

311

Crabbe in all Innocence

A voice said, 'Hello, Elsie.'

He snapped back to the present.

'Ah, Milne. Finished your net practice, have you?'

'No, I've just taken a few minutes off to give you this lot. Perce is bound to go through our pockets after lights out. Be a pal and hide it in your camera case. He'll blow a fuse if he finds this stuff on me.'

Out of his jacket pocket he took a tobacco pouch, cigarette papers and matches.

Crabbe said, 'What if he finds it on me?'

'Oh, you're his golden boy. He won't look in your case. Put it in there... You can't refuse a fellow Chantovian.'

Crabbe couldn't argue with that. The bond between Chantovians was strong. Letting a chap down if you could help him out, just wasn't done. In all honesty though, he'd never taken to Milne, whom he considered rather frivolous, but he took Milne's things anyway although he was loath to break a rule, commit a sin, in such a perfect place.

He said, 'Alright, just this once. But I want you to tell Mr. Pinder I'll be back later tonight. And don't call him 'Perce'. It's disrespectful.'

'Good chap, Elsie,' said Milne, as he set off back down the path.

Alone again, Crabbe put Milne's contraband in his pocket as he looked up at the tomb. It was very high. He'd need a ladder to get up there. A little way along the path he saw a seat, one of several sited at convenient locations around the church grounds, placed as memorials to the dead for the benefit of the living to rest, in peace, whilst their loved ones did the same six feet below.

He left his camera case and rucksack by the tomb and, glancing round to make sure Milne hadn't returned, put an innocent expression on that made him look more like a furtive criminal, and took hold of one end of the seat. He heaved with all the vigour he could muster, expecting that, as at Chantry, the seat would be secured to a concrete plinth. It wasn't, and he easily dragged it down the path to place it by the tomb. Crabbe smiled at his luck again.

For no reason he could think of, the wheels of good fortune were running in his direction, at last. If it were possible for a brain to smile, Crabbe's brain smiled a great beam of delight. He knew he was on the verge of success. Perhaps it was his lucky day. If it was, he was determined to use it to every advantage.

He climbed onto the seat and manhandled his camera case and rucksack up onto the roof of the tomb, where with a little effort, he joined them.

He looked at the angel's face and shuddered. Angels were supposed to look angelic, this one looked like Old Mother Sharkey.

'Must get ready,' he told the angel with an apologetic, 'sure you understand if I get on' nod of the head as he removed his jacket and hung it from a protruding marble feather on one of the angel's wings.

313

Crabbe in all Innocence

He undid the straps on his camera case and set up his tripod humming a happy tune to himself, which was completely at odds with his surroundings and bore no resemblance to the notes penned by the composer, but perfectly reflected his mood, which was currently one of *supreme confidence*.

He glanced over the tomb's edge to make sure he'd left nothing behind, and he noticed – *joys of joys* – a standpipe with an old, galvanised watering can placed inverted, over the tap.

Water! Fresh water. Tea!

There was no need for him to rush. He could take his time, he was English, and an Englishmen always made time for tea. And perhaps a cigarette. He'd never smoked before and he knew full well that boys at Chantry were not allowed to smoke. But this was not Chantry, so he wasn't breaking the rule. He rolled a cigarette, quite successfully, as he'd seen his grandfathers do often. He didn't light it but put it ready for later behind his ear, as Ernie often did.

He opened the rucksack and unclipped the kettle from the primus stove and clambered down the tomb again to fill it with water from the standpipe.

He was smiling again and didn't notice the quality of the distinctly dark water as it coughed and choked its way out from the earth's core.

Back on top of his tomb – by now, he thought of it as his, he set up the primus and brewed a pot of hot but evil-smelling tea. Normally, he would have noticed such a foul odour. He always prided himself on his sharper hearing and keener sense of smell that he thought made up for his poor eyesight.

On this occasion, his sense of smell was monopolised by the foul odour of the water mixed with the reek of paraffin.

He'd unscrewed the top from one of the three metal containers he used, which held either milk, medicinal brandy (emergency use only) or paraffin – he hadn't thought to label them. He took a deep sniff of what turned out to be the paraffin, and unaware that fumes interfere with thinking, actions and judgement, he decided the top of the tomb was the most comfortable place he'd ever find to go to sleep on.

He lay down and resting his head on the rucksack, he gazed up at the strange shapes the clouds made. Just above St. Mary's spire, Mr. Finney was smiling down at him and, over there, above the Speech Rooms, Milne was lighting up a cigarette. Crabbe turned back to distract Mr. Finney away from Milne, but he'd gone. He gave a sigh of relief and passed out.

He woke with a start. Where was he? Alone in the dark? Who'd screamed then? He had.

He froze as he heard the creaking of an old rusting hinge on a once, long-locked door. *Someone was opening the lichgate.*

He leapt towards the guardian angel and did his best to become a second one by squeezing in close and spreading his arms. He looked down and saw a man and woman walking from the gate towards his tomb.

Crabbe put on what he hoped was an angelic expression behind his distinctively non-angelic glasses – not that angels left their cameras and tripods in full view on the tops of tombs either, but he didn't think of that.

With his heightened night senses, the sounds around Crabbe had magnified and taken on an altogether more sinister tone. That lichgate, for example. It had hardly put up a squeak when Crabbe came through it earlier.

For no discernible reason, he felt threatened and found himself gripped with fear. He was in a strange place. A churchyard full of graves, complete with eerie moonlight casting strange, ghostly shadows. It was bound to be a little unnerving. And he was on his own – but for the couple standing below him. He wasn't quite terrified, but not very far off and what was most unnerving was that he was scared even though on the surface of things, there was no real reason to be. In his brain, all he felt amalgamated to produce a sensation of the greatest unease.

'Control yourself,' he said to himself, with his nerves forgetting there were people close by.

'Control yourself,' a female voice rapidly replied.

They're still there! Out of sight of the sweating Crabbe, the couple had sat down on the seat he had kindly provided.

316

Chris Hare

Very gently, Crabbe altered the pious position of his head just a fraction to the left. Just enough to see if there was anyone else at the lichgate. There wasn't. Barely allowing himself a breath, he turned himself within the spread angel's wings so he could see through a gap between its halo and the top of its right ear. He let himself lean forward slightly so that he could see them clearly, sitting there, on *his* seat, by *his* tomb, illuminated by a shaft of soft moonlight.

He was a sailor in uniform and Crabbe blushed as he caught sight of his wife's stocking tops. Her skirt was far too short for a stroll in a graveyard and when Crabbe looked closer, he could see she had made a pretty poor job of eating a choc ice recently and must have tried to put her lipstick on in the dark and missed her lips.

Her hair was blonde and so long it hung down and almost touched the fur of the stole she was wearing which Crabbe thought might be a mink.

The sailor had no hair to speak of, except to say that what he had was cropped very close, in the true navy style. This lack of detail on his head was more than compensated for by the mass of tattoos he sported on both his thick, bare arms.

Above, on the tomb, Crabbe wished he was somewhere else. The couple were clearly arguing about money, which was always embarrassing. But he was here and didn't dare an escape attempt, didn't even dare a move.

Crabbe in all Innocence

He rested his chin on the cold angelic shoulder since he had no other choice but to listen in.

Although he'd missed the first part of their conversation, he soon picked up the thread. The cause of the dispute was obviously something she wanted to buy, but he thought it was too expensive. Anyway, he wanted *something* cheaper. Crabbe had heard about married couples having these kinds of arguments before.

Whatever it was, the wife was adamant, 'That's the price. Take it or leave it!'

After a few more minutes of arguing on their part and pain on Crabbe's Adam's apple's part as a rough piece of marble angel nightie reminded him briefly of Sister Rosemary, the husband gave in and agreed to the price of the whatever it was. With that, they got up and strolled up the path towards the church.

Crabbe watched them with narrowed eyes. He had a feeling he'd missed something: the church wouldn't be open for hours, and they weren't even walking a dog.

Chris Hare

25: CRABBE'S GRAVE

Crabbe was relieved to see them go. He exhaled silently, a breath of deliverance, as he watched them make their way, arm in arm, towards the far corner of the church tower and disappeared from view around the back.

He was pleased the sailor and his wife had resolved their differences and relieved they hadn't seen him. He hated being forced to eavesdrop. It wasn't a thing a decent chap did. And that sailor didn't look the sort of chap that would take that kind of thing very well.

Crabbe disengaged himself from the angel's embrace and tried to recall where he had got up to in his preparations. He couldn't remember, so he started again.

He made sure he hadn't accidently moved the camera and that it was still at the correct elevation and angle. Then he refocused the lens and checked the aperture was $f16$, even though it was too dark by now to see the tiny figures. He struck a match, cupping it in his hands (so a German sniper wouldn't see the light. The Head had told them about that cowardly trick.).

As the flame flared, he could see the aperture was set on $f16$. Which meant all was correct. He fitted the bulb cable release for the time exposure then groped around in his camera case for the tin of flash powder and the scales to weigh it out.

Crabbe in all Innocence

He managed to tip the exact amount into the pan without spilling any, he hoped, and from there, carefully transferred it to the powder tray. Once everything was as it should be, he ate a couple of cheese sandwiches liberally doused in tomato ketchup, (dripping some down his shirt), and settled down to wait the final thirty minutes. Then he remembered the cigarette still stuck behind his ear.

He put it to his lips and struck another match, remembering just in time, that the flash powder tray was lying ready close by. He leaned over the tomb's edge and dropped the burning match which gave out a last flare as it died in the dew. No harm done. He didn't burn the church down or start a forest fire but to flare like that, he realised he must have spilt some paraffin.

On the stroke of ten, Crabbe squeezed the rubber bulb. He heard the shutter click open and gave a smile of satisfaction. Everything was going splendidly, and exactly as planned.

He hung the ping timer by its chain on a stone feather and lit another match. In the flicker, he set the dial to ten minutes and settled down again with his eyes glued to the timer swaying gently to and fro in the moonlight. Exact timing was important – vital to the success of his plan. He would need to repeat the procedure in exactly ten minutes and be ready to set off the flash powder at the end. This would light the foreground and give depth to the photograph, an idea of Mr. Finney's.

Chris Hare

Crabbe watched the dimly lit timer swing side to side, back and forth. He gave a satisfied grunt as he stared. Back and forth, back and fo…

Crabbe didn't *think* he'd ever been hypnotised. He'd heard of it. Cartwright's godmother had sent a book on the subject. Cartwright and the boys he had lent it to went around at break telling people to 'Look into my eyes,' and that they were '…feeling sleepy. Very, very sleepy'. It went on for a whole term, but no one was ever actually hypnotised.

With Crabbe though, it was difficult to tell and now, his eyes really were gradually glazing over and as the clouds darkened and drifted by, unseen and unheard by this new staring form on the marble tomb, the churchyard gradually came to life.

Although the life was not corpses raising up from their graves, which would have passed unnoticed by Crabbe in his trance anyway, but had he been the slightest bit conscious, he would have seen many more couples come whispering and creeping through the lichgate. Most carried torches and flashed them around as if they were looking for certain graves. All the women wore too much lipstick and dressed in short skirts, like the sailor's wife. They all had straight long blonde hair, high heeled shoes and mink stoles too. It was obviously the fashion in Harrow.

In front of Crabbe's nose, the timer gave a soft ping, and he woke from his stupor with a start, initially unaware he was no longer alone and completely unable to comprehend how the last ten minutes had gone by so quickly. He pressed the reset button for the next ten and decided to get the powder ready.

Kneeling down, he saw the scales and the tin, which surprised him. He didn't remember getting them out. He poured the precise amount onto the scales and then transferred it to the tray and as he did, he was struck by a moment of *déjà vu*. He put it down to conducting so many experiments with flash powder in his practice shoots.

Then he heard voices below him again and saw another couple silhouetted against the lights of the streetlamp on the other side of lichgate. He was forced once again, by circumstances, to listen in. From what they were saying it seemed they too, were arguing about money. She, the young lady, was a taxi driver, Crabbe assumed, and he, her prospective new fare. He was trying to negotiate a price to be taken somewhere. They came through the gate and walked past the spot where Crabbe was lying down flat on his stomach above them.

''Ow much to go all the way, love?' the man asked her. Crabbe didn't hear her reply as they moved away. He lay still watching until they neared the church wondering how many other lady taxi drivers there were in Harrow.   In London, all the cabs were driven by men. Fat, greasy-haired men with greasy skin who just sat hunched over the wheel reading the horse racing section of their newspapers as they waited for fares to get in.

From the church door, he heard the man exclaim loudly, ''Ow much?! You're off yer trolley! Completely bats!'

Crabbe ducked, his eyes searching the shadows at the base of the tower for the owner of the voice. His heart was pumping fast now, but it almost burst when the timer went 'ping'.

Bats? Crabbe looked up at the moon and fell calmer. 'No bats. Disappointing, but not the end of the world,' and so he forgot all about the arguing couple.

Time! Balancing the tray on the guardian angel's halo, Crabbe set the fuse and lit it. He ducked down again in case anyone noticed.

Quite a few people did.

Quite a few bats did too. In fact, hundreds of them, who until that moment, had been hanging out peacefully upside down in the belfry. As a blinding flash hit the graveyard and the front of the church with an impressively loud *whoosh*, they all woke up and for an instant afterwards, there was only shocked silence. A small calm before the storm because next, there was sheer pandemonium.

En masse and as one, the bats departed the belfry. The few leaves left on the trees in their immediate vicinity were blasted from their branches. The earth may have stopped moving and people certainly fell off tombstones and all activity ceased.

Crabbe in all Innocence

All those people unnoticed by Crabbe, now stood
erect in various stages of undress and shock before they
began charging around the churchyard in equally
various stages of blind panic in their frenzied attempts
to escape. No one actually saw what created the
explosion. Not even where it had emanated from,
exactly.

Except for Crabbe. Crabbe had thrown himself flat
onto the tombstone, confused again. He couldn't
understand why the powder had gone off with such a
bang. It was as if he'd used two or three times the
correct amount.

His eyebrows were missing. His face covered with a
layer of greasy black soot and ash. He'd been
momentarily blinded so now that when he looked up,
everything was bathed in a sea of soft yellow light.
Even the guardian angel hadn't escaped. She still wore
her halo but now also sported a fine black moustache.

Crabbe raised his head and watched as dozens of
screaming yellow forms rushed by. He had no idea
where they'd come from. They made for the gate and
charged through it, fleeing for their lives down the hill,
waving yellow undergarments as flags of surrender,
just grateful to escape the carnage.

The panic was endemic, affecting Crabbe too, the
perpetrator of the outrage, who alone *knew exactly* what
had happened, and also knew there was no further
danger, that war hadn't been declared and the Martians
hadn't landed at Harrow-on-the-Hill.

But such is the effect of mass hysteria. As soon as most of the crowd had made their escape and were charging away from the scene of devastation leaving only a few bewildered souls wandering among the graves, Crabbe stood up again.

His sight almost back to normal, he hastened to pack his things. With fumbling fingers, he hurried to take the camera down and collapse the tripod as quickly but as silently as he could. He didn't want to draw attention to himself.

When he thought he had everything, he ran his hands over the length of the soot covered marble just to make sure. Satisfied he'd left nothing behind, he lowered his box of equipment, tripod and rucksack by their straps over the far side of the tomb. He didn't want to risk being seen climbing down to the seat on the other side. They landed softly in the darkness and waited for him to follow.

26: LEAP of FAITH

Crabbe realised he'd have to jump and, still clinging to the notion that this was his lucky day, thought he might have a chance of landing without breaking an ankle; that would be the final straw. So, he took courage in both hands and jumped.

That was the final straw.

He made a good landing, both feet together as he'd been taught in gym. He didn't lose his balance, break an ankle, or land on top of his equipment.

He didn't stop either.

Pausing just long enough on the artificial grass and thin wooden boards to give them time to shatter under his weight, he continued on his way downwards.

The plastic grass they use to show off fruit and vegetables in greengrocers' shop window displays looked well enough despite the singeing it had had from Crabbe's burning match – obviously not the real thing, but an acceptable imitation.

They also used it, stretched over wooden boards, to cover freshly dug graves. It doesn't look at all real when laid next to the genuine article, but the casual passer-by was unlikely to notice the difference. Crabbe wasn't a passer-by. He was a dropper-in. A passer-through.

Even if he'd been blessed with excellent vision, he wouldn't have spotted it: it was almost completely dark and he was in the act of saying goodbye to the guardian angel when he jumped, so he wasn't even looking where he was going.

Going through the aperture he had inadvertently created he received some cuts and bruises to his shins and a four-inch rip to his left trouser leg. He was also subjected to a slight battering on the underside of his chin from the broken boards. On reaching the bottom, he received more cuts and bruises to the top of his head as the broken boards dropped in on top of him. Painful and a shock, but not enough to knock him out.

It was the camera case and rucksack that did that.

He drifted in and out of consciousness. Vaguely aware that he was the sole occupant of the grave, in one of his more functioning moments, he attempted to stand. There was a squelching underfoot as he trod on his remaining cheese and ketchup sandwich. He didn't mind: if he was going to be buried alive, he might as well starve to death at the same time. It would bring about his demise all the sooner.

He looked up. There was just sufficient moonlight reflected from the tomb for him to see the opening above and the top few inches of the walls of his grave before it turned into impenetrable stygian blackness.

The grave was long, similar in length to *his* tomb and deeper than he would have expected. *Were they burying a giant?* Crabbe realised that the depth of the coffin would be added to the generally accepted depth of the grave – six feet – making the hole about eight feet deep. Nine or ten, if the deceased was particularly fat. And Crabbe, though tall, wasn't tall enough to see over the top.

But perhaps he could reach up and wave his arms about. You never know, someone might see *something*, if there was anyone left to see.

He tried but to no avail. Could he climb out? He would have to get higher, build a platform to stand on and giving his arms enough purchase to heave himself up.

He took his glasses off and slipped them in a pocket. There was no point in wearing them anyway, he couldn't see a thing down there. He groped around the bottom of the grave, feeling his way and piling everything, camera case, rucksack and broken wooden boards in the centre.

Tentatively, and with hands against the slimy black earth to support him, he climbed up. He gained sufficient height to look over the edge. But there was nothing, or rather no one to see. He looked up the path, towards the church. No sound came to him, not even the rustle of leaves.

Then, behind him, he heard a grunt, then a very wicked word followed by the unmistakeable sound of someone falling to the ground, having tripped over a tripod.

Crabbe twisted round to look in the direction of the grunt and the wicked word.

And there, not five feet in front of him, he saw a face. A face he recognised as belonging to the tattooed sailor he'd seen arguing about money with his wife. He was very muscular and well able, Crabbe thought, to pull him up from the grave.

Leading Seaman George Newing had experienced much during his years of service in the Royal Navy. He had never been far from danger and had witnessed scenes of extreme violence. Scenes that would make an ordinary man shy away and seek somewhere to hide.

His early years on the troubled streets of Liverpool had prepared him for a hard life. A life of violence, first with street gangs and then the awful sights and sounds of total war, of people – *shipmates,* being killed or horribly mutilated beside him. But he'd got used to it and could put up with anything. In the tough world of the Navy, he was one of the toughest.

Until Frankenstein's Monster appeared in front of him from the depths of Hell that is. He gaped at the dark sockets where crazed eyes were caked with mud, at fresh blood oozing from wounds glistening in the moonlight and running down the sides of the disembodied head floating in front of him, just above a freshly dug grave.

His life on the streets of Liverpool and his experiences in the Navy hadn't prepared him for this. He opened his mouth to scream, but only silence came out.

Crabbe in all Innocence

'Good evening. A nice strong sailor. Just the sort of chap I was hoping for,' said Crabbe, with a twisted attempt at a smile.

This time, the sailor was able to scream, which ushered forth unbroken as he rushed from the graveside, kicking the tripod as his panicked legs scrambled for a grip on the damp and uneven ground. He vaulted the lichgate in a single terrified leap to escape the fiends of Hell who, he was sure, were snapping at his heels. Keeping up the momentum, he ran and ran, still screaming but with the noise receding as he got further away, just as it does in naval films that have a bosun's whistle being blown when the Captain comes aboard.

Meanwhile, the particular fiend of Hell who was responsible for the sailor's loss of sanity, slipped from his camera case in surprise. He looked up, thoroughly taken aback by the sailor's reaction.

It was as he was calling out a rather timid, 'Hello, are you still there?' that the tripod dropped, felling him with yet another blow to the head.

He wasn't knocked out, but he was dazed. His head was probably getting used to being constantly battered and had developed its own immune system.

While he was lying on his back the awfulness of his situation came home to him. The reality dawned. If he didn't get out, *this* could be his last resting place: starved to death, or more probably crushed under the coffin of the giant this grave had been prepared for.

It would be *his* grave, not Crabbe's, even though Crabbe had got in there first. It would be *his* tombstone. The carefully carved 'rest in peace' or 'forever in our hearts' wouldn't refer to Crabbe, but to the bloke on top. *No one would ever know he was there!*

His thoughts turned to those he'd be leaving behind: his younger brothers, his sweet little sister. His parents. *His poor, heartbroken family, kneeling and weeping by his graveside!*

No, they wouldn't be! *They would be kneeling and weeping by a complete stranger's grave!*

No, they wouldn't be! *They wouldn't know where he was, and they weren't the sort of people to go around kneeling and weeping at just anyone's grave.*

And school! He had imagined going back to Chantry in triumph as the creator of the definitive photograph of St. Mary's by night. He would give a copy to Mr. Pinder and one to Mr. Finney. And there were his dormers. And he mustn't forget…!

Whoever it was that Crabbe mustn't forget, he forgot, as he realised his photograph would be buried with him and so cruelly denied to the world of art lovers.

He had to get out. He must do *something*!

But what? He wasn't tall enough to climb out unaided, and he certainly didn't have the strength to pull himself up. He wished he'd tried harder at the high jump at Chantry and hadn't been so scared of climbing the wall bars.

Crabbe in all Innocence

Having the strength or not, he was determined to *try*, at least. So, he tried.

Hands grabbing and scrabbling frantically at the sides of the grave, feet kicking, desperately seeking a foothold, *something!*

Nothing. He reached up, *willing* his hands to find, to grab hold of anything solid, a tree root, a clump of deeply rooted grass, someone's old leg bone.

But however hard he tried, he failed.

Exhausted and bitterly disappointed, he slid back down the side of the grave and sat, head in hands, defeated and alone. Waiting for death, he closed his eyes.

An hour or so later, something woke him. A sound.

He was no longer alone. Geoffrey, a tramp who had spent his nights sheltering in the churchyard for years, had also fallen in. In his confused state, Crabbe felt affronted by this sudden intrusion: *this* was his grave. His and whoever was due to be buried on top of him.

Three's a crowd. How many more? Couldn't a chap be left alone by the other chaps to rest in peace?

He opened his mouth to protest to the tramp, who, not unreasonably given his intoxicated state, thought he was on his own.

Crabbe paused and decided against complaining. After all, they were both experiencing the same trauma. *In the same hole,* as the saying goes. And so, with a low-pitched voice that he hoped wouldn't give the tramp a heart attack, he whispered, 'You'll never get out.'

But he did!

Far from killing the tramp with the shock of finding he was sharing the grave with a ghost, the tramp was suddenly filled with the strength of a man half his age. He stopped grappling with the sides of the grave and leapt as if propelled by an invisible spring, coiled and attached to his bottom and then suddenly released.

As the tramp shot up, Crabbe thought he heard an angelic trumpet sounding a long-pitched note, and as he stood to explain, he was assailed by a most malodorous effluvium. An invisible aroma, that hit Crabbe like a heavy door slammed in his face.

He fell backwards, grasping for breath, and was once more alone.

The fight that had been in him, the determination, the feelings of joy, exuberance and approaching success were no more: after the violence he'd suffered that day, he could take nothing else. His lucky day was over, and he reverted to type. He'd failed, let everyone down, had been hurled headway into a grave where, finally, he had been gassed.

He was resigned to his fate.

In the relaxed atmosphere – the dreadful whiff from the gas attack having dissipated, he found that his bed of earth, broken planks, fake grass, camera case, tripod, rucksack and squashed cheese and ketchup sandwich, was really quite comfortable. He no longer wanted to escape. He just wanted to lie there and die, although next time, he thought, he'd bring a blanket. He fell into a deep sleep.

Crabbe woke, blinking in the bright sun, a new and determined mood upon him. Strangely, he knew where he was and what had happened. But he didn't know what day it was. Had he been here since last night or had he been lying at the bottom of the grave a lot longer?

He'd heard of people injured in car accidents and being in a coma for months then coming round in the sincere belief that they'd been unconscious for only a matter of seconds, minutes at the most.

He pondered, and logic told him that what had happened last night, *had* only happened last night. It hadn't taken over a week, even though that was how it felt.

Had the grave been fitted with a mirror, his injuries would have looked very serious, requiring immediate attention at a hospital. But in truth, his cuts, grazes and bruises were all superficial. They *looked* bad, but once the dried blood and tomato ketchup had been washed away and the skin given a few days to heal, he'd look no worse than as if he'd received a slight ragging at Chantry.

He ran his hands over his body, and apart from feeling rather sore in places and stiff almost everywhere else, he didn't think there was any permanent damage. Of course, his clothes were ripped and filthy, completely beyond repair, but otherwise, all things considered, he didn't feel too bad, and so he decided to carry on living.

But how?

He wished he had pencil and paper to help him analyse the situation. He would have done a 'Things I've Got' and a 'Things I Haven't Got' list. Had he done a 'Things I'm Not Good At' list, number one would be 'Getting Out of Graves'.

27: SNAKES and LADDERS

On his imaginary 'Things I Haven't Got' list, his mind wrote 'ladder' at the top, and once he'd formed that thought, could think of nothing else.

He looked up at the pale blue sky and saw a few birds flying free, out of their nests early to lay claim to whatever the bats had missed.

Aloud he said, 'I need a ladder.'

A voice said, 'Do you need a ladder, Geoffrey?'

Whatever sleep remained in Crabbe's brain disappeared as he saw the means of his deliverance appear above, on hands and knees blinking down at him.

'Good morning, err…lovely day!'

'Yes, indeed, beautiful,' said the voice, 'You seem to have grown, Geoffrey.'

'I think there may a little confusion. Probably the light. I'm not Geoffrey. I'm Crabbe, a House Prefect from Chantry. See, I've got a badge.'

Thankfully, the badge was attached to his lapel, but had been painted with tomato ketchup.

'Ah, sorry. I thought you were Geoffrey, our local tramp. He normally sleeps in the churchyard. Forgive me for mentioning it, but I don't think he'd take kindly to your living here. Tramps are territorial, but you'd know that, Geoffrey.'

336

'Are they? No, I didn't know that. And I'm not actually a tramp, I'm a House Prefect. And I'm not Geoffrey, I'm Lancelot, but I'd like to borrow a ladder, just as much as Geoffrey would.'

'Yes, I'm sure. Do you, by chance, know where Geoffrey is?'

'Unfortunately, I don't. But if you'd be kind enough to get me a ladder, we could go and look for him.'

'Good idea.' So saying, the gentleman began to rise and shuffle away. Crabbe could see now that he was elderly, and was wearing the vestments of a vicar, although without the traditional dog collar.

Crabbe began to wonder whether in taking this trip to Harrow, he had unwittingly discovered a community of lunatics.

Despite the fact that he was alone once again, he felt relieved: it seemed certain that someone would find him, someone who wasn't searching for Geoffrey. Someone who would be able to find a ladder and rescue him.

He looked about him and was embarrassed to see the mess he'd made. He was tempted to light the cigarette but refrained when he saw the debris was sprinkled with a thin layer of powder – flash powder that must have come from the tin when it fell in the grave.

Crabbe, ever mindful of the example set by his father, began to tidy everything into a neat pile. It was while he was doing this that the old gentleman returned.

'He's put a seat by it, but he's not up there,' he said, as if Crabbe were the slightest bit interested.

'No? I wonder where he's got to.'

'Who knows? He's a law unto himself, is Geoffrey.'

'Indeed, he is. Decent sort of chap but likes to be free to roam.' Crabbe realised suddenly he had become part of 'lunatic Harrow' and changed the subject back to his escape, 'About the ladder…'

'Oh yes, the ladder. I'll go and get…' He stopped, 'Ooh, manners. We haven't been introduced.' He got down on his hands and knees again and extended his hand.

'We can do that when you've got the … Oh, very well, said Crabbe as the proffered hand grasped air in front of him, 'How do you do? I'm Lancelot Crabbe, House Prefect at Chantry,' he said shaking the old man's bony hand, then adding, just to avoid further confusion, 'I'm not Geoffrey.'

'Neither am I. He's not here. I'm Silas Honeydew, verger at St. Mary's.'

'Oh, *verger?* replied Crabbe, 'I'm sorry, I thought you were the vicar.'

'No, no. We don't have a vicar here.'

'In a church? No vicar?' queried Crabbe, still shaking hands, 'That's most unusual, surely? Who conducts the services?'

'The rector. He's one up from a vicar. Gets more money.'

Chris Hare

'The rector, eh? Perhaps he knows where Geoffrey has got to.'

Crabbe didn't know why he was having this ridiculous conversation and regretted the suggestion as soon as it was out of his mouth. The verger got up, 'Good idea. I'll go and ask.'

'Yes, but could…' Too late. The verger had gone.

Crabbe sat down again and waited. He hoped the verger would return.

He did, some minutes later. 'Still here?' he asked unnecessarily, 'Can't interrupt the rector at the moment. He's doing a funeral.'

The likely truth dawned on Crabbe.

'Sorry to hear that. Would this,' he indicated the ten by four feet area in which he was incarcerated, 'would this be the grave intended for the deceased?'

'Yes,' replied the verger with a smile, 'why do you ask? Do you know him?'

'Mr. Honeybun, I regret I have not had the pleasure of meeting him, but I feel that if I am not released *very* soon, I will be spending the rest of my days in his company.'

'I understand. You'll be needing a ladder then.'

'If you would be so kind,' said Crabbe, with a note of exasperation in his voice.

'You wait…'

'I'll wait here,' interrupted Crabbe, 'you won't forget?'

'Forget what?'

339

Crabbe in all Innocence

'What I've just *told* you.'

'Oh, thanks for reminding me. Once I've taken away the planks and grass, which I see you've collected together, thank you, I've got to toll the bell. Used to be the sexton's job, you know, but we haven't got one at St. Mary's.

If he didn't get a ladder immediately, St. Mary's will be without a verger as well, thought Crabbe. Aloud he said, 'I'll remind you about tolling the bell later, and afterwards, it might be rather nice if we went in search of Geoffrey, we'd enjoy that. Perhaps the rector would like to join in. But first, *please*, the ladder!'

'Good idea. I'll go and get one,' came the reply as if the subject of a ladder had only just been raised.

Crabbe surmised that the next sound he heard would be the doleful ringing of the funeral bell but instead he heard laboured footsteps, accompanied by several grunts.

'Still down there?' called Mr. Honeydew without looking.

'Still here,' replied the rapidly wearing Crabbe.

'Watch out! Here it comes. You'll have to climb out yourself. They're waiting for me to ring the bell. We haven't got a sexton.'

'Fine. Thank you,' Crabbe called while taking hold of the bottom of a pair of stepladders, 'then we'll go a-Geoffrey hunting.' But the verger didn't hear as he was hurrying back towards the church and the stone steps up into the belfry.

Crabbe took his time. His training told him to leave the grave in as clean a condition as he had found it. He set up the ladder in the middle and slowly and with great care, made several trips up to the outside world with his equipment, stacking it neatly under the seat on the far side of his guardian angel's tomb.

He placed the remains of the fake grass and wooden planks at a discreet distance behind a headstone, and it was while doing this that he wondered where they had put the spoil, the earth they had dug to make the grave. He looked about but could see no sign of it. The bell stopped ringing, and he was reminded of the 'meals' bell at Chantry. That thought reminded him of how hungry he was, and from there his mind went to the cheese and ketchup sandwich still lying squashed at the bottom of the grave. Should he leave it there for the worms? No, their next meal was presently being told what a wonderful person he'd been and how everyone was going to miss him.

Crabbe descended once more and began scraping up the remains of the sandwich. It was while thus engaged that he heard a choir singing. The sounds of 'Abide with Me' getting louder, as if the choir singing it was approaching.

Oh glory!

With his hands full of bits of cheese sandwich which had understandably gone stale, and with tomato ketchup (still surprisingly fresh), running between his fingers, he unsteadily climbed the stepladder, using his

341

knees to keep his balance and praying that he would be able to make his escape before the funeral party arrived at the graveside.

His prayers were not answered.

As his head and hands emerged from the centre of the grave, several things dropped at the same moment: his jaw, the rector's jaw, and the widow.

Simultaneously, different noises were also heard; screams from the choir as they fled, gasps from the pallbearers who managed a very slick U-turn with their burden, a tentative 'good morning' from Crabbe, and a cry of outrage from the rector.

There was a collective gape from all the participants remaining at the committal.

Verger Silas Honeydew was not an actual participant at the graveside being still in the belfry. Unaware of what was going on outside, but noticing the absence of bats hanging within, he thought that by now they would be lowering the coffin into the grave and so started ringing the bell again.

Next door to him was the organ loft, fitted with plain glass windows to admit as much light as possible for the organist, Miss Elspeth Woods who obliged by playing the organ on weekdays when the Sunday organist was working.

Unfortunately, the organ loft windows faced north, away from the burial, so she too was unable to see what was going on.

Chris Hare

Miss Wood's sense of timing was slightly at odds with that of Mr. Honeydew, and in her estimation the funeral party would only just now be approaching the grave. She, therefore, embarked on a reprise of the last verse of 'Abide with Me', but played it a lot louder and in a different key. No one would notice. None of the choir ladies knew what a 'key' was anyway.

Below, outside, and allowing for the racket that was coming from above, there was now another stunned silence. The rector was rooted to the spot quite unable to move in the presence of this spectre rising from its grave. An apparition clutching its meal of human flesh, dripping with blood. In one hand, the rector held an open prayer book and in the other, on the end of silver chain, a silver thurible dripping holy water.

Crabbe noticed and wondered whether he should suggest that he might drip a little on the widow, still lying prostrate and completely ignored by those around her. Not that there were many left. The few mourners, being English, were pretending that nothing had gone amiss and were busy reading the inscriptions on nearby headstones.

Hiding behind the rector, an altar boy (that was his title, but he was 65 if he was a day), stood shaking with terror whilst holding a small hand bell that wouldn't stop ringing, along with a lighted candle.

Crabbe took in the scene, waiting for someone to speak. Although it seemed to him, he'd been standing on the top of the ladder for at least ten minutes, really, it had been no more than a few seconds and he now understood why they screwed down the lids of coffins – just in case it was dropped, as the one now being returned at speed to the church almost had been.

The altar boy moved first, raising the candle to see Crabbe more clearly. He did no more as the rector suddenly sprang into life. Dropping his prayer book and raising the large cross that hung round his neck, he screamed, 'Be gone thou foul, evil creature from Hell!'

Crabbe was transfixed and quite frankly, astonished. But even now, *even now, in the worst, most embarrassing situation he had ever experienced,* he thought of Chantry as if it was Gordon standing there hurling insults at him as he had when they had ad-libbed his Royal Messenger scene in *Macbeth*. But this wasn't Gordon. This was a male version of Sister Rosemary.

He managed to speak, 'Sorry, Sister,' and was ignored.

The rector took a pace forward and bellowed, 'Get thee hence! Thou thrice-damned spawn of Satan!'

'I'm Lancelot Crabbe, from Chantry,' Crabbe whispered in a tiny voice as the altar boy threw the candle at him. It missed Crabbe but found the grave. Crabbe watched it drop, so he didn't notice the rector whirling the silver thurible around his head like a mace and chain being swung by a medieval knight.

The mace found Crabbe's left ear as the flame from the candle found the spilt flash powder.

344

There was an explosion inside his head and another under his feet. Crabbe dropped back once more into the grave.

He lay there quite still. Unseeing eyes staring upwards towards heaven, tongue lolling out. He thought of Mr. Red Ted, his parents and grandparents, Miss Peach, Mr. Pinder and Mr. Finney, even Sister Rosemary. And Koshkai. Where was she?

He imagined he saw her face as a tear formed in the corner of his eye. *We don't cry at Chantry.* He blinked it away and closed his eyes.

The Fates smiled down. Another fully qualified Heroic Failure added to their list.

They looked closer. Crabbe was about to breathe his last.

Tick, tock.

Tick…

Crabbe in all Innocence

Tock.

TOCK??

'Atropos, you just tocked,' screeched Lechesis and Clotho in horrified accord. 'You should have cut his thread at the end of the previous page, straight after the last Tick.'

'I know, I know. But I wanted to see what happens. If we let him live, we could get him to the Cottage Hospital. He'll tell them his name's 'Elsie', they'll take him to the Women's Emergency Ward. Then they'll discover he's got an appendage. Wouldn't that be hilarious? Typical Crabbe.'

'What a splendid idea! Let's see for ourselves,' said Lechesis.

'Yes,' replied Clotho, 'let him live.'

And the three Fates agreed to alter destiny.

As only they can.

And Crabbe lived.

Chris Hare

Printed in Poland
by Amazon Fulfillment
Poland Sp. z o.o., Wrocław

76196031R00197